Don

The Bla

Praise for Ana Seymour . . .

"Ms. Seymour has outdone herself again . . . *The Black Swan* is like sipping fine wine—it's intoxicating."
—*Rendezvous*

"Ana Seymour takes her legion of loyal readers into a fascinating new realm of medieval lore."
—*Times Record News*

"Ms. Seymour has captured the historical era and given us a romance filled with wonderful characters and several unique subplots . . . a highly enjoyable read."
—*Romantic Times*

"Exciting . . . The story line is loaded with authenticity . . . The characters are intelligent and warm . . . Fans of this subgenre already know that they see more of the era when Ana Seymour is the author, and this tale enhances her deserved reputation."
—Harriet Klausner

"[Seymour is] again filling pages with her mastery of plotting and the sweet joys found in family, friends, and the simple pleasure life affords . . . It is always a joy to read a novel of this caliber."
—*Under the Covers*

"Readers will be enthralled as they follow spunky Jennie's struggles to keep her family together with a never-give-up determination. Superb."
—*Bell, Book & Candle*

Also by Ana Seymour

THE BLACK SWAN
ROSE IN THE MIST

Irish
Gypsy

Ana Seymour

JOVE BOOKS, NEW YORK

If you purchased this book without a cover, you should be aware that this book is stolen property. It was reported as "unsold and destroyed" to the publisher, and neither the author nor the publisher has received any payment for this "stripped book."

This is a work of fiction. Names, characters, places, and incidents either are the product of the author's imagination or are used fictitiously, and any resemblance to actual persons, living or dead, business establishments, events, or locales is entirely coincidental.

IRISH GYPSY

A Jove Book / published by arrangement with the author

PRINTING HISTORY
Jove edition / August 2002

Copyright © 2002 by Mary Bracho

All rights reserved.
This book, or parts thereof, may not be reproduced in any form without permission.
For information address: The Berkley Publishing Group, a division of Penguin Putnam Inc.,
375 Hudson Street, New York, New York 10014.

Visit our website at
www.penguinputnam.com

ISBN: 0-515-13385-X

A JOVE BOOK®
Jove Books are published by The Berkley Publishing Group,
a division of Penguin Putnam Inc.,
375 Hudson Street, New York, New York 10014.
JOVE and the "J" design
are trademarks belonging to Penguin Putnam Inc.

PRINTED IN THE UNITED STATES OF AMERICA

10 9 8 7 6 5 4 3 2 1

For my irreplaceable daughters,
Kathryn and Cristina

And for their irrepressible father,
who brings out the gypsy in us.

Prologue

October 1567
County Meath, Ireland

"The O'Neill is dead." Cormac Riordan stepped out of the circle of rustling trees and started toward the man sitting by a small campfire in the center of the clearing.

Eamon Riordan looked up at his brother. "Aye, I heard. 'Twas all the news in Fingarry. 'Twill mean war again." Their identical dark eyes met in a sober gaze. The last thing either wanted was a resumption of the fighting that had torn apart their country for so much of the past two decades.

"Aye," Cormac agreed. "With the O'Neill gone, there's no one strong enough to unite us against the English. Elizabeth's men are already swarming over the Desmond lands in the south."

Eamon stood and kicked at a log that had slipped from the neatly pyramided fire. The movement sent sparks swirling in the gusty air. "'Tis all the more reason I should ride south to Killarney and warn Niall."

Only a month ago the third Riordan brother, Niall, had taken his new bride south to reclaim her family lands in the beautiful lake country.

Cormac shook his head. "I rode here to fetch you back. I mislike the thought of you going by yourself. I'd have you wait until Cousin Dermot comes back and can go with you. I wish I could go, but I dare not leave Claire that long."

Eamon gave one of the crooked grins that were a trademark of the three Riordan brothers. Eamon and Niall made gentle fun of Cormac's refusal to leave his wife's side when she was carrying his child, even though she had produced two healthy youngsters with no ill effects. "The way you worry over her like an old fishwife, I warrant Claire was happy to send you after me just to get you out of the house for a couple of days."

Cormac returned his brother's grin. "You may be right, but nonetheless, I'll not leave her till the babe is born."

Eamon walked around the fire to clap a hand on his brother's broad back. "She'll be fine, Cormac. The Riordan curse is over. Claire's given you two healthy sons and no doubt will give you a dozen more the way you keep after her like a randy pup." At Cormac's scowl he continued his teasing. "My poor sister-in-law. No sooner does the nurse appear to take the little ones off to the nursery than you whisk Claire away to the bedroom. I've not been able to hold a decent conversation with the lass in two years."

Flushing in the firelight, Cormac said, "Wait until you are snared by Cupid's net, Eamon. Then we'll see how much time you decide to spend in that precious library of yours."

Eamon gave an exaggerated sigh. "I'll leave the

lovesick moonin' and the breedin' to you and Niall, brother. Give me a warm-hearted tavern wench with fulsome breasts and a naughty smile. Easy loving without the complications." He looked behind his brother toward the trees. "Where's Taranis?"

"I left him tied yonder with your horse, though I'm thinking we should fetch them here by the fire. The countryside's buzzing with English soldiers."

Eamon nodded agreement. "Aye. 'Tis a blustery night and we'd have a hard time hearing anyone coming over the sound of the wind."

The two brothers walked shoulder to shoulder to the edge of the clearing, then moved to single file as they reached the thick woods. "What were they saying in Fingarry?" Cormac asked to his brother's back. "Is there still hope that the rebels can hold together?"

Eamon stopped abruptly without answering his brother's question.

Cormac prompted, "Were you able to speak with the Hennessys?"

"Did you move my horse?" Eamon asked in a low voice.

Cormac answered in some confusion, "Nay, I told you, I left Taranis tethered there right next to him."

Eamon stepped aside to allow his brother a view of the small opening in the trees where the horses had been tied. "Well, *someone* has moved them," he said.

Cormac moved past his brother and looked around, frowning. He walked over to the low tree branch where the horses had been hitched for the night, then crouched down to look at the dirt. "Not moved them," he said after a moment. "*Stolen* them."

Eamon shook his head in disbelief. "You'd only just arrived. How could someone have come here and stolen our horses in those few minutes?"

Cormac stood. "I warrant it doesn't take long to untie two horses."

Eamon strode over beside his brother and crouched to examine the ground. "The bastards can't have gone far. Help me figure out these tracks."

Cormac remained upright. "You think to track them at night? On foot?"

"God's blood, Cormac! We have to do something. The bloody bastards!" he said again. He jumped to his feet and barreled his way through the trees out to the road. Cormac followed him at a slower pace, but when they got to the rutted highway, there was no sign of either horses or horse thieves.

"I can't believe it." Eamon gave a kick to a hummock of grass at the roadside.

" 'Tis the devil's luck," Cormac agreed. "But I can't see that there's much we can do about it tonight. We'd best get some sleep."

"Sleep?" Eamon asked in amazement. "Surely you jest."

"I see little other productive use for our time until dawn. There's not even a moon tonight. Likely we wouldn't see the animals if they walked a yard from us."

Cormac turned back toward the clearing where his brother had built the fire. After a final, futile look up and down the dark road, Eamon followed him.

As the two brothers settled down on the mossy ground, Eamon was still muttering imprecations toward the unscrupulous villains who had robbed them. "I shan't be able to sleep," he said to Cormac.

His brother closed his eyes and rolled over. "You'd be wise to give it a try at least. We may be in for a long walk on the morrow."

•   •   •

He had slept after all, Eamon realized as he opened his eyes to see that the first light of dawn was tingeing the sky. Beside him, Cormac's even breathing told him that his brother had also managed to put aside the previous evening's misfortune long enough to fall asleep.

But now that Eamon was awake, he had no desire to continue dozing. Without waking his brother, he quietly got up, rearranged his clothes, and headed across the clearing toward the spot where the horses had been. He could feel his temper rising again as he neared the scene of the crime. The Riordans had always taken great pride in their horses. Eamon's mount, Rioga, and his brother's big stallion, Taranis, were two of the best horses on the estate. It seemed impossible that they had simply vanished into the night.

It had been too dark the previous evening, but with the light of day he intended to make a thorough search of the dusty ground where the animals had been tethered in hopes of finding some clue as to the identity of the thieves.

Breathing hard with renewed indignation, he almost missed the flash of color. Someone was there among the trees. He stopped just in time before stepping out and revealing himself. Whoever it was appeared to be heading toward the exact spot where the horses had been tied . . . and was leading a horse. *Taranis*. The color that had caught Eamon's eye had been a bright red-and-blue bandanna tied around the head of what appeared to be a young lad.

Eamon had left his pistol and sword back by the fire with his saddlebags. He drew a hunting knife from his belt and scanned the trees for other miscreants, but the boy appeared to be alone. Eamon thought briefly of going to awaken his brother, but realized that the thief might escape while he turned his back. Stealthily he

crept up behind the boy and clamped a long arm around
his neck.

His captive choked and sputtered and kicked scrawny
legs as Eamon lifted him clear off the ground and
growled, "What are you doing with that horse, you little sneakthief?"

The only answer was a strangled coughing as if
Eamon's arm was cutting off the boy's air. Eamon
scanned the trees once more for signs of any confeder-
ates, then eased his hold and set the boy back to the
ground. "Don't try to run," he warned. "And don't
holler out for help from your thieving friends, or I'll slit
open your gullet like a filleted trout."

The boy continued to cough for several moments,
then finally said, "I was puttin' this 'un back."

Though it had appeared that the thief was doing precisely that, his actions made no sense to Eamon. Fur-
thermore, this was not the burly horse thief he had
envisioned the night before. The boy's shoulders were
so puny, Eamon could snap him in two without even
thinking. He loosened his hold further and turned his
captive around so that he could see his face.

Thick reddish lashes rimmed bright blue eyes in a
dirty, thin face. Thin, and too pretty to belong to any
boy. "You're a wench," he said in disbelief.

"If yer thinking 'twill be easy to have me, ye'd best
think again. I . . . I bite." The girl gave a defiant tilt of
her head. Despite her brave words, he could see the
beginning of tears. "I . . . bite," she continued. "I bite,
and . . . and I scratch like a demon."

"Do ye now?" Eamon asked with a smile. He
dropped his hold on her and stepped back. Now that he
knew she was a girl, he could see that she was not quite
as young as he had assumed, though she still looked to
be little more than twelve or thirteen. He reached

toward her and snatched the bandanna from her head. Auburn hair tumbled past her shoulders. He noticed that she flinched when his hand neared her and that there was a sizable bruise on her right cheek. "I don't intend to hurt you, lass," he said gently. "But I'd have you tell me what you're doing with my brother's horse."

"I told ye. I was bringing him back."

"Were you the one who took him in the first place?"

She nodded warily and braced her body as if waiting for a blow.

"Where's the other one—my horse?"

"Yonder," she said, indicating the direction with a nod of her head.

"Were you intending to bring him back, too?"

She hesitated a moment, then shook her head. "Nay."

Eamon stared at her in disbelief.

"I shouldn't have taken both," she continued. "I only need the one."

For a moment Eamon wondered if he was in fact still sleeping and was dreaming the whole encounter. "You've come to return my brother's horse because you decided that you only wanted to steal one of our horses? And I happen to be the lucky one?"

She looked slightly indignant. "Ye should be grateful. I'm returning the best 'un," she said. She reached to give Taranis's neck a stroke. "He's a beauty," she added. Her tone held an awed reverence.

Eamon had no argument with the girl's judgment of horseflesh. He was fond of Rioga, but his brother's mount was the finest horse in all of Ireland. "Who are you?" he asked her.

"They call me Maura."

"Well, Maura, would you like to explain to me why you decided to steal my horse? Do you know what they do to horse thieves?"

"I reckon they hang 'em mostly."

Eamon gave an exasperated shake of his head. "Doesn't that bother you?"

"Nay," she said, her blue eyes unblinking.

"I trow 'twould take very little effort for the hangman's rope to break that scrawny neck of yours." He reached his hand toward her, but stopped when once again she flinched at the movement. "I said I'd not hurt you, girl. How is it that you claim to have no fear of hanging, yet you recoil from me like a fawn facing a wolf?"

The girl shrugged, and for the first time Eamon felt a pang of sympathy. She was young to be on her own, young to be risking death. "Where do you live?" he asked.

Once again her tiny shoulders hunched. "Nowhere. Everywhere," she said. "I live in the woods."

"Have you no family?"

This time she answered too quickly, "Nay, I've no one. I'm alone."

Eamon hesitated, trying to decide what to do. What he *should* do, he told himself, was truss the chit up on the back of his horse and deliver her to the nearest sheriff. But something about the way her gaze met his so directly made that idea unpalatable. She was, after all, little more than a child.

"I'll tell you what we'll do, Maid Maura of the Woods," he said finally. "You'll show me where I can recover Rioga, and then my brother and I will ride on our way and endeavor to forget this misadventure."

She appeared to be considering his offer.

Eamon gave a snort of disbelief. "I'm doing you a favor, lass. I could turn you into the authorities for the bad night you gave my brother and me."

"I need the one horse," she said after a minute. "I've

brought ye back one, because 'tis the way of my people not to take more than we need."

"I thought you said you didn't have any people."

Her gaze shifted away from him. "I don't," she said.

"You talk in riddles, lass, and I've not the time to stand here all day listening to them. Now, you'll show me where you've left my horse, or I'll call for my brother to help me tie you up in a neat bundle for the local magistrate."

She looked up at him, then nodded. "I'll take ye to yer horse."

"Wise decision," he said dryly. "Which way?"

She pointed to the opposite row of trees. "Just beyond there."

Eamon nodded and started walking in the direction of her hand. When she didn't appear to be moving alongside him, he looked back, saying, "You lead the way."

The half turn of his head was just enough to allow him to see the rock coming toward him. Oddly, his mind focused on the fact that her hand was so small it could barely surround the big stone. Then everything went blank.

The relief was obvious in Cormac's tone. "Come on, little brother, that's right, open your eyes. It takes more than a knock with a pebble to keep a Riordan down."

Eamon blinked hard. His head was on Cormac's leg, and he could almost swear that his brother had been holding him enfolded in his arms. He discounted the idea. Embraces were not customary in the all-male Riordan household, unless they were part of a wrestling contest.

Both brothers suddenly seemed self-conscious at their uncharacteristically tender scene. Cormac put an arm behind his brother's back and lifted him to a sitting position. "Are you feeling better?" he asked.

Eamon's head cleared as he sat upright, but there was a tremendous ache between his shoulder and neck. " 'Twas a boulder, not a pebble," he said grumpily.

Cormac put a hand on the spot. "Here, right?"

Eamon winced with pain. "Aye."

"You're lucky he didn't hit you on the skull. It could have killed you."

"She probably couldn't reach that high."

"She?"

Eamon moved aside his brother's hand and rubbed the spot himself. It felt as if the entire base of his neck had swelled into a huge lump. "Aye, she. A tiny she-devil from the bowels of . . ." He broke off and looked around with a sudden thought. "She's left Taranis. We can go after her."

"Taranis is fast, but there's no way he could catch a single rider on Rioga with us riding double."

"Then you wait here while I go after her myself." He struggled to stand.

"You're not going anywhere, and I'm not leaving you here until we're sure you've suffered no ill effects," Cormac said firmly. "How many others were there?"

"She was alone."

Cormac glanced at the lump on his brother's neck, but remained silent.

"Go ahead and say it," Eamon challenged.

Cormac shrugged as if to indicate that he would refrain from his normal brotherly banter, but then he appeared to be unable to resist asking, "How big did you say she was?"

"I'm going to catch the little thief, Cormac." He let his brother help him up, then swayed as waves of nausea hit his stomach. "I'm riding after her."

"Nay, you're not." The mocking twinkle was gone from Cormac's eyes.

"You can't stop—" Before Eamon could finish speaking, he clutched Cormac's arm for support, then turned to one side and doubled over while his stomach emptied itself of the remains of the previous evening's supper.

"We're going back to Riordan Hall," Cormac said tersely.

"What about my horse?" Eamon asked, wiping his mouth with a shaky hand.

"We've horses aplenty back at Riordan Hall," Cormac answered, "but I've only two brothers. We're going home where we can summon a doctor."

Eamon let Cormac ease him down to sit leaning against a tree while his brother collected their things and packed them on Taranis. Then he fought off the nausea once again as Cormac helped him mount.

"Can you ride?" Cormac asked.

"Aye," he answered glumly.

"I'll send men back to find her, Eamon. We'll get Rioga back. 'Tis you I'm concerned about for the moment."

"She'll be leagues away by the time anyone can get back here."

"If she is, so be it. 'Twill teach you a good lesson never to turn your back on a woman."

Eamon refused to return his brother's smile. "Aye," he said. "If I ever see that little wretch again, you can be sure I'll be watching my back."

One

Tara Hill, October 1574

Maura had never thought to return to Tara Hill. When she'd fled the Gypsy camp seven years before, she'd wanted to travel as far away as possible and never come back. The grief had been too fresh. She'd been unable to see any reason to stay when she'd lost the only real family she'd ever had—her beloved father, Giacomo.

Now as she looked out over the familiar plains of Tara, she realized that the years had dulled the ache of his loss. She felt a rising excitement at the thought of seeing all her old friends. The old grandmother of the troupe, Nonna. Her son, Giorgio, who had rocked Maura like a babe in his arms as she wept over her father's grave. Giorgio's son, little Momo. He'd been Maura's constant shadow. The lively youngster would be nearly grown by now.

In a way they *had* been her family, though she'd always felt slightly set apart from the rest. Her hair and eyes had told her she was different long before her father admitted that her mother had been Irish, not Romany. It had been a search for her mother's heritage that had first brought Giacomo's caravan to Tara Hill. And it was that search that had brought Maura back.

She could feel her heart pumping as she walked up a small hill that gave her a view of the bare landscape. It had been a bad year for rains, and the wind that blew over the grasses still held hints of the hot, dry summer that had just ended. After seven long years away it felt like home.

She knew that she'd be able to find Giacomo's family if they were still anywhere in the area. Romanies had a special sense about that. Only now, of course, they weren't Giacomo's family any longer. The side of her neck pulsed as her heart beat faster still. It was Pietro's family now. Pietro with his narrow dark eyes and filthy, roving hands.

Seven years ago she'd been a child. She'd run away from him in blind panic. But she was a grown woman now, one who had learned to take care of herself on the streets of Dublin and the back alleys of Liverpool. She reached down instinctively to touch the knife she always kept in the side of her leather boot. If Pietro refused to recognize that she was no longer an easy victim, she had ways to convince him.

Cormac Riordan reached a sly hand underneath his wife's billowy petticoats and rubbed his palm along her leg.

"Nay, lout, you'll not be starting things up again. I've just got myself set back to rights," Claire Riordan complained, but her smile refused to match the words.

"We've time for another wee tussle, *chara*," Cormac murmured, sliding against her on the rough blanket they had been using for a picnic with their three children at

Tara Hill. The children had been led away by their uncle
Eamon for an expedition to Cliodhna's Glen, which had
been a favorite childhood hideaway of the three Riordan brothers. Cormac had wasted little time in taking
advantage of the rare moment alone to coax his wife to
join him in the shelter of a thicket.

"Nay, we do not have time, husband," Claire insisted, even while she tipped her head to allow Cormac
to nip gently at the underside of her neck. "Eamon and
the children could appear at any moment."

Cormac gave an exaggerated sigh and sat up. "I suppose you're right. That is, if the rascals haven't escaped
from him to set out on some adventure of their own." At
Claire's look of alarm, he put his hand on her cheek.
"'Tis a jest, *chara*. Eamon can handle them."

The two parents exchanged a look of shared doubt,
then Claire jumped to her feet. "Perhaps we should go
looking for them."

Cormac reluctantly joined her, reaching down to roll
the blanket around his arm. "They'll be fine. Eamon has
often had them in his care."

"Aye, but Ultan gets rowdier every day. I swear, he's
dearer to me than my own heart, but he has me at my
wit's end."

Cormac slipped his free arm around his wife as they
started walking out of the shelter of the bushes, scan-
ning the horizon for some sign of their missing progeny.
"He's just an active lad. Bright and curious. He needs
schooling—something to challenge that quick mind of
his."

"Aye, and just how are we supposed to accomplish
that when he's run off every tutor in Kilmessen?"

"Ultan's too smart for the country lads of Kilmessen.
I'm considering sending to Dublin for a proper tutor.
Mayhap to London."

"London?" Claire asked in awe.

"Aye. Ultan will be head of the Riordan clan some day. He may as well begin learning about the world."

"But he's just a little boy."

"'Tis none too early to start. Especially since the little rascal has begun running circles around every servant in the place. And around his mother, as well, at times," Cormac added, giving Claire an affectionate squeeze.

"And around his uncle," Claire added, pointing down the hill to where their three children were trooping toward them. "There are the children, but where's Eamon?"

Eamon had exhausted his vocabulary of epithets to describe the manner of fool he considered himself. Even so, he reckoned the language was nothing compared to what he would hear from his brother.

He gave another tug at the rope that held him securely tied to the tree branch. He couldn't imagine why he had agreed to Ultan's pleadings about a game of Robin Hood. The wily youngster had been amazingly clever about disguising his intentions, right up to the moment he pulled the rope tight around the branch and stepped away with his infectious boyish laugh.

"Robin and his merry men have got you now, Uncle Eamon. I mean, Sheriff!" he'd cried. "We'll leave you tied to this tree while we go to Nottingham to rescue the Maid Marian from wicked Prince John."

"I thought *I* was Maid Marian," his sister had said.

"Nay, Eily. You're too little to be Maid Marian," her brother declared. The girl had nodded solemnly and made no further protest.

Eamon shook his head. His young nephew was already showing the signs of leadership that would stand

him in good stead when he became head of the powerful Riordan clan. But authority was hard to accept from
a nine-year-old.

Lord, he hoped the boy had led his little brother and
sister directly back to his parents, as he had promised.
If not, Cormac would really have his hide. He leaned
over the rope and began to gnaw at it with his teeth.
How could such a little boy tie such a big knot? he
wondered.

"Would you like some help with that?"

Eamon blinked. For a moment, he wondered if the
long afternoon in the sun was causing him to see things.
The vision in front of him looked like one of the woodland faeries, come down out of Cliodhna's Glen. Her
thick reddish-brown hair billowed around delicate features—bright blue eyes and a nose that tipped slightly
upward.

She was watching him from some distance, her head
cocked as though considering whether she should come
closer.

"I'd be obliged," he told her, giving his bound hands
a shake. "My—er—nephews and niece—we—er—we
were playing a game. . . ." He let his voice trail off as he
realized how foolish his explanation sounded.

The vision took a step forward, then stopped. "'Tis
a bit rare to see a man trussed up like a horse," she admitted. "How do I know you've not been put there because you're a dangerous character? Mayhap 'tis not
safe to let you loose."

"I assure you, mistress, I'm not at all dangerous. In
faith, since I've been left in this position by a young
boy, I would say that I come close to being the least
dangerous man in Meath County."

She smiled at that and started walking closer. The

smile made a dimple deepen in her right cheek. Her
eyes sparkled like the pond at Cliodhna's Glen.

"Where is this fearsome nephew of yours?" she
asked, looking around.

"That's what I need to find out, and the sooner the
better. God knows what mischief he's up to now. So if
you would be so kind . . ." He motioned again with his
bound hands. "The knot is complicated, but I've a knife
in my boot you could use to cut it."

After one last moment of hesitation, she moved toward him. The complicated tangle of rope seemed to
melt away as soon as she touched it. "There," she said,
brushing her hands.

He looked at her, amazed. "You know something of
knots, mistress," he said. "I'm in your debt."

"Nay, 'twas but a simple thing."

He looked at her more closely. There seemed to be
something familiar about her, but he was sure that if
he had ever seen anyone this lovely in County Meath,
he would remember it. Her clothes were an odd diago-
nal cut, as if she came from another country, and the
inflection of her speech was slightly different, though
she spoke like a member of the upper classes. "You're
not from here," he stated. "Are you visiting one of the
neighboring estates?"

"Aye, I'm visiting," she said simply, taking a step
back from him.

"Visiting whom?" he pressed. "I'd like to call and
extend proper thanks, but I must see that the children
have safely—"

She was studying him, and suddenly seemed to grow
pale. "I should leave, as well," she said. "I'll be missed."

She turned her back on him and began walking
quickly across the clearing.

"Wait!" he called to her. "I didn't get your name or—"

Without turning back, she said, "Forgive me, sir, I'm quite late." Then she lifted her oddly cut skirt and started to run.

Eamon stared after her, perplexed, as she disappeared into the woods, much like the faerie he had first imagined her to be. His first impulse was to run after her and demand to know who she was and where she was staying, but the thought of his charges made him abandon the idea. His first task was to make sure that Ultan, Dylan, and Eily had come to no harm. Then he could worry about the identity of his mysterious woodland rescuer.

Maura continued running long after there was any danger of pursuit. The man had not followed her. Perhaps his story about having been tied up by children was true, and he'd gone in search of them. If so, she was glad that she had stopped to spit in the stream she'd passed that morning. It had brought her luck, just as Nonna always said.

Although she could as easily say that it had been bad luck that had brought about the encounter in the first place. What ill fortune had ordained that upon returning to County Meath she would come face to face with the man whose horse she had stolen all those years before? He hadn't recognized her, of course, but she'd had the feeling that if he'd had enough time, he eventually would have been able to find the dirty face of the little urchin thief in the woman she had become.

She would have to be more careful. Once she got back with the Romanies, she would settle in to life in the caravan and stay out of sight of all the Gajos, at least until she was ready to once again begin the hunt for her mother's people.

She felt a twinge of regret. The Gajo was a handsome man. His dark eyes had lit with a special warmth when he'd spoken of his nephew. He had a crooked grin that she'd never quite forgotten all those years away. More than once during those years, she'd thought back on that morning with remorse. At least now she knew that her victim had suffered no lasting hurt from the blow she'd given him. At the time she'd thought that she had no choice. She'd had to get away from Pietro. The Gajo's horse had meant freedom.

She sighed and began to walk more quickly. Her instinct was telling her that the way to find her family was to continue along the small river she'd encountered. West, following the setting sun up into the hills. The path had suddenly become so certain that it was all she could do to keep from breaking into a run.

She found them exactly at sundown—a neat little semicircle of wagons arranged around a fire pit built of rounded stones. It was exactly as she had remembered. For a moment she had the odd feeling that she'd never been away. She'd crept out of the camp before dawn that brilliant autumn day. Now she was returning to the glow of a harvest sunset, and it was as if the seven years between had never happened.

A young man stepped out from behind the nearest wagon. He wore a scarlet tunic and shiny black boots up to the thigh. Maura drew in a quick breath as she recognized the dark curly hair and handsome features. "Momo," she whispered.

The man looked her way and froze. His black eyes widened as he stared at her, then a smile broke across his face and he began to run toward her. "Maura!" he cried.

Before she knew what was happening, he'd swept her off her feet in a whirling embrace. He kept repeating her name, "Maura, Maura!" as he planted heavy kisses on both cheeks. "Ye've come back!"

Laughing and breathless, she managed to extricate herself and hold him away so that she could study his face. "Is it possible?" she asked. "This can't be my little Momo?"

He flushed. "No one calls me *little* anymore, Maura. I've grown up."

"Aye, I can see." She could see. The little boy of ten who had been her constant companion before she'd left now towered over her. Though he still had the leanness of youth, his shoulders were broad, and his chin was shadowed with the stubble of a beard.

"I'd thought ye'd gone forever, Maura," he said. "But my grandmother always said that ye'd be back. She had a vision."

"Nonna was right, as usual. Is she well? And Giorgio?"

"Father is well, but Nonna has had the cough for nigh on two years now." His eyes darkened. "We don't know how much longer she'll be with us."

Maura felt a wave of sorrow. She'd never known her mother, and though she'd been mostly content with the love of her father, there had been moments when she'd longed for the voice and touch of a female. During those times she'd sought out Nonna.

"I shouldn't have stayed away so long," she said.

"She'll be happy to see ye, Maura," Momo said gently, taking her hand and giving it a squeeze.

Maura looked over at the camp as if hoping to see the old woman running toward her, arms outstretched.

"She rarely ventures out of the wagon these days,"

Momo explained. "But I warrant the sight of ye will re-
vive her."

"I'd expected to find you here," Maura said, letting
her gaze wander over the site, "but 'tis something of a
miracle, nonetheless. This looks like almost the exact
spot where we were camped when my—" she broke off.

"When yer father died," Mom finished for her. "Aye.
We've wandered a bit over the years, but Pietro always
seems to lead us back to Tara Hill."

Maura winced at the sound of the dreaded name. "So
Pietro still leads you?"

"Aye, and he still speaks of ye. Mayhap 'tis in search
of ye that he brings us back here every fall."

Maura shook her head. "I hardly think so. I was little
more than a child when I left here."

"Aye, but ye were Giacomo's daughter, and some
say that Pietro will never be content until he possesses
everything that was Giacomo's."

Maura's eyes shifted to the familiar square cart at the
far end of the circle. Her father had built the cart with
his own two hands, and it had been her home for most
of her childhood. "He lives there now?"

"Aye."

"And has taken no wife?"

Momo hesitated. "No *wife*."

She noted her friend's odd inflection. "He has a
woman, then?"

"Aye, a poor little thing he brought home one day
after the Burley market fair. She speaks little and
mostly stays in the wagon. I've tried to question her to
see how she's faring, but she refuses to speak much."

Maura frowned. None of this sounded like the happy
Romany camp she remembered from her childhood
days. They had truly been a family, then, though few
were blood kin. Suddenly she realized that, though it

was suppertime, the camp looked deserted. Where were the women bustling around preparing their meals, the children running in and out of the wagons, the men chopping wood or tooling their leather goods?

"Where is everyone?" she asked.

"My father is hunting," Momo said. "I stayed to care for Nonna."

"Hunting?" It was not a normal activity for the Romany men. Food had usually been obtained by trading for horses or horseshoeing or for the leather and tin goods they fashioned.

Momo shrugged. "Scavenging, more like. Rabbits, shrew, dead birds, whatever they can find. Food is not as easy to come by these days."

Her frown growing deeper, Maura turned toward the circle of carts. Now that she was looking at them carefully, she realized that there were only a handful left, fewer than half the number there had been in the old days. " 'Tis not like it used to be," she said almost to herself.

"Nay," Momo agreed. "Nor are ye, Maura. Yer speech is different."

She smiled briefly. "I had to learn Gajo speech to survive in a Gajo world," she said.

"Well, ye're back in the Romany world now."

"Aye. Will you take me to see Nonna?"

Before she finished the question, a big man stepped from between two wagons into the fading twilight. "Damned if the old hag didn't get it right this time," he said. "Ye did come back."

Even now Maura could feel her skin crawl at the sound of the familiar voice, but she straightened her back and forced herself to answer coolly, "Aye, Pietro, I'm back."

The man walked toward them, studying her boldly

from head to toe. "I always said ye'd be as fine a wench as they come when ye filled out."

Maura ignored his comment. "Momo is going to take me to see Nonna," she said.

"The old lady can wait. Have ye no better welcome for an old friend?" He took a step closer. His smile flashed the gold front tooth, the same tooth that had often appeared in her bad dreams.

"We're not friends, Pietro, nor ever have been. I came back because of the others and because I felt some responsibility to my father to see what had become of his people."

"They're my people now, Maura. I'm the leader here, so if ye've come to stay, ye'd best start acting a bit more friendly like."

At her side, Maura could feel Momo bristling. "She's just arrived, Pietro. Leave her be," he said.

The last thing she wanted her first night back was a fight. "You're right, Pietro," she said, her tone conciliatory. "You're the leader here. I respect that position. But I've been walking all day. I'm tired and I want to see Nonna. I'll speak with you and the others in the morning."

For a moment Pietro looked as if he was going to continue his insistence, but finally he shrugged and said, "Aye, tomorrow will be soon enough."

Somehow he made the simple words sound ominous. The confidence Maura had built up about being able to deal with the loathsome man was fading. When Momo reached for her hand, she grasped it firmly and held it all the way to his wagon.

Her words to Pietro had been the truth, she told herself. She *was* tired. Tomorrow the little camp would not look so dismal and Pietro would not look so menacing. She'd dealt with worse characters than Pietro in her travels, and without the friends to help her that she could count on here.

"Don't worry about him," Momo said in a low voice. "I'm a man now—old enough to protect ye. I don't intend to let him bully ye like he did before ye left."

The fervor in his voice made Maura wonder exactly how much the ten-year-old Momo had understood all those years ago about Pietro's "bullying."

"I'm not worried," she said. "I don't intend to let Pietro ruin my homecoming."

"All the same, ye should know that ye have my support against him, if need be. I'm not the raw boy I was when ye left."

She gave him a grateful smile. "Nay, Momo, you're not." She pointed up to the closed door of the wagon. "Now scamper up there and warn your grandmother that I'm here so she doesn't go into a fit at the sight of me."

She watched as the nimble youth followed her instructions. As he had said, he was no longer a raw boy, but neither was he a match for Pietro's burly strength. She'd have to be careful not to let Momo get ideas about becoming her champion against the troupe's leader.

Almost as soon as he had closed the wagon door behind him, it opened again and his curly head popped out. He looked at her with a grin. "Nonna says if ye waste any more time before getting yerself in here, she's not too old to take a switch to ye."

Maura smiled and hiked her skirts to climb the rickety wooden steps into the wagon. She'd deal with Pietro tomorrow, but for the moment she intended to enjoy her reunion with the only family she'd ever known.

TWO

"I could take the lad with me to Ulster," Eamon suggested. "'Twould at least give you and Claire a rest for a few weeks."

"I need no rest from my own son," Cormac said grumpily. "And if I did, I'd hardly be likely to entrust him to his uncle. No doubt he'd have taken over the captain's helm before the ship left Dublin—with you trussed up in the hold."

The two brothers were alone sharing a late-night drink in the lofty Riordan dining hall. Before dawn Eamon would leave for a sea journey to visit Riordan cousins in northern Ireland and Scotland.

Eamon grimaced. "I fear I'm never going to be forgiven for my performance as the Sheriff of Nottingham."

"Nay, I don't blame you. The lad's a handful. Everyone says it. But it doesn't help matters when you fill his head with adventure nonsense like your Robin Hood tales."

"Ach, you're gettin' stodgy in your old age, brother.

The stories are harmless. Every troubadour in the country sings of the exploits of the outlaw band. Anyway, 'tis what interests the boy. If you'd rather have Ultan's nose buried in ancient Latin tomes, you'll have to find him a tutor."

Cormac took another pull on his mug of ale. "Aye. 'Tis what I've been telling Claire. I'm thinking about sending to London, since no one from Kilmessen seems to be able to handle the lad."

"You'd have a bloody Englishman teach my nephew?"

Cormac shrugged. "A professional teacher. The boy will be head of this family one day. I'd like him to have a more formal education than I had. And mayhap 'twould not be a bad thing to learn more about English ways."

"Since the blackguards have taken over most of the estates in the south by now," Eamon agreed. "Though many say 'tis not a situation we should tolerate much longer."

Cormac pushed back his carved master's chair and rose with a sigh. "I mislike the thought of renewing the struggle. We've had more war than peace in our lifetime, and what good has it brought us? The English queen still sends her lords to seize our lands and meddle in our affairs."

"They'll never seize Riordan lands," Eamon said fervently.

"I warrant we've the backing of too many of the Midland families for them to try that," Cormac agreed. "Nonetheless, 'twill be good for you to visit the Riordan kin to be sure our support is solid."

"'Twould be good for Ultan to meet his family as well," Eamon said.

Cormac shook his head. "Nay, the boy's still too

young. A tutor's the solution for him. We just have to find one the little imp won't send packing."

Eamon swallowed the last of his ale, then stood beside his brother. "I wish you luck," he said. "Now to bed with ye! I swear if I had a woman like Claire awaiting me upstairs, I'd not be wiling away the evening getting drunk with my lout of a brother."

Cormac's grin was tired. "Ah, brother, 'tis little enough you know of the ways of the marriage bed. With three lively youngsters to herd all day, poor Claire is half asleep before we even finish the evening meal."

"Aye, and the flush on her fair cheeks when you two emerge from your room each morning is due to the sun coming in through the master windows, eh?"

Cormac's grin broadened. "I'll thank ye to keep your eyes off my wife's cheeks, flushed or otherwise, brother, lest I have to knock your head sideways on those square shoulders of yours."

Eamon reached over to cuff his brother's arm. "I'd never be disrespectful of Claire, and well you know it."

Cormac grabbed his brother's wrist and clasped Eamon's arm with his own. "I know. Claire loves you like her own brothers, and we both wish you a safe journey. Come back to us soon."

Eamon nodded, slightly self-conscious at his brother's sudden show of emotion. "I'll be back before the Christmas holidays. I'd not deprive the children of their visit from the Lord of Misrule."

Cormac briefly added his other hand to his grasp of Eamon's arm, then released him. "'Twould not be Christmas without you," he agreed.

Maura boosted herself up on the barrel in the corner of Giorgio's crowded wagon and tucked her legs underneath her. The perch was not quite as comfortable as it

had been when she was smaller, but it gave her a familiar sense of home and family. How many hours had she
sat there listening to Nonna's stories?

"Don't think that we're not pleased to have ye back,
Maura," Giorgio was saying. "'Tis just that we're worried." He sat across from her on a rough bench that was
built into the side of the unique wagon. Nonna was on
her bed, and Momo had a seat similar to Maura's on top
of some wooden boxes full of the few belongings the
family carried with them.

"Don't talk nonsense, Giorgio," Nonna said. Her
voice was reedy and weak, but the twinkle Maura remembered was still in her dark eyes. "We're pleased to
have her back, and that's an end to it."

"'Twill not be an end to it if Pietro decides he still
wants her," Giorgio said darkly.

Maura hunched over her folded legs, rocking
slightly. "I'm not afraid of Pietro anymore. I've grown,
and I've learned to care for myself. Besides, Pietro has
his own woman now. What's her name?"

Momo answered, "They call her Aislin."

"She's not Romany, then?"

"Nay, she's an orphan waif from Burley," Giorgio
explained. "I reckon she came with Pietro out of desperation because she had nowhere else to go."

Maura felt a pang of sympathy for the unknown girl.
She herself knew something about feeling desperate
and without choices in life. For one thing, it had turned
her into a horse thief and an assailant. Her thoughts
went back once more to the man she'd seen earlier that
day near Tara Hill. Over the years she'd managed to go
long periods without remembering that horrible day
when she'd turned into a true thief. But seeing her victim had brought it all back. The guilt would probably
never totally leave her, even though, like poor Aislin,

she'd felt she had no choice at the time. The horse had allowed her to get away from Pietro. The sale of the horse in Dublin had given her the money to live until she could find ways to make a living in the non-Romany world.

Maura looked around at the three dear faces in the wagon. Nonna and Giorgio had not undergone the transformation that Momo had, though both looked older. The always diminutive Nonna looked even smaller, and the sun-bronzed face Maura remembered was now pale. Giorgio had added some bulk to his stocky chest, and there were now streaks of silver in his black hair.

No doubt they all would be shocked to know what she had done in order to escape all those years ago. Giacomo's family of Romanies had always lived by the Kris, the strict moral code of her people. They took only what they needed, and they repaid in kind for anything they took.

"I must meet the poor girl," she said. "Is Pietro treating her well?"

She could see the doubt in all three of her companions' faces. Momo finally said, "He treats her like a servant, ordering her about at all hours of the day and night."

Giorgio's voice was grave. "I fear this is not the happy family it was when yer father was alive, Maura."

Tears filled Nonna's eyes. "I've told Giorgio that he needs to become head and force Pietro to leave, but he says 'tis not the Romany way."

"Pietro is family," Giorgio said.

" 'Tis like keeping a rotten apple in the barrel," Momo argued, with an angry glance at his father. "Eventually 'twill poison all of us."

Maura was silent for a long moment. She'd come

back to the family for selfish reasons—to find out about her own mother—but now she wondered if another destiny had brought her back. Her father would be heartsick to see what had become of the family he had led so well for so many years.

"I'll talk with this Aislin," she said firmly, "and if Pietro is mistreating her, I'll deal with him."

"'Tis time someone did," Momo agreed, with another glance at his father.

Giorgio looked uncomfortable. "Both of ye are too young to understand tradition. Pietro is the leader, and he must be respected."

"I'm not too young," Nonna argued. "And I say when the leader is not setting a good example, 'tis up to the members of the family to tell him so. If Maura's come back to help us, then we should be behind her."

"I'm with ye, Maura," Momo said, jumping down from his seat on the boxes. "Come, I'll introduce ye to her. To Aislin," he clarified with a flush.

Maura noted his expression with wonder. Was Momo old enough to be infatuated with a young woman? She answered her own question. Of course he was. But *Pietro's* woman? She felt a shiver of disquiet.

"It's getting late," she said. "We'd best wait until morning."

Momo was insistent. "None of us have seen Aislin for two days. I'd like to know that she's all right."

Maura looked at Nonna, who nodded. "'Twould not hurt to go meet the child."

Without further argument, Maura slid off the barrel and followed Momo to the wagon at the end of the semicircle. Her sense of dread increased with every step. She'd been so happy all day at the thought of seeing her family again, but suddenly she felt a premonition that her return to Tara Hill would bring some kind of disaster to the once close-knit band her father had so loved.

As if confirming her fears, Momo turned to her as they reached Pietro's wagon and whispered, "Pietro will not like us coming here."

"I've come to see Aislin, not Pietro," Maura answered with more calm than she was feeling.

Momo knocked on the closed door of the wagon. When there was no response after several moments, he knocked again and called, "Pietro!"

After a third try Maura lost patience and pushed past him to grasp the door latch. "There may be some reason he doesn't want us to see her," she said, remembering the bruise she'd had for days after Pietro had knocked her to the ground for refusing his advances.

She pulled the door open and peered inside. Pietro was sitting against the far end of the wagon, holding a jug of ale to his lips. On the wagon's narrow cot was a slight girl with hay-colored hair and a thin, pale face. With alarm, Maura noted that the girl's lips were bluish, and there was a pile of bloody rags at the foot of the bed.

"What have ye done to her, ye bloody bastard?" Momo cried from behind Maura.

Pietro took a drink from his bottle, then said, "I've done nothing. She's just lost the brat she was carrying. "'Twas not my whelp—she already had it when she came here."

The girl turned her face toward the wall as if hiding shame. Maura climbed into the wagon and went to sit next to her. "You poor thing," she said. She turned angrily to Pietro. "Why didn't you ask some of the women for help?"

He shrugged. "She didn't want anyone to know. 'Twas her choice."

Maura reached to take the girl's chin and turn her back to look at her. "Don't worry," she told her gently. "You don't need to go through this alone. No one here will blame you, Aislin. I'm going to help you. My name's Maura."

"I know," the girl said in a barely audible voice. Her gaze flitted briefly to Pietro, then she looked again at Maura. "Thank you," she whispered.

Maura had never dealt with a human miscarriage, but she'd seen them in the horses she'd cared for. Within moments she'd cleared Pietro and Momo out of the wagon and recruited the help of Nonna and Zara, one of the few remaining women in the camp. Though Nonna was little physical help in her own frail state, the experience of her many years and her calm manner helped as the three women tended to the sick girl and made her comfortable.

It was nearly dawn before Maura climbed wearily out of Pietro's wagon. She'd sent Zara and Nonna to bed earlier, but had stayed beside their patient until she was satisfied that the girl had fallen into what seemed to be a normal sleep. Maura herself had been up walking since before dawn, and she could feel the exhaustion in her back as she turned to make her way to Giorgio's wagon.

"Will she live?" asked a voice out of the dark.

Maura turned to see Pietro sitting on the ground, his back leaning against the big red wagon wheel. Maura was surprised that he had stayed awake out of evident concern for the woman he had taken into his life, but his next words dispelled any charitable feelings.

"If so, 'twill be a miracle. The stupid wench must've bled for a full day without telling anyone."

"You could've fetched Nonna," Maura accused.

"She didn't want a fuss."

"So you let her almost die."

She could see him shrug in the dark. " 'Twas what she wanted."

Maura was too tired to argue or to tell Pietro what she thought about his neglect. She turned to leave, then froze as he continued softly, "I reckon the little baggage won't be much good to a man for a while. I'll be needin' to find myself a new woman."

Maura's stomach did a flip-flop as she remembered that tone of voice from years before. She whirled back around to face him. "Whatever the circumstances, you took that girl in. Now she's your responsibility. You'd better concentrate on seeing that she gets well and forget about your own base needs."

It was too dark to see the expression on his face, but she knew what it was. It was the same smile that had haunted her dreams for seven years.

Willing herself not to lose control, she turned away from him and forced herself to walk at a normal pace back to Giorgio's wagon.

Eamon sat up in his bunk so swiftly that he nearly cracked his head on the low ceiling of the bunk just above him. It was the middle of the night, and the *Seawitch* had been at sea for several hours, but it wasn't the sudden choppiness of the channel that had awakened him.

He'd been dreaming, though the scene had been as real as it had been that morning seven years ago when the little horse thief had brought the stone crashing down on his head. But this time the face of the thief was not the dirty urchin he remembered from that morning. It was the face of the beautiful woman he had seen yesterday in the woods—the one who had rescued him from his embarrassment and had then disappeared like some kind of ghost.

"She was the one!" he said, clapping a hand to his mouth as he realized that he'd spoken the words aloud. He froze in the darkness, hoping that he hadn't awakened any of the ship's officers who were sharing their quarters with him.

After a few moments when the only sound he heard was gentle snoring, he relaxed and lay back against the bed. Could it be true? he wondered. He'd always held out the hope that he'd encounter his young assailant again, but somehow he hadn't considered that in all this time she would have changed. He certainly had never imagined that she'd grow into a mature woman with rounded breasts and high cheekbones and liquid blue eyes the color of the sky. Naked underneath the thin ship's blanket, he could feel himself swelling at the memory.

He whispered an oath. There was no doubt that the woman was beautiful enough to fire the blood of any man, but who the hell was she? She was a thief, he reminded himself. Perhaps worse. She could have killed him with that rock. How many others had she bashed on the head and robbed?

There was no doubt about it—she was a dangerous, conniving thief, who had probably cultivated that considerable female allure in order to attract more victims. God's blood, it would attract him readily enough, if he didn't know the truth about her.

Ignoring the insistent throb of his now thoroughly aroused body, he turned toward the wall and forced himself to close his eyes.

Aislin was slow in recovering from losing her child. Maura suspected that the girl had not been well-nourished to begin with, and the strain on her body of losing the baby had added to her poor condition. Fortunately, Pietro appeared to be behaving himself. He'd not followed through on his threat to go looking for another woman, and had kept out of Maura's way when she'd come each day to his wagon to care for his ailing mistress.

"An angel come to earth is what ye are," Aislin told her on the fourth day after the miscarriage. Her faded blue eyes were shining with gratitude.

"I'm no angel, Aislin, just a friend," Maura told her. "I know what it is to be without friends in this world."

"Ye've not told me yer story. Pietro said that ye ran away from the band after yer father died, but ye don't seem to me like the runnin' kind. What was it that caused ye to leave?"

Maura hesitated. Part of her wanted to warn Aislin that the man she had chosen to be her savior was in reality as dangerous as whatever life she had come from— the life that had left her alone and with child. Yet the girl appeared content with Pietro and seemed not to notice his lack of attention.

"I reckon I was running from a lot of things," she answered finally. "I was near crazed with grief when I lost my father."

"Momo told me that your mother is also dead."

"Momo?"

"Aye, he comes to talk with me sometimes."

Maura hoped that Momo was careful about spending too much time with Pietro's woman. She resolved to talk with the boy about it.

Turning her attention back to her companion, she said, "Aye, my mother died long ago."

"Momo says that she wasn't a Gypsy. She was a Gajo like me."

Maura smiled at her friend's use of the Romany word for anyone who was not one of them. "Aye, she was a Gajo."

"Did ye not know her, Maura? Or her people?"

"Nay. My father never knew where she had come from. He only knew that he had met her at Tara Hill and that she was the most beautiful thing he'd ever seen in his life. He fell in love with her instantly and never stopped loving her until the day he himself died."

Aislin sat propped on pillows on her narrow cot. She shook her head sadly. "Love can be very sad, can't it?"

"So Nonna tells us in her fanciful tales. For myself, I wouldn't know, and I have no interest in finding out."

Both young women giggled, and for a moment they were like little girls sharing a secret. Aislin reached out a hand and Maura took it. "I'm so glad you're here, Maura," she said. "Every time I talk with you, I feel a little better."

"You've color in your cheeks now. Before long you'll be up and about again."

A slight shadow crossed the younger girl's face. "Aye."

"Is something wrong?" Maura asked.

"Nay, 'tis just—" The girl appeared to be considering, then stopped and shook her head. "Nay, 'tis nothing. Anyway, I'm glad you've come back."

Maura was glad, too, she decided as she made her way from Pietro's wagon and headed down to the stream. It was wonderful to be with Nonna and Giorgio and Momo again, and she had the feeling that Aislin could become a good friend.

It was nearly dark, but she had time for a quick bath before starting to help Giorgio and Momo with supper. She knew that the others in the camp thought her frequent bathing was strange, but after years in the filth and grime of the city with no way to get clean, she'd resolved that once she returned to the country, she'd never be dirty again.

She was humming as she approached the water, a Romany song that her father used to sing. One of the joys of her homecoming had been the recapturing of all the lovely folklore of her people—the rousing ballads, the haunting love songs, the adventure stories and poems. Her father had been a masterful storyteller, and Nonna was almost his equal. Maura had loved them all, and had missed the long evenings by the firelight sharing the Romany magic.

She swayed as the music took her into a tale of a love lost and a betrayal avenged. The words wove themselves into her mind so firmly that she failed to see Pietro sitting on a rock overlooking the stream. "I've been waiting for ye," he said as she walked directly beneath him.

She gave a little start of surprise and looked up. "Aislin is better," she told him, struggling to regain her composure.

He jumped down from the rock, landing directly in front of her. "I don't care about Aislin," he said. His voice had the oily tone she dreaded.

"She's the only thing I care to discuss with you, Pietro. So if you're not interested, I'll be leaving."

She turned to walk away from him up the path, but he grabbed her arm and pulled her back. "'Tis ye I want, Maura. I've always wanted ye, and now I intend to have ye."

His face was bent close to her, his mouth set in a determined smile. She pulled with all her strength and freed herself from his grasp, then brought her hand up to slap him across the face. "I should have warned you,

Pietro. I'm no longer the helpless young girl you once attacked."

He took a step back, rubbing his cheek, but his smirk only broadened. "So be it. I like my encounters rough." He leaned close to her. "And will ye scream when I take ye?"

Maura swallowed down a wave of sickness. "I'll scream for help, Pietro, as I should have done all those years ago instead of running. Shall I scream now? Shall I bring the rest of the camp to see just how evil you are?"

Pietro's smile faded. "Are ye willing to risk yer friends just to preserve yer precious honor?"

"You may be the strongest man in camp, but you can't stand up to everyone. 'Tis time we got together to end your bullying. We'll fight you, if need be."

Pietro's eyes narrowed to crafty slits, and his tone became silky. "Why, Maura, I don't intend to fight anyone. I'm the leader of this family, remember? 'Tis my place to see to everyone's welfare."

She looked at him, confused. "If you want to see to everyone's welfare, then you'll leave me alone."

Pietro looked as if he hadn't heard her. " 'Tis a heavy burden to be responsible for everyone. Especially when one member of the family is an old lady who could easily fall and stumble the next time she walks out in the woods to tend to her needs. And one is a callow boy whose temper ignites all too easily when he sees me enforce some necessary discipline on my woman."

Maura felt a bitter taste at the back of her throat. "What are you saying, Pietro?" she asked, but she already knew the answer. She had thought that she would be able to handle Pietro if he tried to renew his attentions to her. But she hadn't considered that her return to the camp could cause problems for the others.

"I think ye understand me, Maura, my little pet." He reached his hand out and caressed her cheek. "I'm the leader here. If I'm happy, then the family is happy. If I'm not happy, then"—he shrugged—"who knows what may happen?"

"My father's fears were right, Pietro. You're not fit to be head of this family."

Pietro turned and started walking away from her. "I'm in no hurry, Maura. Ye may have some time to think about it. But in the end I will have ye. Or ye won't like the consequences."

Maura watched him walk up the path to the camp, whistling the same tune she'd been singing so happily only moments before.

Three

After her encounter with Pietro, Maura had lain awake much of the night, trying to decide what she should do. Finally, in the hazy hours of early morning, she'd been comforted with the clearest vision of her father she'd had in years.

He'd looked at her with the buoyant smile that had brought so much joy to his little band, and then he'd repeated the advice she'd heard so often when he was alive. "When you need an answer to a hard question," he'd tell her, "go to the most quiet place deep inside your heart. The answer will be waiting for you there."

The memory of his warm, calming voice had brought her peace, and when she had looked into the quiet deep inside herself, she'd known that she had to leave the family that had once been his. She had no doubt that Pietro was capable of carrying out the threats he'd made. But beyond that, she had the strong sense that she no longer belonged here. The family her father led was no more. This was Pietro's family now, and it had no place for her.

Once the decision was made, she was able to get a couple hours of sleep before she awoke to the sound of Momo stirring. She waited until he left, then she sat up, collected her few things, and quietly climbed out of the wagon.

Outside in the campsite Momo was crouched down, building up the fire from the previous evening. He smiled at her, but the smile faded as he saw that she held the small bundle she'd carried the day she arrived. "What are ye doing up so early?" he asked, his face somber.

She walked toward him. "You may already know, my friend," she told him with a twist of her mouth. "You've always known what I was going to do before I did myself."

Slowly he straightened and stood facing her. "Ye're leaving again."

"Aye," she said.

His black eyes flashed as he glanced toward Pietro's wagon at the end of the row. "What's he done to ye?"

"Nay, Momo, 'tis not like that. Pietro hasn't touched me, I swear it."

"Then he's threatened ye, or he's—" He broke off, helplessly.

She reached a hand out to him, and he took it in both his own. "I don't belong here anymore, Momo," she said gently. "I came back to find my father's family, but Giacomo's family no longer exists."

He held her hand so tightly that her fingers throbbed. "'Twill get better, Maura. My father thinks it's against the Kris to go up against Pietro, but I don't share his opinion. I've been waiting to act because Nonna's been so sick, and I haven't wanted to—"

"Exactly," Maura agreed. "I don't want her to be upset, either, and if I stay, she will be. I'm sure of it."

"She'll grieve if ye leave."

"She has you and Giorgio. You were her world until I came back."

"She never forgot ye, Maura."

Maura felt a deep ache in the middle of her chest, but she kept her voice firm. "Momo, you must tell her that I've gone to look for my mother. Tell her that I'll soon return, if you think 'twill give her comfort."

Momo released her hand and took a step back. "But 'twill be a lie, won't it? This time ye're never coming back."

In the light of the day her choice did not seem as clear as it had seemed in the middle of the night. "Honestly, Momo," she said, "I don't know. I only know that something is telling me to leave here before bad things happen. Maybe once I've found a place to settle, I'll come back to tell you where I am. We'll see each other again. I'll see Nonna again. You can tell her that."

Momo studied her face for several moments. Finally he said with a slight smile, "I'll not have to tell her. Nonna always knows what's to happen, remember?"

The tightness in Maura's chest eased. She smiled back at him. "Aye, then perhaps she'll be the one comforting you. We'll leave it in the hands of the fates."

"Ye'll not wait to say goodbye to her?"

Maura shook her head. "I want to be gone before—" She paused, considering her words. She'd awakened with an urgency to be gone before Pietro could find some way to stop her from leaving. But she didn't want to say anything that would cause Momo to go up against the ruthless Gypsy leader. Finally she said simply, "Call me a coward, if you like, but 'twill be easier to leave before the others wake up."

Momo looked to the east, where the bright orb of the sun was just appearing above the trees. "Ye'd best be getting on, then," he said. He averted his eyes, and she could see his pain in the deliberate set of his jaw.

She went up on tiptoe to plant a kiss on his cheek. Her eyes swept the little circle of wagons one last time. "Take care of them, Momo," she whispered.

His gaze shifted to meet hers for a long moment. Then he nodded. "I will."

Maura stepped around him and started across the clearing. When she reached the trees, she paused and looked back at the little camp through a blur of tears. Momo gave a forlorn little wave.

Once again she was stealing away with the first rays of dawn, leaving her friends for the uncertainty of a world that she already knew to be anything but friendly. She drew in a long breath, then turned quickly and headed into the woods.

By afternoon she was already regretting her decision. She'd acted impulsively. Her father always used to say that it was her one fault. "Are you with me, Papa?" she whispered, looking into the quiet waters of the small pond at her feet.

After several hours of walking, she'd come across a sheltered clearing in the middle of thick woods on top of one of the hills south of the plains of Tara. The coolness of the place had seemed inviting after a day in the sun, and she'd decided to sit there. Perhaps she'd stay the night, though she had already finished the little bit of bread and cheese she'd brought with her from the camp.

She'd be hungry by morning if she didn't move on to a place where she could spend one of her precious coins to buy more food. Still, she lingered by the tranquil pond in the middle of the glen. There was a crumbling stone ruin on the far side of the water, directly across from where she was sitting. It appeared to be some kind of altar, perhaps left from the ancient times when Druids met under the moon.

In her life with the Gypsies, she'd often felt more drawn to those ancient worship sites than she did to the present-day churches and the priests with their superior airs who were so quick to condemn the old Romany beliefs.

A slight breeze sent a ripple across the water, and Maura felt a corresponding tremor along her back. "Is it you, Papa?" she asked again. "Are you frowning at me for leaving without saying goodbye to Nonna?"

It *had* been cowardice, she decided. She'd returned to the Gypsy camp because she'd been certain that she could face up to anything Pietro might do to her. But she hadn't known what it would feel like to worry about someone else's safety. That was new, and she hadn't dealt with it well.

"You would have known what to do about Pietro," she said to the water.

"Are you talking to yourself or a faerie?" asked a young voice from a few feet behind her.

She turned around with a start. The speaker was a boy of about eight or nine years. He had black hair and dark eyes that shone with intelligence. She smiled at him. "I suppose I was talking to myself," she answered.

He nodded and walked toward her. "I only wondered because there are faeries here, some say."

"Ah, well, I can see that this might be a place where they'd like to come. 'Tis a lovely spot."

The boy nodded and, without asking, sat down beside her on the slight bank. "It's called Cliodhna's Glen," he told her.

"Cliodhna, the goddess?"

"Aye. I believe she comes here herself sometimes, though my father says 'tis fanciful thinking."

"There's nothing wrong with fanciful thinking, if you ask me," Maura answered. She could already tell that the child was more thoughtful than most youngsters his age.

He smiled at her for the first time. "'Tis the first time I've ever heard an adult say that."

"The way I see it, if it's fancy, then 'tis in your mind. And Nonna, who is one of the wisest adults I know, always used to tell me that anything the mind can imagine is possible."

The boy's eyes widened. "Do you believe that?"

"Aye," she answered. "Though sometimes 'tis hard to keep that belief." She hadn't held enough belief in her own possibilities to stay with the Gypsies.

"What do they call you?" the boy asked.

"Maura. And you?"

"Ultan. For my grandfather who was killed before I was born."

"'Tis a proud name, then."

That seemed to please him. "Aye. One day I'll be chief of the clan like he was and like my father is now."

Maura was starting to get the idea that the boy came from a powerful family. She should probably leave before any of his relatives came looking for him. She knew from past experience that people were never happy to find Gypsies around their children. It was one of the reasons that she had rarely admitted to her Romany origins in the years she had lived away. She supposed once again she would have to keep that secret, though it galled her. She was proud to be Romany, as her father had been and his father before him. She was every bit as proud of her heritage as the boy sitting next to her was of his.

"Chief of the clan, eh? That will be a big responsibility," she said, looking down at the slender boy. She remembered well when Momo was that age, with those same big eyes that were so full of ideas and plans and questions that they were never quiet. "So tell me, Ultan. What are the things you would like to do when you become head of your family?"

The boy's jaw dropped. "Do you really want to know?" he asked.

"Of course."

"In truth, I have a lot of ideas. For one thing, I'd have a regular meeting of all the kin. . . ." The words tumbled out as if he'd been saving up his thoughts, waiting for someone to be interested enough to tell. She listened intently, occasionally nodding to express particular approval.

When the rush of words trickled to a halt, she pronounced solemnly, "You'll be a wise leader for your family one day, Ultan. Your father and mother must be proud of you."

He looked a little doubtful, and his gaze shifted away from her toward the water. After a moment he said, "I warrant they would be if I wasn't such a bad boy."

Maura frowned. The child sitting beside her appeared to be lively, bright, sensitive, committed to his family and his future. She couldn't imagine what would cause him to think that he was bad. "What do you mean by a bad boy?" she asked carefully.

"It seems I'm always wanting to do something I'm not supposed to. I run away sometimes." He looked back at her warily, as if waiting to see the disapproval take over her expression.

"I run away, too, sometimes," she said.

"You do?" Once again he looked surprised.

She nodded. "I warrant we all run away at times. The

problem is that running away can cause pain to the people we run away from."

"Like my mother," he agreed gloomily.

"Aye. Like your mother. She loves you very much, Ultan, so if you run away, she's worried that she might lose you, and her heart begins to ache at the thought of never seeing you again."

"I thought she was mostly just angry with me."

"Nay, it might look like anger, but 'tis fear. And pain."

His face screwed up in an attempt to hold back tears. "I didn't mean for her to feel that way."

"Of course you didn't. You're a curious, lively boy and you want to see things and learn things. But I believe that you are also smart enough to be able to do all that in such a way that your mother doesn't have to suffer while you're learning. Don't you think so, too?"

He nodded. She could see a hard swallow travel the length of his thin neck.

"So does that mean you'd better be getting back home, Ultan?"

He waited another minute while he appeared to be recovering his composure. Then he said, "Aye, not home, but back to O'Donnell House. 'Tis my mother's family home. We came for a visit—my mother, my brother and sister and I. 'Tis not far."

"And you slipped away to visit your special glen?"

His thick black eyelashes swept guiltily downward. "Aye."

Maura stood, shook out her skirts, and reached a hand out to him. "It so happens that it's time for me to go, too, so how about if I walk with you as far as O'Donnell House?"

He smiled. "I'd like that. You can meet my mother."

Maura hesitated. Her natural instinct was to refuse

his suggestion, but she had to return to the Gajo world at some point. She might as well stop avoiding it. "I'd be happy to meet your mother, Ultan, and tell her what a fine son I think she has."

The boy beamed. He took her hand and let her pull him up, then he continued to hold it as they began walking out of the clearing. "I think my mother will like you," he said happily.

Claire O'Donnell Riordan was the most beautiful woman Maura had ever seen. She'd had three children, yet her figure was as slender as a girl's. Her near-violet eyes were warm and kind.

"How can I repay you, mistress?" she asked as she scooped Ultan up in her arms and hugged him. He squirmed with slight embarrassment until she set him down.

"There's nothing to repay, Lady Riordan," Maura answered, keeping her tone light and poised. Growing up, she had been told to keep away from Gajo people, which had made her self-conscious when she had first been out among them. But with practice, she had learned how to move in their world, speak their language, and maintain the air of confidence that was necessary to be accepted as one of them. "I was merely walking this way, and Ultan kindly let me accompany him home," she told the woman with a smile.

Claire's grateful look showed she understood that Maura had deliberately accompanied Ultan to be sure he reached home safely. Now that her relief in seeing him was ebbing, her tone to her son became more reproachful. "Where did you run off to, Ultan? Your grandfather Raghnall was just about to send out his men looking for you."

"I wanted to see if Cliodhna had come back to her glen," the boy answered, his eyes down.

"Now, sweetling," his mother said gently, "you know your father has said that's unlikely."

Ultan lifted his gaze to his mother's face and observed in a brighter tone, "Maura says that anything the mind can imagine is possible."

Claire looked over to Maura. "Maura? That is you?" she asked.

Maura gave a little curtsy such as she had seen in the big city. "Aye, my name is Maura." As Claire appeared to be waiting for more, she continued. "That is— Maura . . . Maura Roman."

Claire's smile was bright. "And I'm Claire Riordan. I'm so pleased to meet you." She reached a hand down to smooth her son's disheveled hair back from his forehead. Addressing him, she said, "I think what Mistress Roman told you was very wise, Ultan. I hope you will remember it. But that doesn't excuse you for running off without telling anyone. Do you know how worried we've been?"

The boy gave a grave nod. "Aye, I do. Maura says that when I run away, your heart hurts you."

Claire smiled. "Well, she's right."

"So I've determined that I'm not going to do that ever again."

Claire looked over at Maura with amazement. "It appears I owe you more than one debt."

Maura shook her head. She crouched down to look directly into Ultan's eyes. "And will you also remember what I told you about what a fine leader I think you're going to make for your family some day?" she asked him.

"Aye," he said. "I'll remember."

She nodded and started to rise, but before she could

do so, Ultan put his thin arms around her neck in an embrace.

Claire watched the exchange thoughtfully. When Maura had stood and was ready to turn to leave, she asked her, "Might I inquire a bit more about you, Mistress Roman?"

Maura looked up warily. This was the time when she became cautious, the time when her Gypsy background might be revealed, bringing with it unfair accusations of all sorts. "Aye, milady," she answered.

Claire asked her if she was in the neighborhood visiting friends or family, and when Maura answered negative to both questions, she pressed further. "My son seems so taken with you. Have you had employment working with children before?"

The question was not what Maura expected, but as the woman asked it, she felt a shifting in her midsection, as if her reply was going to be of major importance in the course of her life. The calling of destiny, Nonna would say.

"Do you mean like a nurse?" she asked carefully.

"Ultan is too old for a nurse, of course, but he is in need of a tutor."

"Could she, Mama?" Ultan burst out, jumping up and down in excitement. "She would be ever so much better than those dull men from Kilmessen."

Claire looked from her son to Maura, her expression doubtful. Though she spoke aloud, she appeared to be going over the arguments in her own head. "'Twould not be customary to have a woman, of course. Cormac has been saying for a while now that he would arrange something, but so far he's done nothing about it. The boy's obviously taken with you."

The odd, shifting sensation in her midsection became stronger. "I have had some experience with children," she said quickly. It wasn't such a lie, she told herself. She had spent endless hours with Momo, teaching him the Gypsy ways, telling him the old tales.

Claire's face brightened. "And you read, of course?"

Maura could feel the heat rising from her neck, but she managed to keep her expression even as she agreed, "Of course." She couldn't believe she'd uttered such a monstrous lie. How long did she expect such a thing to keep from being revealed?

Ultan gave another little jump. "I want Maura to be my teacher, Mama. And I promise, I double swear, that I'll never run away again."

Claire already appeared to be having second thoughts about the impulsive idea, but she gave Maura a nervous smile and asked, "And—er—your family background? That is, how is it you're here alone?"

The first lie had been difficult. The second was easier. "My father was a village schoolmaster, milady," she said. Was that a genteel enough occupation for a fine family like the Riordans? she wondered. "I—er—he left me little when he died, and I've had to make my way in the world." That much, at least, was true.

Claire gave her a last long study. Finally she asked, "Are you interested in a position, mistress? Would you like to become my children's tutor?"

Maura's stomach was definitely unsettled and there was a rushing behind her ears. Destiny, indeed, she thought with something akin to panic. Then she looked down at Ultan's excited face.

It was true. He was not that much different than Momo. She remembered how she had loved the hours she and the boy had spent together weaving the old tales into clever songs and poems. The ruse couldn't last, of course. Before long the Riordans would discover that she was no more a tutor than she was Queen of England. But for the moment it might work. It would give her a place to stay while she decided her next step. And it would give her time to be sure that her new young friend no longer thought of himself as a "bad boy."

"Aye, milady," she answered with a smile. "I'd very much like that."

Four

For Maura the days at O'Donnell House had gone by in a blur of happiness. The other two Riordan youngsters had proven as delightful as their older brother.

Dylan, the carefree seven-year-old, had Ultan's intelligence, but approached life with much less seriousness. Whereas Ultan thought hard about his family and the future, Dylan was more interested in watching the newly born bunnies his grandfather had penned at the back of the O'Donnell barn or exploring the countryside around Tara Hill.

The Riordan daughter, six-year-old Eily, had neither of her brothers' seemingly insatiable need for exploration. Dark-haired and with her mother's intense blue eyes, she was the darling of the household, yet was not the least bit spoiled by the attention. Like a flower taking in sunshine, she seemed to gracefully absorb all the love given her by her mother, her O'Donnell grandfather, her aunts and uncles, and she radiated the love back to them in full measure. Maura found it a marvel, especially in a child so young.

"Eily is a gift," Claire had told Maura. After only a few days in the little girl's company, Maura had to agree. She'd already come to love all three of the children, she realized with a touch of sadness as they said goodbye to the O'Donnell relatives and started out toward Riordan Hall. Surely this deception of hers couldn't last much longer. Most likely, as soon as she met Lord Riordan—the husband Claire talked of so fondly—she would be recognized as a fraud and sent on her way.

"You've been very quiet the whole trip, Maura," Ultan said, observant as always. "Are you ill? 'Tis not much farther."

She smiled at him. She was riding in a cart with the children while Claire had chosen to ride home on her own horse. Ultan and Dylan sat along the bench on the opposite side of the cart while Eily was curled up asleep, her head on Maura's lap. Maura's hand rested on the girl's soft hair.

"I may be a little nervous," Maura admitted. She'd discovered that whenever possible, it was best to tell Ultan the absolute truth. Which made it all the more difficult that she'd had to tell so many lies since her arrival at O'Donnell House.

"What are you nervous about? Meeting my father?"

As usual, Ultan's perception was acute. "A little, I warrant. Your mother herself admits that your father may not be pleased that she has hired a woman to tutor you children."

"Papa will like you," Dylan said, munching on a sweetcake that the O'Donnell cook had packed for the two-hour journey. "We like you and so he'll like you." In his young mind the logic was unshakable.

"I hope so," Maura said. She didn't want to trouble the children with her worries. She knew that her re-

maining time with them might be short, so she wanted
to enjoy it as much as possible.

"I'm a little worried, too," Ultan said abruptly.

This surprised her. "Worried that your father won't
like me?"

"Of course not. I'm worried because now that we're
going to be home again, Mother says we must start our
studies in earnest."

Maura had been relieved that Claire had suggested
that the real lessons wouldn't start until they had left
O'Donnell House. But now that they would be at Riordan Hall, she was sure that some kind of formal cur-
riculum would be expected. One that she couldn't
possibly hope to provide.

Dylan frowned. "Does that mean you won't be able
to tell us any more stories?" he asked Maura.

"I don't think so," Maura answered, though in reality she had no idea what the arrival at Riordan Hall
would bring. "Stories have always been considered a
good way of teaching."

Dylan finished his sweetcake and began happily
licking each one of his fingers. "I'm ever so glad. Your
stories are much better than when Master Tuttle tried to
teach us."

Eily was stirring and looked up with sleepy eyes.
"Are we home?" she asked, sitting up.

The cart had turned from the main highway onto a
rutted road lined on each side by a grassy bog, dry with
the brown and gold colors of autumn. At the end of the
raised pathway she could make out a large, turreted
house made of gray stone.

Ultan and Dylan had jumped up from their seat in
excitement. "Aye," Ultan told his sister. "There's Riordan Hall. Is it not a grand place, Maura?" he asked her,
beaming with pride.

"Aye, Ultan, very grand," she assured him, but her heart was sinking. She had never so much as been inside such a home. How could she possibly think that she could belong there?

Ultan seemed to sense her apprehension. He leaned over and gave her hand a squeeze. "Don't worry, Mistress Maura. You'll be happy here, and everyone will love you."

Her throat was too full to give him any answer but a smile.

Claire had ridden ahead of the cart carrying Maura and the children. She and Lord Riordan were both waiting on the front steps of Riordan Hall when the vehicle came to a stop at the end of the driveway. Claire had evidently told Cormac about Maura, since he did not seem surprised to see her with his children. He gave her a courteous nod of welcome, but his main attention was for the three youngsters. They jumped off the back of the cart in unison into his big arms, which easily managed all three, though Ultan and Dylan soon wiggled to the ground. Eily stayed in her father's embrace and happily allowed him to carry her up the entrance stairs.

Maura watched with a troubled smile as the father and daughter disappeared into the entrance hall. Lord Riordan was every bit as handsome as Claire had described, but something about his striking features seemed familiar.

"Come on in, Maura," Claire said, gesturing from the doorway. "Welcome to Riordan Hall."

Maura climbed the stairs slowly. There had been something about the way Cormac Riordan had smiled at her that triggered an alarm in her head. Had she met him before? she wondered. Surely he was not one of the men she had fended off on the waterfront of Dublin when she'd worked a short stint there in a tavern?

Then it came to her, and she could feel the blood draining from her face. She *did* know that smile, but it had not been on Cormac Riordan's face. It had been on the face of the man she had met in the woods the day she had arrived back at Tara Hill—the man she had previously knocked out while stealing his horse.

She reached the top of the stairs and swayed slightly. Claire gave her a look of concern. "Are you quite well, Maura?" she asked. "Did you become ill on the journey?"

"Nay." Maura put her hand on the doorjamb to steady herself. All at once it made perfect sense. That day in the woods, the man had mumbled about his nephews—adventurous lads who had left him in that compromised state. Who else would it be but the curious and restless Ultan and his little brother? The man had had a brother—she'd almost stolen the brother's horse as well, she remembered, before her conscience had made her return it.

Claire was watching her with concern. "We must get you to bed, my dear," she said, putting an arm around her shoulders.

Her kindness only made Maura more miserable. She could almost hear Nonna's cackling laugh those evenings around the campfire when she would look into the flames and say, " 'Tis beyond our powers to fight the twists and turns of fate. It takes us where it will, and just when we've thought to turn away, it takes us back again."

"I've told them to prepare your room," Claire was saying. "We'll put you right to bed with a mug of hot ale."

Cormac and the children were nowhere in sight, but

Maura needed no second look at the man to know that her assessment of the situation was correct. "Does Lord Riordan have a brother?" she asked Claire as she let the noblewoman lead her up the broad curving front stairway of Riordan Hall.

"Aye. He has two, Eamon and Niall. Niall's not here. He lives in Killarney on his wife's family lands."

Maura felt a brief surge of hope, but it died almost immediately. She'd seen her horse-thief victim at Tara Hill only a few weeks ago. "Where does his brother Eamon live?" she asked, anticipating the answer with a heavy heart.

"Here at Riordan Hall, normally, though he's not home, either, at the moment. He's on a journey."

Once again the hope surged. If her former victim would stay away, she could keep up the ruse for a while longer. Perhaps if she were here long enough, she would feel comfortable enough to ask Claire to help her make inquiries about her mother. It was a fantasy she'd begun developing as she lay awake at night, contemplating the turn of fortune that had brought her to the Riordans. If she could just find her mother's family, perhaps she could be truly accepted as one of these people.

They'd reached the top of the stairs, where a wide hall led to two different wings of the huge house. "Your room is in the east wing near the children," Claire said, turning left down the hall.

Maura followed her, feeling shaky. She straightened her shoulders trying to regain her calm. Why should she care? she asked herself, trying to put her predicament into the proper perspective. If Lord Riordan's brother came home, she'd simply slip away, as she had so many times in the past.

This time, however, the thought of leaving was painful. How had this family become so important to her in such a short time? she wondered.

Claire walked to the end of the hall and opened the door to a small room with a window at one end. "I hope you'll be comfortable here," she said.

Maura stepped into the room and looked around. It had a small fireplace with a settle to one side, a wash-stand, a large chest, and a tall, inviting bed puffed high with a feather quilt. Maura's eyes widened. "This is for me alone?" she asked.

Claire smiled. "You may find yourself with frequent visitors, if I know my children, but, aye, 'tis yours."

Maura closed her eyes and thought about the cramped quarters of the Gypsy wagons, the stuffy attics of the taverns where she had worked, the squalid poor-house where she'd been forced to live for months in Dublin one winter when she'd taken ill.

"Will it do?" Claire asked.

Maura opened her eyes and smiled at her mistress. "Aye, milady. I'm much obliged."

Claire nodded, then started to leave. "I'll leave you to rest then, Maura, but I'll have Molly the cook bring you up a tray of supper just in case you get hungry. She can answer any question you may have about the garderobe and such matters."

Then, with a final smile, she went out the door and shut it after her. Maura stood alone in her new quarters, still unable to believe that she had an entire room all to herself. Even at O'Donnell House, she'd slept in the servants' quarters with the other single women of the household.

There was a fire already burning on the grate. She walked slowly over to it and sat on the settle, feeling a little dazed. At O'Donnell House with Claire and the children, she'd been happier than she remembered being since the death of her father. Now the Riordans had welcomed her into their home and given her a room that would be very proper for one of their own kinsmen.

But the welcome was given under false pretenses. How long would it be before she would have to see Claire's smile turn to horror and disgust when she found out the truth about the young woman she'd entrusted with her children? Shall I run away again before they find out who I am? she asked, staring into the fire. Nonna used to say that the firelight spoke to her. But Maura heard nothing, and she saw no answer to her questions in the dancing flames.

Maura had thought that sleep would be difficult, but when she had finally left her seat by the fireside and climbed up into the big bed, she'd slept soundly. When she awoke, the sun showing through the room's tiny window was already high in the sky. ·

The tray that had been brought to her the previous evening by a smiling, roly-poly woman was sitting on the big chest, untouched. Last night her troubled thoughts had left her with no appetite. But now as she half-slid from atop the puffy mattress, she could feel her stomach rumbling in complaint.

She walked over to the tray, picked up a dried piece of bread, and began to gnaw on it while she made herself presentable for the day—her first and what could be her last day at Riordan Hall.

She'd come to O'Donnell House with only the frock she was wearing, making up yet another story for Claire about losing all her possessions. Claire and her sister, Eileen, had immediately found a number of dresses for her to wear.

At first it had seemed odd to be wearing Claire's fine clothes. But the dress she'd brought from the Gypsy camp was worn and tattered, and little by little she'd grown accustomed to the soft fabrics and fine fit of her new wardrobe.

She knelt beside the small trunk that had traveled in the cart with them from O'Donnell House and chose the brightest dress she could find—a brilliant blue. If this was to be her only day at Riordan Hall, she'd face it with a bold color.

Would she be expected to start the children's lessons immediately? she wondered. Swallowing down the last piece of bread, she took a deep breath and smoothed her dress with moist palms. There was no help for it, she told herself. It was, as always, in the hands of the fates. And it did little good to delay any longer finding out what they had in store for her.

Resolutely she opened the door to the hall. Sitting across the hall from her room like a trio of birds on a fence were her three students. When they saw her, they jumped to their feet. "Mama said we weren't to wake you, but we've been waiting here for you to wake up," Ultan explained.

"Waiting *ever* so long," Eily added.

Maura smiled. "You could have knocked on my door. I wouldn't have minded."

Dylan shot an angry look at his brother. "I *told* you so," he said.

"Mama said no," Ultan snapped back. He looked at Maura a little uncertain.

She nodded. "Aye, that's a good lad. If your mother says no, then you mustn't."

Eily skipped over to grasp Maura's hand. "We're to take you to Papa," she chirped.

Maura felt a roll of her empty stomach. "Now?" she asked.

Ultan nodded. "Aye. He's waiting for us in the library."

The trip from the east wing to the downstairs library at the back of the big house seemed long, but it wasn't for lack of lively companionship. The children chatted cheerily about their homecoming, detailing how each of their pet animals had fared in their absence, how Molly the cook had prepared suet pudding for dinner just to please them, how Aidan the stablemaster had declared that Ultan had grown so much he needed to find him a real horse to replace his pony.

Finally they reached the double doors of the Riordan library, a separate room that had been built on the west side of the house at the suggestion of the children's Uncle Eamon, who they evidently considered to be the scholar of the family. Ultan explained to Maura that while his uncle kept his collection of books, his father used the library mostly for household accounts and to meet with his bailiff and other household retainers. The information gave her a small ray of hope. If the children's father was not scholarly himself, it might be some time before he noticed her own lack of learning.

"Is your uncle Eamon away for some time?" she whispered to Ultan. But before he could answer, the doors to the library opened. Lord Riordan stood just inside the doorway, regarding them with his lively dark eyes and that crooked smile. He motioned the group inside.

"I hope they didn't disturb you this morning, Mistress Roman," he said to Maura. "Lady Riordan said you were not well after your journey."

"I'm fine," she assured him hastily. "And I find your children delightful. They would never be a disturbance."

One black eyebrow went up. "You might receive some argument about that around the estate," he observed with a twinkle in his eyes. "But I'm glad you feel that way. And they seem to be equally taken with you. 'Tis a happy situation, though a bit unconventional." He looked at her, his expression sobering. "My wife says that you have had experience teaching children."

Maura hesitated. "I've . . . er . . . I have, in fact, worked with a boy just about Ultan's age."

Cormac appeared to relax. "Ah, excellent." The children had left the two adults talking in the doorway and had made their way inside the room. While Eily watched, Dylan and Ultan were climbing a tall step stool that was propped up against the far wall where a number of leather books rested on a high shelf. Cormac turned around and shook his head. "Nay, the library is not a playfield, as well you know, boys."

"We're going to look at the Robin Hood book," Ultan told his father.

" 'Tis their favorite," Cormac told Maura. Then to the boys, he added, "Soon you'll be *reading* the Robin Hood book for yourself, lads. Mistress Maura can take it to the nursery for your reading lesson. But you must be careful with any of the books you use, or you'll have your uncle Eamon to reckon with. Now climb down from there."

Obediently the boys climbed down from the stool. Cormac turned back to Maura. "You may use any of those texts," he said, waving toward the shelf full of books. "Just take them one at a time. You'll have to watch how the children handle them. They've not yet learned the value of things."

Maura nodded, her gaze fixed on the bookshelf. There had to be at least thirty of them, she figured. Thirty books. She never in her life had so much as held one in her hands.

"It appears to be a wonderful collection," she said finally.

"Aye, 'tis my brother Eamon's pride. When you've read them all, he'll be pleased for the excuse to purchase new ones."

Eamon. She heard the name like some kind of guilty refrain in the back of her head. Brother Eamon. Uncle Eamon. The man she had robbed. "Er—when do you expect your brother to return, Lord Riordan?" she asked.

Cormac's face brightened. "I've a message from him this very morn. He's lingering in Dublin another week, then we should see him back here."

Forbidden to climb, the children had once again surrounded Maura like a ring of Maypole dancers. "Can we begin with Robin Hood, Mistress Maura?" Ultan asked, pulling on her hand. "It has wonderful drawings of Robin fighting the wicked sheriff."

"He whacks him with a pole," Dylan added.

"And Maid Marian," Eily contributed.

"He doesn't whack Maid Marian, silly goose," Dylan corrected her.

All three children began telling the story at once as Cormac threw up his hands and walked across the room to pull a big red book off the shelf. Giving it a quick dusting with his hand, he rejoined the group at the door and handed it to Maura. "It appears you have your first lesson prescribed for you, Mistress Roman. It might not be as scholarly as Latin and sums, but there's always time for that."

Maura took the heavy book from his hands and looked down at it with awe. In her world, stories came from people, not from books, but the idea that this cold, dry paper could contain the same magic that Nonna and her father had produced around their campfires was amazing and wonderful. Of course, she hadn't the slightest idea how she was supposed to extract that magic when she'd never read a word in her life.

"Much obliged," she said. Then she bobbed an awkward curtsy and let the children lead her away to the nursery.

"Nay, 'twas the *rain* that Lallah brought back, not the sun," Ultan argued to his brother.

Dylan looked at Maura, who nodded. "Aye, 'twas the rain."

"Tell us the story again, Mistress," Dylan said, his fine Riordan features marred by a frown.

"Aye," agreed Eily, clapping her hands. "Tell the story of Lallah."

Maura smiled at the threesome who sat grouped around her on the floor in front of the nursery fireplace. In an effort to change the room from a nursery to a schoolroom, Claire had had benches brought in and had put the children's playthings into two large trunks that were now pushed up against the wall at the end of the room. But Maura had found that the children preferred sitting beside her next to the cozy fire, rather than sitting at their benches. She herself found the position strangely comforting. It was almost as if she was back at the Gypsy camp, although now she was the one doing all the storytelling.

It had been three days since Lord Riordan had given her the Robin Hood book. She and the children had looked all through it, peering at each carefully inked drawing. When the children had been put to bed each night, she'd spent hours going over the scripted letters, and amazingly enough, she'd found that she could decipher a few of the words. She could recognize the name

Robin Hood, and she'd had the children try to spot it on each page.

But for most of their schoolroom time, she'd reverted to doing what she knew best—the stories and songs of her childhood, and so far, her pupils had been rapt with attention.

The story of Lallah was one of the children's favorites. As she began the by-now familiar tale, the children eagerly joined in the tale.

"Then Lallah went to find the rain," Maura continued.

"To the Land of the Moon and the Sea," Eily supplied.

"Aye, when she went to the Land of the Moon and the Sea, the sky began to whisper to her," Maura continued.

"And the wind," Dylan added.

"Aye, the sky and the wind. And after a time she realized that the sky and the wind were telling her stories."

"So she brought the rain back to her people, and she became a storyteller," Ultan finished.

Maura put her hands on her hips and said with mock sternness, "Now, if you all know the story already, why am I telling it to you?"

Eily stood and put her arms around Maura's neck. "We like the way you tell it, Mistress."

She was returning the little girl's embrace when a deep voice from behind her said, "I like the way you tell it, as well."

Maura turned around quickly, then felt the blood drain from her face. Standing in the doorway, his broad shoulders nearly filling the frame, was Eamon Riordan.

Five

"*Uncle!*" *the children* cried, jumping up in unison and racing across the room to their uncle's embrace.

"How are my three poppets?" he asked, lifting each one in turn for a squeeze.

"Did you see any pirates?" Ultán asked. "Did you bring back a sword?"

"Did you have a shipwreck?" Dylan added.

"Whoa! One at a time!" Eamon tried to concentrate on giving a proper greeting to his niece and nephews, but his mind was on the woman who sat still as a statue on the flagstone hearth.

When his sister-in-law Claire had told him about the wonderful new female tutor they had found for the children, he'd somehow suspected that it was none other than his mysterious apparition from the woods the day before he left on his journey—the same woman who had once stolen his horse and left him knocked out cold on the ground. He'd wasted no time in heading up to the nursery to confirm his suspicions.

If her pale face was any indication, the new tutor

seemed to realize that he had remembered who she was. What a brazen wench she must be to think she could come into his very household and teach his own nephews after what she had done to him.

The children were still vying for his attention.

"You three are to eat supper at the big table tonight," he told them, "and I've promised your papa and mama that I'll tell you all my tales. I've a little surprise for each of you, but you'll have to wait until then. Now, who is going to introduce me to your new teacher?"

Ultan and Dylan each grabbed one of his arms and dragged him across the room toward the woman, who still sat as if nailed to the ground.

"This is Mistress Maura," Ultan said proudly. "She tells wondrous stories, Uncle Eamon."

"Aye, so I was hearing." He looked down at her. "I've no doubt she's quite a storyteller."

Finally she moved, giving herself a little shake, then untangling her legs and rising. Her hands nervously smoothed down the sides of her blue skirt, but she held her head high and looked him directly in the eyes. "I'm pleased to make your acquaintance, Master Riordan," she said in a formal tone, as if she were lady of the manor.

The wench had courage, he'd give her that. And she was as beautiful as he remembered from that day in the forest. Her hair was neatly tucked away in a cap, but there was a sparkle in her blue eyes and a look of determination in the set of her full mouth.

"I'd thought you might not be so pleased," he said.

The color was flooding back into her smooth cheeks. "Children," she said, her voice giving no hint of any distress she might be feeling. "I believe we've finished the day's lessons. You may run outdoors for a few minutes before supper."

The children looked at Eamon. "We'll see you at supper, Uncle Eamon?" Ultan asked.

"Aye," he answered, smiling. "Now do as Mistress Maura says and go play outside until 'tis time." He waited until the three had barreled out of the room, the boys challenging each other to a race down the front stairs. Then he turned to their new teacher and said, "They are a lively crew."

"Aye, but they are dear children."

"We are in agreement on that point, Mistress . . . - *Maura*? Is that your real name?"

She nodded. She was still holding her chin high, emphasizing the tilt of her nose, but the light in her eyes had dimmed.

"I grant you I have limited experience with horse thieves, but 'tis my belief that they are not past using false names upon occasion. Is this—" He indicated the schoolroom with a wave. "Is this your real occupation, as well?"

She appeared to hesitate, then she lifted her chin even higher and said, "It is now."

His anger began to surge anew in the face of her continued calm. "It is when you are not stealing horses, don't you mean?" he demanded.

"Nay, 'tis not what I mean. I don't steal horses."

"And I suppose you're going to tell me that you don't make a habit of going around and bashing innocent victims on the head, either."

She continued to face him bravely, but he could see a distinct look of misery in her eyes. It almost made him feel a pang of sympathy until he forced himself to remember the exact circumstances of their first encounter. "I've always wondered if you intended to murder me that day," he said grimly.

When she didn't answer, he sauntered past her to one

of the new benches and sat, his legs sprawled in front of him. Then he looked up at her and said, "You're not going to deny that it was you."

She lifted a hand to her throat, which, he noticed, was still slender, not a likely candidate for a hangman's rope. "Nay, I won't deny what you already know to be true," she said after a long moment. "I was the one who took your horse."

"And coshed me on the head and left me for dead. Don't forget that part."

She shook her head. "I aimed for the neck, not the head. I didn't want to hurt you."

He smiled briefly. "Ah, you aimed for the neck. Shall I be thanking you, then?"

She stood in front of him straight and tall, without flinching. "Of course not. I did you a grievous wrong, but I had my reasons."

"Perhaps you'd care to share them with me." He was finding her composure increasingly irritating. Whenever he'd thought of the loss of his horse, he'd imagined what it would be like to find his little assailant again. This was not at all the picture he'd had of how it would be. The scene he had envisioned had the culprit remorseful and groveling and begging for mercy.

"Nay, I'd not care to share them," she said. "You'll have to accept my word that my case was desperate and the reasons were good ones."

He let out a snort of disbelief at her audacity. "Do you think that makes it right to steal?"

She cocked her head as though considering his question, then she made a wide motion with her arms. "You live in a fine house, Master Riordan. I trow you have many horses, equally as fine as the one you rode that day?"

"Aye, but—"

She continued without letting him speak. "At that time, on that particular day, I needed that horse more than you did. Some day you may need something, and if fate wills, 'twill be my duty to give it to you." Her face brightened. "I freed you from the tree that day, remember?" Then she paused, considering. "Though I warrant 'twould not yet be considered sufficient payback for a fine horse."

Eamon felt as if he'd just had another blow to his head. "You needed my horse more than I did?"

"Aye."

He looked up at her and shook his head in disbelief. "Truly, I've never met anyone like you. You steal my horse, then you come into my household and represent yourself as a teacher for my nephews and niece—"

"I didn't know 'twas your household. I'd not have accepted Lady Riordan's offer if I'd known."

He straightened up on the bench. He'd discovered what he'd come up to the nursery to learn. The new tutor was, indeed, a horse thief, or at least a former horse thief. She'd even admitted it. So why was he still sitting here discussing the matter with her? What was preventing him from dragging her downstairs and exposing her treachery to his brother and Claire? Nothing, he told himself firmly, getting to his feet.

Her big eyes regarded him gravely. The only clue to any agitation she might be feeling was the whiteness of her knuckles as she held her hands tightly clasped in front of her. She stood without moving like a prisoner at the dock awaiting sentence.

Eamon took in a deep breath. "My sister-in-law says that Ultan has become quite taken with you," he told her. "She says you've managed to make him behave, which I'm finding ironic, all things considered."

She loosened her lips long enough for a fleeting

smile. "Because I'm such a sinister character myself? I assure you, Master Riordan, my behavior on the day you first met me was not at all representative of my character."

Eamon shook his head in bewilderment. He'd just completed a long journey. He'd arrived home expecting to spend a peaceful evening playing with the children and catching up on all the mundane news of the estate. The last thing he'd expected was to find that a woman he knew to be a criminal had insinuated her way into his family and into the heart of his beloved nephew.

He hesitated so long that when he looked over at her, he could see that her expression had become slightly more hopeful. She was evidently intuitive as well as audacious.

"Do you continue to steal horses?" he asked dryly.

"I haven't stolen one for weeks," she answered with a hint of a smile.

He scowled back at her. "You may not have meant to kill me, but my neck was sore for days," he said. The words came out sounding peevish.

"I apologize. Truly," she added.

How could she stand there without moving so much as a muscle, he asked himself, when he felt jumpy all over?

"If I refrain from telling my brother about you right now," he said finally, "it doesn't mean I won't tell him eventually."

"Aye, I understand."

"Nor that I've forgiven you. Rioga was a good horse and worth a lot of money."

"Six pounds ten," she answered.

"I beg your pardon?"

"Six pounds ten. 'Twas the sum they paid for your horse in Dublin."

Eamon stared at her, incredulous. "And you simply stand there and tell me that?"

"Aye. 'Tis the debt I owe you, in this world or the next. Six pounds ten. Minus freeing you from the tree."

Eamon's head had begun to pound. He'd awakened well before dawn in order to reach home early. "We're not finished with this, mistress," he said. "But I'd not mar my homecoming by disappointing my nephews and niece with the news that their tutor is a criminal."

She nodded, but offered no thanks.

"I warn you," he admonished sternly. "Don't try your thieving tricks in this household, or I will see that you're turned over to the sheriff."

Her only answer was another nod.

Eamon studied her, hoping that he wasn't making a mistake. She didn't appear sinister, but then, he'd thought the same thing the day she had hit him with the rock. He gave one more exasperated shake of his head, then turned to leave the room.

Maura waited until the schoolroom door had closed behind him, then she sank down on the hearth. She'd managed to maintain a pretense of calm as she had stood in front of him, but now that he'd left, she could feel the trembling beginning deep inside her.

She should have packed her things and left before Eamon Riordan had ever arrived home, but each day she'd told herself that she might have one more day to be part of this wonderful household. Now Eamon had surprised her by arriving ahead of schedule, but miraculously, it appeared that he wasn't ready to expose their past history. What made him decide to protect her? she wondered. He had every reason to be resentful, even to hate her.

Perhaps he'd merely told her that he wouldn't expose her in order to put her off guard. Perhaps he was this very minute sending for the magistrate to take her away for trial. But somehow she didn't think so. Eamon Riordan had a directness in his dark eyes that told her that he was not a man for subterfuge or falsehoods.

Little by little the quaking in her middle subsided. *'Twas fate made me choose Eamon Riordan's horse to steal,* she told herself, *and fate that brought us together all these years later*. She would wait to see what fate had in mind for the next act of her life's play.

With that decision, she stood again, and headed off to round up the children for supper.

"So you met Mistress Roman?" Cormac asked as the two sat down at the Riordan dining table.

Eamon glanced at his brother to see if there was any special emphasis behind the words, but Cormac's expression indicated that the question was straightforward. "Aye," he answered. "I met her. She was telling the children a story."

"She seems to tell a lot of stories," Cormac observed with a slight frown. "I've yet to see much evidence of hard studies, though I suppose they are still getting to know each other. Mayhap that 'twas the problem with the tutors from Kilmessen. They tried to do too much too soon."

"If she does nothing but tell stories, 'tis no wonder the children like her," Eamon said, his tone harsher than he intended. He was feeling guilty for not telling his brother what he knew about the new teacher. After all, these were his brother's *children*. Cormac would no doubt be furious to think that Eamon had allowed them to continue in the company of a thief.

"She's teaching them to read, as well. I've seen them going over the Robin Hood book." Claire's voice came from the doorway and Cormac turned around with a smile of welcome. His face as he watched her enter held an expression of love that hadn't altered in the nine years of their marriage. Even though Eamon had seen it many times, the look never stopped amazing him. It made Cormac cease to resemble the authoritative, headstrong older brother he'd known when he was growing up.

"Teaching them to read, is she?" Cormac asked. "Excellent. It appears you made a wise decision after all, my dear, in spite of my doubts."

Claire walked to the head of the table and planted a kiss on her husband's cheek before she sat in the chair he had pulled out for her. "I trust it doesn't gall you to admit that women can be as wise as men, husband?" she asked him sweetly.

Eamon smiled. He enjoyed watching the banter between the lord and lady of Riordan Hall. They managed to spar without either one giving quarter, yet since the early days of their marriage when they'd had a family feud and various other problems to sort out, he'd never seen true anger between them. He loved them both dearly, and he loved their three children equally as much. He'd never do anything to cause any of them hurt, which was why he couldn't get his mind off the decision he had made to stay silent about Maura.

"Did you check on Mistress Roman's background before you employed her, Claire?" he asked abruptly.

She looked up at him in surprise. "She's told me something about herself, the poor thing. Her father was a village schoolmaster. Both her parents are gone now and she's alone in the world. I trow 'tis a blessing for her as well as for us that she happened on Ultan that day at Tara Hill."

There was a commotion on the stairway as the children clattered down. "Pray, don't speak of it further,"

Claire said hurriedly. "I've asked her to join us at the table with the children tonight."

Eamon gave an inner groan. The peaceful home-coming supper he'd anticipated during his long day's ride was not going to be possible if he had to spend the meal sitting across from his former assailant. His beautiful former assailant, he corrected as Maura walked into the room holding Eily's hand.

Jesu. She was dressed for evening with her hair loosely arranged in a thick braid. He recognized her dress as an old one of Claire's that his sister-in-law had abandoned with a good-natured complaint that child-birth had enlarged her bosom. The low-cut frock molded to Maura's trim breasts perfectly. Claire motioned her to a seat directly across from Eamon.

Eamon studied her from across the table as she spread her skirts and sat. The feeling that he had had in the schoolroom of her standing at a prisoner's dock was gone. She moved gracefully and appeared to be totally relaxed, as though she had dined at the master's table of a great manor every day of her life.

Her father was a schoolmaster, Claire had said. Yet when she was still little more than a child, she'd been desperate enough to steal his horse. Eamon frowned. Mistress Maura was a mystery, he decided. And for the sake of his brother and his brother's children, it was a mystery that he would do well to solve.

"Did you not hear the question, Eamon?" Claire was asking.

"I beg pardon, sister," he said, suddenly aware that he had been staring rudely across the table.

"I asked if you heard any news of further English encroachments when you traveled north," Cormac repeated.

Eamon reached for his mug of ale to take a long,

steadying drink and gather his thoughts before answering. His mind had been on the new tutor, not on the war. " 'Tis peaceful for the moment, but no one expects it to stay that way. There's talk of a new rebel movement, trying to gather the remains of the forces that fell apart after the O'Neill's death."

"Which families are behind it?" Cormac asked, leaning toward Eamon with intense interest.

Maura sat back on her chair and watched as the two brothers launched into a discussion of the possibilities for a renewal of the conflict that had racked Ireland for years. She recognized some of the family names, but she understood little of the background of the struggle. For the Romanies, it made little difference if the Irish ruled or the English. The Romanies themselves would still be outcasts, never accepted by the regular populace.

"It may depend on who finds the O'Neill's gold," Eamon was saying.

"Is it a chest of Spanish gold like the buccaneers' treasure?" Ultan asked, abandoning the rule that children should be silent at the table.

Eamon turned to his nephew with a smile. "I reckon 'tis much like a buccaneer's treasure, lad," he confirmed. "In fact, your father and I were with the O'Neill in the rebel camp when he received the gold years ago, before you were born. That was after your mother helped to save it from being captured by the English. Did you know that your mother was a heroine to the rebel cause?"

Ultan looked over at his mother with wide eyes. Maura herself gave her employer a surprised look. Claire seemed so settled as lady of the manor and mother to her children. It was difficult for Maura to think of her being involved in some kind of intrigue with English soldiers and rebel gold.

Claire gave an embarrassed shake of her head. "Nay, as it turned out, I did very little to help anyone's cause," she told her son. "In fact, I was rather a problem to everyone, as your father will confirm."

"I was ready to throttle her for her mischief," Cormac agreed, but he smiled at her fondly.

Maura looked from Cormac to Claire. Their love was so evident with every look and touch they exchanged. She watched it with a pang of envy. In the isolated world of the Gypsies, she'd never thought much about finding love for herself, and she'd certainly not ever bothered to look for it when she was scrabbling to earn her living in waterfront taverns. It had taken all her energy to keep the men at a distance and fend off the ones who would not be convinced that she had no intention of selling her body.

Involuntarily she glanced across the table at Eamon. He was watching his brother and sister-in-law with an expression that revealed a similar kind of envy. Had he no sweetheart for himself? she wondered, then pushed the notion aside. It was none of her concern whether Eamon Riordan had a dozen sweethearts. Her only concern was how much longer he would be willing to let her stay on in his house under what he knew to be false pretenses.

"'Tis impossible to mount an army without money," Cormac was saying. "Queen Elizabeth has powerful resources, and if the families in the north intend to attempt another uprising against her, they'd best be sure they have the men and the arms to do it right this time."

Eamon nodded agreement.

The children had been sitting patiently, listening to their elders' talk of war, but Maura could tell that they were getting restless. Once again Ultan risked a reprimand by speaking up. "Uncle Eamon, you said you would tell us about the pirates."

Emboldened by his brother's example, Dylan added, "And what about the presents?"

None of the adults scolded the children for their interruption. Eamon smiled at them and said, "Ah, well, let me see those plates. There'll be no presents for children who haven't finished their suppers."

In a frenzied rush that Maura thought would likely lead to stomachaches in the middle of the night, the three youngsters shoveled the rest of their food into their mouths and jumped up from their benches.

"We're finished, Uncle Eamon!" Dylan cried.

"Finished!" Eily echoed, her mouth totally full of root mash.

Eamon looked over at Claire. "May we have your permission to leave the table, sister?" he asked. "The gifts are in my chamber."

"Aye," she answered with a smile. "As if I could stop them."

Eamon stood and started out of the room with the children clamoring behind him. When they reached the door, Ultan stopped and pulled on his uncle's arm. "May not Mistress Maura come with us to see the gifts?" he asked.

Eamon looked back at Maura, his expression unreadable. There was a flicker in his dark eyes that made Maura's heart suddenly skip.

"Aye," he said after a moment. "Mistress Maura may come."

Six

The children raced up the stairs ahead of the two adults and were already ensconced on Eamon's big bed when he and Maura arrived. The room was sparsely furnished, and the lone bench was covered by a blanket.

Eamon glanced at it, then looked at Maura. "Would you care to join your charges on the bed, mistress, since 'tis the only seat available at the moment?"

"Aye, Mistress Maura, join us," Ultan urged, moving to one side to make room for her.

Eamon watched as she walked across the room and gave herself a little boost onto the high mattress. His mouth twisted in a rueful smile. This was the first time he'd ever invited a woman to his bed at Riordan Hall, and it was not for the purposes he usually had in mind when he took a woman to bed.

The minute he let the thought enter his head, he knew it was a mistake. Under normal circumstances, Mistress Maura Roman, or whatever her real name was, would very much fulfill his qualifications for a desirable bed partner. But these were anything but normal circumstances.

"Where are the presents, Uncle Eamon?" Ultan and Dylan were chanting in turn. He could see Maura's body rock back and forth as the two youngsters jumped up and down on each side of her. Far from being upset at their antics, she seemed to be enjoying them.

"I warrant you've waited long enough," he told them, smiling. "But according to the laws of chivalry, the lady is always first, which means that the first gift will be for your sister."

He started walking toward the covered bench, and Ultan slipped off the bed to follow behind him. "I can give it to her, Uncle," he offered.

Eamon reached under the blanket and pulled out a delicate pink fan, painted with flowers and butterflies. Ultan viewed the offering with disappointment.

Eamon laughed. "I said 'tis for your sister, Ultan, not you. Now hop back up on the bed and wait your turn." Then he walked over to put the fan into Eily's tiny hands. She held it as if it were one of the butterflies depicted on it.

"Oooh," she breathed, eyes dancing. Then she carefully handed it to Maura. "Is it not beautiful?"

When Maura had duly admired the fan and Eamon saw that the boys were growing impatient, he walked back to the bench and threw off the blanket to reveal two half-size longbows and two quivers full of short arrows.

Dylan and Ultan jumped to the floor with shouts of excitement and raced over to retrieve them. "I know just how it works, Uncle!" Ultan exclaimed. "'Tis in the Robin Hood book." He pulled an arrow from the one of the quivers and began to fit it in the notch of his new bow.

"Hold, boys!" Eamon shouted. "You can't just start shooting off arrows in the middle of the house—"

Before he could finish his statement, Ultan's arrow had zinged off the bow and shot across the room. Fortunately it hit the far wall with little force and fell harmlessly to the ground.

"Now, this won't do!" Eamon began. "If you can't use them properly, I'll have to take them back."

Maura jumped off the bed and walked over to put a calming hand on Ultan's shoulder. Gently she plucked the bow from his hands, asking, "May I see it, Ultan?"

Reluctantly the boy let her have it.

She turned it back and forth, with an admiring cluck, then said, "You're right, 'tis exactly like Robin Hood's bow. What a wonderful present your uncle has brought you."

Ultan beamed. "May I have it now?" he asked.

Maura handed it back, but kept hold of one end of the bow. "Of course, 'tis yours. But I need to remind you about something."

The boy's face looked wary.

"You remember that the first task of Robin Hood was not to shoot his arrows, was it?"

She looked at Dylan to include him in the question as both boys shook their heads.

"What was his first task?"

"To take care of the people of Sherwood," Ultan said in a low voice.

"Aye, to take care of his people. Just as your first task is to be sure that your people—the people of Riordan Hall—are cared for. Which means you can't go around shooting arrows that might hurt someone here."

Ultan looked up at his uncle with a forlorn expression. "Can't we shoot them?"

"Of course. We'll shoot them tomorrow. I'll set up a

target for you behind the stables, and we'll shoot them as long as you like. But until then, you must only look at them. Like Mistress Maura says, you don't want to hurt anyone."

With the rules established, the smiles returned to the boys' faces, and they took several more minutes examining their new weapons while Eily looked on with some envy, fanning herself vigorously to show off her own prize.

Finally Eamon said, "I warrant 'tis past time for my poppets to be asleep."

In unison the three looked to Maura, who nodded. "You may run down to show your gifts to your parents, then 'tis to bed with you."

Calling final thank-yous and good-nights, the three trooped out of the room, each holding his or her gift. When they had disappeared down the hall, Eamon looked at Maura and said, "They listen to you well."

"I'm their tutor. They have to listen."

"Tell that to the procession of hapless lads from Kilmessen who tried to tame them before you came."

"Mayhap they prefer listening to a woman."

"Mayhap they prefer listening to *you*."

It was true. In just the short time he'd seen his nephews with Maura, he'd been amazed at how taken with her they seemed. He wasn't sure what kind of spell she'd cast on them, but, as he gazed at her eyes sparkling in the light of his room's big fireplace, he realized that he was feeling the pull of it himself.

His voice harsher than he had intended, he said, "My sister-in-law tells me that your father was a poor schoolmaster. He must have been *very* poor if he sent his young daughter out to steal horses."

Maura hesitated before answering quietly, "My father was dead by the time I met you that day."

Her answer softened his tone. "And your mother?"

"My mother died when I was born."

Perhaps the story she had told to Claire was true. If her father had died when she was still young, leaving her without resources, she might have been driven to desperate straits. She'd already told him that she'd sold his horse in order to live. What else besides stealing had she been driven to do? The thought was unexpectedly painful.

"I never knew my mother, either," he found himself confiding to her. "Childbirth has been notoriously hard on Riordan brides."

"Aye, 'tis one of the moments when a woman must truly trust herself into the hands of fate."

The hands of fate. Eamon remembered that she'd mumbled something similar in a previous conversation. It was an odd manner of thought, especially for a scholarly schoolmaster's daughter. But it seemed to fit her.

She looked around as if suddenly aware that the two of them were alone in his bedroom. Eamon had been aware of it all along. "I should go," she said.

"Do you put the children to bed?"

"Nay, their old nurse, Fiona, does that, and Lady Riordan usually goes in to kiss them good night."

"Claire is a wonderful mother."

"Aye. The children are lucky to have her."

They exchanged a look as they realized that the shared loss of their own mothers was a tenuous bond between them. Then Maura started toward the door. Eamon grasped her bare arm just below the short sleeve of her dress. He'd merely wanted to stop her from leaving, but when he touched her, his fingers seemed to burn against her soft skin.

Good Lord, what was wrong with him? Perhaps his brother's teasing was right. He spent too much time in his new library and not enough with the willing maids of Kilmessen. What other explanation could account for the heightening of his senses as he stood next to Maura, smelling the wild scent of herb that seemed to cling to her? By Judas, she was his nephews' tutor, not some woman put here for his sensual pleasure.

He dropped his hold on her arm and made his voice stern. "I'd like to know more about your background, mistress, in exchange for my promise to keep your career as a horse thief from my brother."

She bit her lip, and glanced longingly toward the door, but after a moment, she turned to face him without flinching. "Since you claim to have doubts about whatever story I tell you, what good would it do? 'Twould merely waste my time in the telling and your time in the listening."

The logic was irrefutable. After a moment he answered, "I can tell you one true thing, Mistress Roman. I've never met a woman quite like you."

She cocked her head. "An old woman I used to know always said that each soul has its own pattern. We are none of us alike, nor are our paths through life ever the same."

"Then let me just say that the pattern of your soul appears to me to be less conventional than most of the souls I come across."

Finally she smiled, and Eamon realized that he had been waiting to see that smile again.

"Will that be all, Master Riordan?" she asked.

The green dress made her hair look almost red and deepened the blue of her eyes. While it was true that he felt an obligation to find out more about her, at the moment he simply wanted to continue to listen to her, continue looking at her. But he could think of no plausible reason to keep her standing in the middle of his bed-chamber.

"Aye," he said. "Perhaps we'll talk further in the morning."

"I'll be with the children all day."

"Ah, of course. Well, tomorrow at supper, then."

"Normally I take supper in the schoolroom with the children. Tonight was a special occasion for their uncle's homecoming."

She seemed to show little inclination to speak with him again, and for no logical reason, he found her in-difference irritating.

"Then perhaps I'll see you passing back and forth to the garderobe," he said testily.

The corners of her mouth quirked, but she made no reply.

After another long silence, Eamon waved his hand at her. "Take yourself off, then," he said. "I've been awake since well before dawn and am in need of sleep."

She paused and appeared to be considering whether a curtsy was in order, but in the end she simply nodded her head and turned to leave the room.

By the time Maura reached her bedchamber, her fore-head and her hands had broken out in a sweat. Once again she'd managed to maintain her coolness in front of Eamon Riordan, but tonight it had been even more diffi-cult than that afternoon in the schoolroom.

It was obvious that the middle Riordan brother dis-trusted her. She suspected he was uncomfortable with his decision to keep what he knew about her from his brother, and that he intended to be vigilant to ensure that she would cause no harm to the household.

But it was not Eamon's distrust that had her skin moist and her breathing altered. It was, in fact, some-

thing entirely new to her that she herself didn't quite
understand. It had something to do with the way he
looked at her. When he'd touched her just now, his
strong hand surrounding her slender arm, she'd felt an
awareness of her own body that was quite extraordi-
nary. She could swear that her breasts, which had fit so
perfectly into Claire's old dress, had seemed to swell,
and she'd felt an odd hollow in the pit of her stomach
that was not entirely unpleasant.

"I think you left some things out of your stories,
Nonna," she said aloud with a rueful smile. A fire was
already burning cheerily in her room. She sank down
beside it and hugged her knees. Life is a banquet,
Nonna used to say—some things are sweet, some sour,
some juicy, some dry. Maura had a feeling that she'd
just been given a glimpse of one of the most tempting
of life's dishes—a rich, succulent platter that belonged
only on the tables of nobles such as Eamon Riordan.
Such fare was not meant for her. She'd do best to stick
to the hearty peasant stock that she knew—bread and
cheese and thick, fresh cream.

Smiling a little at her own culinary fancy, she leaned
over to throw some sticks on the fire and began to sing
one of the fireside songs that had always comforted her
in the old days.

Maura's head throbbed. She'd managed little sleep
the previous evening after her talk with Eamon Riordan, and she'd gotten up early, as usual, to try to plan
one more day of "lessons" for the children. She knew
that her subterfuge was nearly at an end. She couldn't
keep going day after day pretending to teach, when in
reality the marks in the big Robin Hood book were only
a little more clear to her than they had been when she
first saw it.

She sat in the schoolroom, looking at the closed book as if it were an enemy across a battlefield. How did one begin reading anyway? she wondered. If it were a skill that could be acquired by force of will, she'd surely have it by now.

Maybe today the letters would make more sense. Resolutely she opened the book and peered at the page. R-O-B-I-N. H-O-O-D. Those she could do. And if the one word was *hood*, then surely this one must be *good*. Two *o*'s. *Oo. Good. Hood. Oo*. Lost in concentration, she formed the sound with her mouth and said it aloud. "Oo." What else sounded like that? *Book?* Robin Hood didn't have books. What about *l-oo-k*? Eagerly she ran a finger down the page, searching for another pair of *o*'s. "Aha!" she cried, spotting the combination with an *l* and a *k*. Carefully she formed the word. *"L-oo-k."*

" 'Tis not so hard after all," she said. "Mayhap I can do this."

"I trust this is some kind of game you're preparing for the children," said Eamon's voice from the doorway.

Maura whirled around in her seat, nearly tumbling off the little bench. "You startled me," she said.

"My apologies." He strolled over to stand next to her and looked down at the book in her hands. "I've been trying to figure out what you are chanting. Is it a game?"

Maura closed the book. "Of sorts. I-I need to begin teaching the children to read."

"Your methods would appear to be . . . unusual."

She couldn't be sure from his expression, but she had the feeling that Eamon Riordan knew very well that what he'd just witnessed was no game, nor yet a method of teaching. In a way, it was for the best. She'd hoped to stay on a bit longer, but it would be a relief to stop pretending.

"I wasn't preparing a lesson," she said, looking up at him. "I was trying to read myself."

To her surprise, Eamon laughed, though the sound held little humor. When she bristled, he said, "Forgive me, Mistress Roman, but you must see that 'tis the height of absurdity. How did you come to sign on as a tutor when you knew very well that you cannot even *read*?"

"I was in a desperate—"

He held up his hand. "In a desperate case. I know, I know. It seems I've heard that tale of yours before. But truly, this is beyond belief. Did you think no one would notice that you were doing little more than telling stories to the children?"

"Nay, but I'd not thought to stay long."

He looked puzzled, then suspicious. "Then why did you come here at all? Perhaps you wanted to stay only long enough to see how you could steal something valuable from my brother's household?"

Maura closed her eyes and tried to control her anger. As much as it hurt, Eamon Riordan had every right to think her a common thief. Opening her eyes, she answered calmly, "Whatever you may think of me, Master Riordan, I would do nothing to hurt these people who have been so kind to me. I had thought to stay only long enough to help Ultan learn that he was not such a bad boy as he was beginning to believe."

This seemed to give him pause. "I can see the change in him," he admitted after a moment.

"So perhaps my job is done. I'll gather my things and be gone before dinner." She stood, placing the book carefully on the bench behind her.

"Nay, wait. The children will be tremendously disappointed if you leave."

"I won't go without saying goodbye."

He seemed to be struggling with some kind of decision. "Perhaps you can stay on a bit longer."

"As you just said, 'tis pointless to continue to fill their lessons with storytelling. They are happy enough, but they must begin their book learning."

Eamon walked over to the tall schoolroom windows and looked out to the grounds below. He stood there for a long minute, before turning back to her. "I draw a great deal of pleasure from my books," he began.

"Aye, so the children have told me."

"I want my nephews and niece to know the joy of books, as well."

Maura nodded, waiting for him to continue.

"Perhaps I could join your lessons for a time," he said.

She gaped at him. "Here in the schoolroom?"

"Aye."

"Would that not be exceedingly odd?"

Eamon shook his head. "Nay, I've read to them often. I've even thought of offering to instruct them myself when Cormac and Claire were having such difficulty finding a tutor, but I didn't think my brother would approve."

Maura remembered something. "I believe you had read them the Robin Hood book that day they tied you up in the woods."

That brought a smile. "Aye, the little devils. I find pleasure in working with them. 'Twould be no hardship, at least through the Christmas season. There will be little enough work to do around the estate, and likely there will be no renewal of the hostilities until spring."

Maura could hardly believe what he was offering. "Why would you do this for me?" she asked. "Why don't you just tell your brother who I am and send me on my way?"

"I don't know," he said bluntly.

There was that odd flicker again in his eyes. The instincts that had protected her all those years on the waterfront suddenly surfaced. "I'll not lie with you," she blurted.

His head jerked back. "I beg your pardon?"

"If you're offering to help so that you can take me to your bed, then the answer is nay. I'll be getting my things and leaving today."

There it was—that crooked smile. She knew at once that she'd made a mistake with her accusation. Eamon Riordan was not a waterfront sailor. It had no doubt never crossed his mind to think of bedding a poor tutor in his brother's household. Her face flamed in embarrassment. "Forgive me," she stammered. "'Tis just that I've known men to be—" She gave a kind of hopeless flutter with her hands, trying to pull the words together. "Forgive me, Master Riordan," she repeated more firmly. "You are a gentleman, and I'm sure that such a thought never has entered your head. I apologize for making the implication."

His smile stayed in place. "So you would be willing to give our joint lessons a try?" he asked. "You'd like to stay on?"

"Aye, I'd be grateful."

"Then 'tis settled. I'll join you later this morning."

Her cheeks were still burning. "Very good, sir."

"I have only one condition for the arrangement," he said. "What's past is past, but from now on I expect you to tell me the truth."

She hesitated, then nodded her head in agreement.

He started to leave, then paused and turned back to her. "As long as we're going to tell the truth, Mistress Maura, I should clarify something."

"Aye?"

"I do consider myself a gentleman, as you said, and I expect nothing in return for helping you."

She smiled. "Aye, once again, I apologize for suggesting—"

He held up a hand. "But 'twould not be entirely accurate to say that the thought had never entered my head."

With that he gave a nod, turned on his heel, and stalked out of the room. Maura watched him leave, her mouth gaping.

Seven

Eamon found himself grinning all the way down to the dining hall. He wasn't sure why. He'd just discovered even more incriminating information about the woman whose past he was keeping from his brother. The situation should have him concerned, yet all he could think about was that after breakfast, he would once again be joining her in the schoolroom.

Cormac was already sitting at the table reading a letter. His expression was grave. "What is it?" Eamon asked his brother.

Cormac looked up. "'Tis from Niall. He says more estates in the south have been given over to English lords. Elizabeth's favorites are vying for estates in Killarney, especially, since 'tis known for its beauty."

Eamon made an effort to put Maura out of his mind so that he could concentrate on the serious matter of the ever-present possibility of war. "Are the O'Malley lands in danger?"

Their brother Niall was living with his wife, Catriona O'Malley, on the Killarney estate that had been restored to her when the treachery of her English guardian had been exposed. It would be ironic and tragic if she lost the estate again, this time at Elizabeth's command.

"Niall doesn't say. I'm sure they're worried, as is everyone. 'Tis more fuel on the fire, of course."

Eamon took the seat next to his brother and reached for a slab of bread. "If Shane O'Neill were still alive, we'd already be at war again."

"Aye," Cormac agreed. "The rebels continue squabbling among themselves, and it has kept them from action."

"Someone has to take on leadership again."

"I reckon 'twill be the one who finds the O'Neill's gold."

Eamon frowned. "The money is that important?"

"Paupers don't become generals. You can't field an army without supplies and weapons."

Eamon shook his head. "Then mayhap 'twould be best for the gold to stay lost forever. I can't believe it will benefit anyone to start the fighting up again."

"No one wants to fight, Eamon, but would you let all the great Irish estates be seized by the English, one by one? Would you see Elizabeth holding court at Tara Hill where the great Irish kings once ruled?"

Eamon gave a sigh. "Nay. Do you think I should go to Killarney to be with Niall?" Normally, he would have welcomed the thought of traveling to spend time with his brother, but at the moment the idea did not appeal to him. What was worse, he knew that the reason for his reluctance was sitting upstairs in the schoolroom. He could still picture how she had looked when he had come upon her this morning—peering intently at the big book on her lap, her mouth carefully forming the sounds she was trying to learn. The memory made him smile again.

"Into what kind of pleasant reverie have I lost you, brother?" Cormac asked.

Eamon looked at his brother, embarrassed. "'Tis nothing. I was thinking how much I enjoyed seeing the children again. I might spend a little time with them and the new tutor, if you and Claire have no objection."

Cormac studied his brother. "Of course we have no objection, but I'm wonderin' if 'tis truly the children that's put that mooncalf look in your eyes or if 'tis the comely tutor herself."

"Perhaps both," Eamon admitted.

Cormac looked a little worried. "You'd best have a care, Eamon. We know little about her."

We know more about her than you think, brother, Eamon reflected. *And none of it good.* "Don't fret, Cormac," he said. "I'm not likely to forget."

Eamon had been coming to the schoolroom every day faithfully for a fortnight, and Maura found each session more exhilarating than the last. Without revealing her ignorance to the children, he'd managed to allow her to continue with her stories and songs, while he had taken over the task of teaching them to read. Their familiarity with the Robin Hood book was proving to be a tremendous help, and they all were beginning to decipher a number of words. Ultan could read most of the page, and to Maura's amazement, so could she. The skill was not at all as difficult as she had imagined, once the tiny scripted letters began to make sense.

"I've brought a new book today," Eamon said, entering the room with the long strides that Maura had come to know.

The children jumped up from their seats on the hearth to run over to their uncle. Ultan peered at the book, then frowned. "'Tis Latin," he said.

"Aye," Eamon agreed. He ran his fingers under the words of the title as he pronounced, *"Grammatica Latina."*

"We like Robin Hood," Ultan said.

"So do I," Eamon said patiently, "but you don't want to keep on reading the same book over and over. There's a whole world of new things to learn."

Ultan turned his back on his uncle and went to sit on the hearth, his arms crossed. "Soldiers have no need for Latin," he mumbled.

His face had a sulky expression that Maura hadn't seen since her very first days in the household. The children had been allowed to stay up past their usual bedtime the previous evening waiting for Cormac to come home from a short trip, and Ultan's grumpiness was partly due to lack of sleep. But she also suspected that Ultan was sharing some of her own sentiments. They were doing well with the Robin Hood book—she and the children both. They were proud of their progress. But Latin was another matter. Latin conjured up thoughts of learned monks in faraway universities, men who devoted their lives to study. She herself felt doubt about whether she could ever master such a subject, and she suspected young Ultan was feeling the same.

She leaned toward him and put a hand on his shoulder. "Soldiers may not need Latin," she said, "but brave men are willing to take on a new task and see what advantages it may give them, even if they can't know what those may be."

Ultan looked up at her. His eyes were so like his father's and his uncle's. She wondered how she hadn't seen the connection immediately when she had first met the child at Cliodhna's Glen. Would she have offered to accompany him home if she had realized that he was kin to the man she had robbed?

"Do you think we need to learn Latin, Mistress Maura?" Ultan asked.

"Aye," Maura said firmly. "And we'll make the learning an adventure, as surely as Robin Hood is an adventure of a different sort."

With that established, there was no more argument from the children. Eamon gave her a look of gratitude as the three youngsters dutifully sat on their benches around a desk and watched as Eamon opened the book to the first page.

To the surprise of both adults, the Latin lessons proved to be a great success. The children were soon challenging each other to remember the odd words that up to now they had only heard spoken by the priests at the big church in Kilmessen.

Maura's fear of the new subject had disappeared almost immediately. To her amazement, the Latin words were little different than the Romany language she'd spoken growing up. If Eamon wondered at the ease with which she mastered the subject, he didn't comment, though occasionally she'd see him watching her with a glint of admiration in his dark eyes.

She tried not to catch those moments, since they always unsettled her, often making her trail off in the middle of a sentence.

The truth was, she admitted to herself when she retired to her room each night, Eamon Riordan had so taken over her mind that she could think of little else. It wasn't just his darkly handsome looks that attracted her. It was the way he moved, the way he smiled, the patient way he dealt with the children, the gentle teasing he used when he was trying to coax one of them to work harder.

She'd become infatuated with him. And she hadn't the least idea what to do about it. She remembered that one of Nonna's sayings was "The fish must not love the bird, for their worlds can never meet." She and Eamon were as different as a fish and a bird, and she had best remember it.

The children had been dismissed to play in the yard before supper, but Maura had stayed to continue her translation of an Ovid poem. Eamon sat back on his stool and watched her, since she needed no help from him. It was obvious she had a special gift for the language. The Latin words flowed from her lips as easily as if she'd been speaking them her entire life.

Her eyes gleamed as she read the words. Her hair had pulled loose from its cap during the long day of studies and curled delicately around her neck. Eamon took in a breath that turned ragged. Maura, intent on her book, didn't notice.

He should leave, he told himself. Most of the time over these past two weeks they had been with the children, who served as distractions from the improper thoughts that occasionally tried to creep into his head. But in the few moments he spent alone with the vibrant young tutor, he was finding those thoughts increasingly difficult to banish.

She finished the last line of the poem and looked up at him. "'Twas all correct, was it not?" Her smile of triumph was totally endearing.

"Aye," he confirmed, "it was correct. Well done." Without thinking, he leaned toward her and kissed her cheek.

The gesture surprised them both. Maura jerked her head back and lifted a hand to the spot his lips had touched.

"Forgive me," Eamon said immediately. "'Twas done without thinking."

She didn't look offended. In fact, her eyes had widened with an expression of wonder that did nothing to slow the racing of his heart.

"I should leave," he said quickly.

She nodded.

He stood and started toward the door, then paused. "I've not offended you?"

She looked up at him, cheeks flushed. "Nay, I—" She hesitated. "Nay, you've not offended me."

He studied her for a moment more. He remembered her determined look the day he had first offered to help her. She'd been adamant that she wouldn't return his kindness with sexual favors. At the time he had been amused, knowing that he would never put a woman in such a position.

He still wouldn't, he told himself firmly. The trouble was, she no longer had the look of a woman putting up barriers. In fact, her slightly misty gaze and husky tone gave every indication of the exact opposite.

"Until the morrow, mistress," he said abruptly, then he stormed out of the schoolroom and didn't stop until he had reached the stables. The stable man, Aidan, was at the far end of the long building and looked up with surprise as Eamon threw a saddle on his stallion.

"Would ye like some help, Master Eamon?" Aidan called.

"Nay," Eamon called back with a wave. He swung himself up on the big animal's back, then turned him out the open stable doors and up the hill toward the setting sun. Perhaps, he thought grimly, a long, hard ride in the twilight would help him put his unruly notions regarding his nephew's tutor out of his head.

Maura closed the big book with a little sigh of regret. Tomorrow the children began an eighteen-day holiday for the Christmas festivities, which meant that the daily sessions in the schoolroom with Eamon were at an end for the moment. She wasn't sure what was expected of her during the holiday. With no lessons to give, she did not know how she would occupy her time. She supposed a normal tutor would have taken the opportunity to travel to his or her own home, but Claire knew that Maura had no home to go to, and she had made no mention that Maura should make any plans to leave the household for the Christmas season.

She would read, of course. Every day the task became easier to her, and she had already made her way through three of the books in the Riordan library. Undoubtedly she would also join the children in some of their activities. She knew that they enjoyed her company, and they asked for her to be included in everything they did.

She had not joined the adult activity in the household, which was to be expected. She was, after all, a servant, not a member of the family. Besides, whenever she was in Cormac's presence, he seemed to have more questions for her, and it was increasingly difficult to stay vague about her background. She suspected that he disapproved of the amount of time his brother was spending in the schoolroom, but if so, his brother's opinion had not seemed to deter Eamon. He had come faithfully every day.

It had been three days since the afternoon he had impulsively kissed her, and neither one had mentioned the incident. He'd come the next morning and the lessons had proceeded normally as if nothing out of the ordinary had happened between them.

Still, Maura had not forgotten it. When she lay in her bed at night, she could still feel the brush of his warm lips against her cheek.

"Maura, you're still here."

Maura gave a guilty start as the mistress of the household entered the schoolroom. "Aye, milady," she said. "Did you want something?"

Claire glanced at the heavy book on Maura's lap. "Ah, you must be pleased to be putting those aside for a spell. I haven't told you how pleased Lord Riordan and I are with how the lessons are progressing. Eamon says that the children are learning fast, and 'tis all thanks to you."

Maura flushed. "Master Riordan is too kind, for he's done much of the teaching himself."

"The children adore him. But I imagine he can be distracting at times."

"Er—distracting?" Were her developing feelings for Eamon becoming obvious to her employers? she wondered.

"Aye, keeping the children from their studies. He loves to play with them."

"Ah, distracting for the children," Maura said, relieved.

"Aye. If you feel 'twould be better not to have him there, you have but to say."

"Nay, I—"

"Of course," Claire continued, " 'twill no doubt not be an issue after the holidays. The men will be beginning their talk of war again, and Eamon will be wanting to visit the Riordan kin in other parts of the country."

This was disappointing news to Maura, but she merely said, "He's welcome in the schoolroom whenever he's available. He's far more learned than I," she added truthfully.

Claire laughed. "Aye, Eamon loves his books, but he's fun-loving as well, as you shall see when he plays Lord of Misrule."

Maura hesitated, then asked, "Will it be suitable for me to stay here during the holidays?"

Claire looked surprised. "But naturally. Where else would you go?" Her expression grew sober and she lay a hand on Maura's shoulder. "I haven't given up trying to find information about your mother's family. I've asked a number of the neighboring families if they know of any tales of a young woman who disappeared twenty-some years ago, but so far no one has come up with any possibilities."

Maura had told her employer a careful version of the story of her mother. She'd said that her mother's family had been unhappy over her chosen husband's humble status and had refused to allow the marriage, causing her mother to run away from home. For the most part, the story was true. Maura had simply omitted that fact that the real opposition had been to her father's Gypsy heritage.

"I'm grateful, Lady Riordan," Maura said, realizing with amazement that it had been several days since she'd even thought about the quest to find her mother's identity.

"So in the meantime I want you to consider yourself part of our household. I hope you'll join us for dinner tonight. My sister, Eileen, is arriving for the holidays. You remember Eileen from our stay at O'Donnell House?"

Maura nodded. Though she'd been uncertain of her place with the Riordans when she had first moved into O'Donnell House, she remembered that Eileen O'Donnell had been kind to her. Claire's sister was an attractive young woman, but her beauty was quite different from her sister's. Whereas Claire was tall and striking, Eileen was shorter, rounder. Her hair was dark like Claire's, but instead of hanging sleek and straight, it tumbled from her headdress in riotous curls. Her face lit up frequently with a sweet smile that dimpled both her cheeks.

"I'd be pleased to join you," Maura told her with a smile.

"I've always fancied a match between Eileen and Eamon, though up to now neither one has shown the inclination. Mayhap the Christmas season will work its magic this time."

Maura forced her smile to stay in place. "The children will be at dinner, as well?" she asked.

"Aye, we eat together as much as possible for the holidays, so you should just plan on joining us at table, unless something changes."

"Very good, milady," Maura agreed.

Claire gave a final look around the schoolroom. "'Twill be good for you to get out of these confines for a few days, Maura. We'll see you this evening in the dining hall."

"Aye, milady."

There was a heavy feeling in Maura's chest as she watched Claire leave the room. Her employer was as warm and generous as anyone could want, but Maura was not sure that her insistence on including Maura in the family Christmas would turn out to be a good thing. She may be part of the household, but she was still a servant of uncertain origins.

Growing up in the Gypsy camp, she had never celebrated Christmas, and the Riordan children's enthusiasm had made her curious about the holiday festivities. But at the moment Maura wished that she were curled up in the tiny sleeping cupboard under her father's wagon or even back in the Dublin waterfront tavern. Anything would be better than spending Christmas at

Riordan Hall watching from a distance as Claire tried to match her eligible sister with Eamon.

The meeting with Eileen had not been as difficult as Maura had feared. When they had all come together at the supper table, Eileen had greeted Maura with genuine warmth, as if they were old friends. She seemed to give no mind to the difference in their stations.

"Perhaps we'll need to steal Maura away from you one of these days, Claire, now that Conn is producing a brood of his own," she told her sister. The oldest O'Donnell brother had married a McClatchey the previous year, and his strong young bride had now presented him with twins.

"I'll not let you take her," Claire replied firmly. "Nor will the children."

Ultan bobbed his head in agreement, and when his mother gave him a nod of permission to speak, he blurted, "Mistress Maura is staying with us *forever,* Aunt Eileen."

Ultan was seated on one side of Maura and Eily on the other with Dylan beside her. Across from them Claire had placed her sister next to Eamon. A number of other Riordan cousins had joined the group, and Maura had been duly presented to each one, but she knew that she would never be able to keep the names straight except for one cousin, Dermot, who was visiting from the Riordan family in the north.

She had paid particular attention to Dermot, partly because he bore such a close resemblance to Eamon and Cormac, but mostly because when Claire had introduced him, he'd lifted Maura's hand and bowed over it like a courtier greeting a noblewoman. Maura had been immensely impressed, and had found her eyes wander-

ing to the handsome young man from time to time
throughout the evening.

She'd tried to avoid watching Eamon, who had spent
much of the meal talking in animated tones with Eileen
O'Donnell. To Maura's eyes, it appeared that Claire's
desire of a match between her brother-in-law and her
sister might be a distinct possibility.

Much of the talk during dinner was of the English
encroachment. Claire expressed some regret that Niall
and Catriona had felt it unwise to leave the O'Malley
lands long enough to travel to Riordan Hall for the
holidays.

But as the ale flowed more freely, the conversation
became more cheerful. Cormac and Eamon took turns
telling tales of their days growing up in Riordan Hall
without female supervision or influence. Their antics
had been infamous in the county, but now that they'd
grown to a much more sane adulthood, the stories drew
gales of laughter.

"Mayhap 'tis time the children were off to bed,"
Cormac said finally, "before they learn entirely too
much about the example set by their father."

The three youngsters looked disappointed, but made
no complaint as their mother nodded agreement. "Run
upstairs and find Fiona, dearlings," she said. "I'll come
up in a few minutes to tuck you into bed with dreams of
almond tarts and plum pudding and all the sweet things
to come over the next few days."

This brought the smiles back to their faces as the
three obediently stood and walked in procession out of
the dining hall. When they had left, Cormac suggested
to his brother, "Why don't you and Dermot join me in
the great room for a glass of port?"

Eamon shook his head. "I've promised to show Mistress Eileen my library."

"At this time of night?" Cormac asked with a snort. " 'Twill keep until tomorrow."

"Husband," Claire said firmly from the other end of the table. "Let your brother decide for himself. If he wants to show my sister his *library,* then your port can wait."

Cormac frowned, then looked from his brother to Eileen and back to his wife, who was giving a significant little nod. "Ah," he said, comprehension dawning. "By all means, Eamon, show Eileen the library. No doubt she'll find it fascinating. And don't bother to hurry. I find the hour's growing late for port."

Dermot threw his younger cousin a teasing glance. "Nay, don't hurry on our account, Eamon, but I, for one, shall be waiting in the great room in case all those dusty tomes leave you with a thirst."

Eamon stood, shaking his head good-naturedly at both his brother and cousin. Then he held Eileen's chair and took her elbow to help her rise. "I'll meet you there later, Dermot," he said.

" 'Twas a fine meal, sister," Eileen added. "I'm so very happy to be here with you all." Her glance encompassed the entire table, including Maura. But Eamon did not so much as look Maura's way as he tucked Eileen's hand into the crook of his arm and led her out of the room.

Eight

Maura had spent the entire day trying to avoid running into Eamon. When she'd been unable to rid her mind of the picture of him disappearing with Eileen, she told herself that this foolish obsession with the brother of her employer had to stop. If she had anywhere else to stay during the holidays, she would, but as it was, she would just have to do the best she could to avoid his company. Claire had said that after Christmas he would probably be leaving for other business, and that would take care of the matter.

She had progressed in her studies much faster than the children, so she was sure that she would be able to continue teaching them for a while yet. They had yet to tackle mathematics, at which she was likely to be hopeless, but with the fine library Eamon had collected, she could cover almost every other subject.

The children had spent the first day of holiday helping their mother and Molly the cook with the house decorations. They'd brought in cut boughs and holly branches that had filled the great room and the dining hall with fresh, pungent fragrance.

Maura had stayed to one side, not wanting to intrude on what was evidently a family tradition between Claire and her children. When Eamon had entered the room, once again in the company of Eileen, she'd slipped away to her own room, where she was working on a copy of Ovid's *Metamorphosis*. It was much more difficult than the Latin grammar text, but surprisingly, she was having a great deal of success deciphering it.

Engrossed in the text, she almost didn't hear the knock. Normally, she left her door open whenever possible so that the children would feel free to enter. Perhaps they'd come looking for her. She set the book aside, rose from the bed, and walked over to open the door. But it was not the children standing on the other side. It was their uncle.

"Oh!" she exclaimed in surprise.

"I trust I didn't wake you, mistress," he said.

"Nay, I was just—" She waved toward the open book on the bed. "I've borrowed one of your books."

He walked in and gave the volume a glance, then whistled. "You may have left learning till late in life, but once you started, you've taken the thing in earnest."

"I like Latin," she said. "I like the way the words sound when I say them."

"I like how they sound when *you* say them, too," he agreed with a grin. "For myself, I've a devil of a time twisting my tongue around them."

She folded her hands to keep them still. *Why was he here?*

"I came to find you," he said, as though he had heard her silent question. "You disappeared just as all the fun was beginning."

"I—'twould seem to be a family thing," she stammered.

"'Tis a family thing, and you're part of the family now, especially for the holidays."

"Nay, not really. Nor would they want me to be if they knew my real story. I'm not sure that I've expressed this to you, but I'm grateful to you for helping me to stay here."

"I'm the only one who knows about your life of crime, you mean," he said, his eyes twinkling.

Even though he was obviously teasing, the words stung. Her chin went up. "Aye."

"As Lord of Misrule, I preside over the Christmas festivities, and I hereby declare that Mistress Maura Roman is absolved of any past misdeeds."

To her annoyance, she could feel her eyes misting. "You are the one with the weightiest grievance against me."

"Then 'tis perfect, for that makes me the best one to wipe the slate clean." He reached out to grasp her hand. "Now, come, join us downstairs for a glass of wassail."

Her throat was full, and she still had no desire to spend more time watching him court Eileen O'Donnell, but after his proclamation, she decided it would be churlish to refuse. "Very well," she said. "I should freshen up first. Then I'll come down."

He dropped her hand and his expression became serious. "You sound as if you are dreading the prospect. Are we such poor company, then?"

"Oh, no! You know how much I love being with the children, and I love to watch them with Lord and Lady Riordan."

"Then perhaps 'tis I who am driving you away." When she made no immediate reply, his eyes widened.

"I was attempting humor, mistress. I trow 'tis not truly my company you resent?"

"Nay," she answered, but her eyes betrayed her.

"So I am the one you are fleeing." She could see the hurt in his expression. "I had thought you liked me. Working together with the children, I thought you enjoyed it as much as I did."

"I did."

"So what's changed? What's gone wrong between us?"

Once again she could feel the stinging of tears. Angrily she blinked them away. "Prithee, Master Riordan," she pleaded. "Do not ask me. I'll join you and the rest of the family in a few minutes, I promise."

He looked into her eyes for a long moment, then his expression changed subtly. He turned around and walked to the open door, but instead of leaving, he pushed it firmly shut. Then he walked back to her and, shoving aside the Latin book, pulled her down to sit beside him on the bed. "I once told you that the only condition I would impose for helping you was that you tell the truth. So tell me the truth, Maura. Why do you suddenly find my company undesirable?"

He held her wrist so that she couldn't move away from him. Feeling trapped, she answered without thinking. "I wonder that you should care, since 'tis apparent you have sufficient company to keep you entertained."

He looked confused for a moment, then a slight smile tipped his lips. "Are you referring to Mistress Eileen?"

"You seem to be enjoying her visit."

Maura tried to look away again, but he seized her chin with his fingers. "You're jealous!" he proclaimed with a grin.

"I—" she began, then stopped. How could she deny

what her own words had made obvious? "Jealous would imply that there is something between the two of us, which, of course, is folly. I'm a servant in your brother's household and—"

Before she could say another word, he put his hands on her cheeks and turned her face toward him. "Mistress Maura, you are *jealous*," he said again. "And do you know how I am certain that you are jealous?"

She shook her head.

"Because I had the same feeling when I saw Cousin Dermot press his lips to your hand last night. I wanted to smash his face in."

Her eyes widened in surprise.

"I want to be the only one whose lips can touch you," he said. There was just time to see the flare of passion in his eyes before he bent to kiss her. His lips were warm and dry, then hot and liquid as he used his tongue to open her mouth. His hands slipped from her cheeks into her unbound hair, and he tipped her head to deepen his onslaught. After a few heady moments, his kisses moved along her chin and found a tender hollow just underneath her ear.

Maura rested her head against his hands and let the sensations wash through her. These were nothing like the rough kisses Pietro had tried to force on her, nor the drunken busses of the sailors at the tavern. These were like nothing she had ever experienced.

In the end it was Eamon who pulled away. She was totally lost in the new sensations. He could have kept her there forever. But once the contact was broken, reality came flooding back. What had she been thinking? Why hadn't she protested or pulled away or slapped his face?

Eamon was breathing hard, and his eyes had narrowed. "This time I'll not apologize," he said soberly.

"You can no longer deny that you feel this thing between us. If your words about Eileen hadn't told me,
your response to my kiss would."

He was right. She did feel the pull between them, but
that didn't mean that it made any more sense than it had
made before he came up to her room. Her voice was
shaky as she said, "When you agreed to help me, I
warned you that I'd not repay your favors with—"

"That's not what this is," he interrupted her angrily.
"I think you know well that I'm not asking for a return
for my silence about you. Neither of us expected that
this would happen."

Deep down she didn't truly believe that he was trying to take advantage of her, but that didn't alter the im-
possibility of the circumstances. "I think it would be
best if you left."

"Do you truly want me to leave?" he asked.

His gaze bored into her and she sensed that he knew
exactly what she wanted. The thought made her voice
sharp. "I'm sure by now Mistress O'Donnell has missed
your presence at the festivities."

"I don't give a figgy pudding if she's missed me or
not," he snapped back.

They still sat side by side, their bodies almost touching. Part of her wanted to slip closer to him again, but
she steeled herself and said, "If Mistress O'Donnell is
to be your wife, you'd best have more of a care for her
feelings."

"Wife! What put that fool's notion in your head?"

"Her sister . . . Lady Riordan said you would—"

Eamon muttered an oath under his breath. "My sister-in-law is ever trying to arrange the world, but she
knows nothing about what I want. Nor, evidently, about
what her sister wants." When Maura looked confused,
he explained, "Eileen has spent most of this visit asking

advice about her infatuation for a certain Master Harrian, who has yet to gain her father's approval."

"Oh," Maura said flatly, but she felt a flood of relief.

Eamon grinned at her again and took her chin with his fingers. "You may as well stop fighting it, teacher—you're jealous as hell."

He looked as though he was going to start to kiss her again, so she pulled away and hurriedly stood up. "Fine, I'll admit it," she said, trying to prevent her voice from cracking.

"*Macushla,* I was teasing." He rose to stand facing her.

The endearment started a tear out of the corner of her eye. He brushed it with his finger. " 'Tis no easy thing, Maura," he said gently, "this coming together of a man and a maid. I did not kiss you because I thought I had the right or that I simply could because of your position in this household. I kissed you because it was not within my earthly powers to stop."

His words only added to the heaviness that was gathering in her chest. "Mayhap I was wrong to think that you would take advantage of me while courting another woman, but tell me this, Eamon Riordan, if we continue on this path, what can happen between us?"

He did not pretend that he didn't understand her question, but he apparently had no better answer to it than she did. "None of us knows what will happen in the future," he said with a touch of irritation.

She smiled sadly. Nonna often could tell the future, but of course, Eamon knew nothing about Nonna. It was bad enough that he knew Maura had once been a horse thief. What would he say if he knew that she was a Gypsy instead of the impoverished daughter of a schoolmaster? she wondered.

"We can't foresee the future, but you and I both

know that we are of two different worlds—worlds that have no meeting place."

He put his hands on her upper arms. "Then how did we come to meet?" he asked, giving her a gentle shake. "What are we doing standing here together, wanting to feel our lips touching again?"

She took in a long stream of air. "Can you honestly say that you could ever forget the difference in our stations?" She paused to give her words time to reach him. "Do Riordans customarily marry horse thieves?"

She could see the answer in his eyes, and it made her throat close. "I think you should leave," she said again.

"You're wrong, Maura. 'Tis not impossible. When the time comes for me to marry, I'll not be choosing a bride for her station or her wealth or her family." He paused a moment, then continued, "Yet I have to admit that I've not truly thought that I wanted a bride of any sort."

The last was said with such a rueful smile that she couldn't keep from smiling back. "I warrant you'd not be the first gentleman to woo first and worry about the consequences later. But we women are the ones who bear those consequences, sometimes for a lifetime, so I'll thank you to not come around my room anymore with that crooked smile of yours, for I swear it puts my head in a muddle."

He took a step back from her, relieving the tension that their closeness seemed to generate. His expression was contrite, but there was still a bit of mischief in his eyes as he said, "You did kiss me back. Admit at least that much."

"I'll admit it if it will make you go away."

"You'll not come downstairs with me?"

"Don't ask me," she pleaded. "I'd prefer to be here by myself tonight."

"Would you have me go alone to Mistress Eileen?" he mocked.

"You can go to the devil for all I care. Just stop confusing me."

He cocked his head, studying her, then said finally, "Aye, 'twould be best if I leave you now."

She thought he was about to turn to leave, but instead, he pulled her into his arms and took her mouth in another thorough, searching kiss.

It was over almost before she could recover from the surprise. "You kissed back again," he said smugly.

Then he turned on his heel and left the room.

Maura was left once again to gape after him. Toward the end of their conversation, she'd thought that something had been decided between them. She'd made it clear that she was not a servant whose virtue was ripe for the plucking. Eamon was not ready for marriage, even if she did believe his protestations that the station of his future wife did not matter to him. Therefore a relationship between them was impossible.

So why had he kissed her again? she asked silently, looking toward the crackling fireplace. Once again, the flames refused to answer.

The Riordan legend held that the custom of appointing a Lord of Misrule was begun in the household by one of the tragic young brides who had subsequently died on Twelfth Night, just as the Christmas festivities were ending. But in spite of the grim story, the Riordan children over the years had urged that the tradition be continued, and for several years Eamon had taken the role of the mischievous jester who pretended to rule over the holiday celebrations.

Unlike in the old days, when the festivities still held the stamp of ancient Druid days, the modern lord was a harmless enough fellow. Eamon's chief duty was presiding over the ceremonial decoration and the banquet that followed on Midwinter Day, three days before Christmas.

This year Eamon had prepared his typical outrageous costume complete with crown to wear for the evening and had arranged with Molly to have a little figure baked into each Christmas tart to surprise the children. But he was having trouble keeping his mind on the celebration. He hadn't seen Maura since he'd visited her room the previous evening, and he hoped that the encounter would not make her decide to stay closeted for the duration of the holidays.

The Christmas log was burning brightly in the huge great room fireplace; the Yule candle had been lighted in the front window; and he and his nephews had just finished nailing the garlands of yew and holly around the dining room when he decided that he would wait no longer.

"Have you seen Mistress Maura today?" he asked Ultan as the boy climbed down from the chair he'd used to reach the top of the doorway.

"Nay." Ultan frowned. "I wonder why? Do you think she's sad because it's Christmas and her own family is dead?"

Eamon put a hand on his nephew's head. "I warrant she may be," he said. "Perhaps I should go find her."

"Dylan and I can all go," Ultan suggested.

Dylan, standing just behind his brother, agreed. "Aye, we'll go find her. She's missing all the fun. 'Tis almost time for supper."

Time for him to don his jester rags, Eamon realized, but he said, "Nay, you boys run to ask your mother if there is anything further to be done in the house. I'll see to Mistress Maura."

"You will tell her to come to supper, won't you?" Dylan asked.

"Aye, I'll tell her."

"You can *order* her to come, Uncle," Ultan suggested with a giggle. "You're the lord for tonight."

Dylan joined in his brother's laughter. "Aye. Mistress Maura has to do whatever the Lord of Misrule tells her."

The notion sent a jolt of lust to his midsection. He'd had vivid flashes all day long of how it had felt to feel her lips surrender to him. Though he had yet to clear the confusion in his mind over the questions she had raised the previous evening, he knew with utter certainty that the matter was not done. There would, at least, be more kisses. She wanted it as much as he.

"Is something the matter, Uncle?" Ultan asked.

"Nay. Go find your mother. I'll see you at supper."

"Will you have a patchwork vest like last year?" Ultan asked.

"And a scepter with an apple on the end?" Dylan added.

"You'll just have to wait and see," Eamon told them with a smile. "Now let me go get Mistress Maura."

"Why, there she is now!" Ultan cried.

Eamon turned to see Maura descending the big stairs. She saw him immediately, and her face flushed. He, too, felt a rush of heat, though not in his face.

Ultan and Dylan went running out into the hall and up the stairs toward her. "We've been wondering where you were, Mistress Maura," Ultan said. "You've missed the decorating."

She smiled and held out a hand to each of them to let them escort her the rest of the way down the stairs. "Then you'll have to give me a tour of the manor and show me what you've done," she said.

Eamon had the feeling that she was trying to avoid being alone with him, but he said, "The boys are about to see if their mother needs any more help, but I would be happy to show you our handiwork."

Maura and her escorts had reached the bottom of the stairs, and she stopped a few feet from him. Dylan and Ultan obediently dropped her hands. "We shall see you at supper, Mistress Maura," Ultan said. Then he and his brother raced around the corner toward the back of the house.

Maura looked over at Eamon. "'Tis not necessary for you to show me the house. I merely said that to please them."

"Ah, but it would please *me* to show you, teacher." He reached his hand toward her, and after a moment's hesitation, she stepped forward and took it. He drew her into the doorway of the dining room and gestured with his other hand to show off the room.

"Oh," she gasped. "Truly, 'tis lovely. And the smell!" She took in a deep breath.

Eamon watched her with a smile. She was wearing a dress of watered green silk decorated with slashes of red. "You look much like a garland yourself tonight."

She flushed again. "'Tis Lady Riordan's frock, of course. She's been overly generous with me."

"It never looked lovelier on her," he told her.

"I—'tis kind of you to say so," she stammered.

Eamon had never known Maura to be reticent about speaking her mind, but it appeared that when it came to gallantries she was at a loss for words. Of course, if she had been raised in the home of a schoolmaster, she'd have had little opportunity to witness such social exchanges.

He drew her one step further into the room and pointed above her head. She twisted her neck to follow the direction of his gesture. Above the door was a small uprooted holly tree. "What is it?" she asked.

He answered her with a grin. "Don't you know? 'Tis a kissing bush. Any female standing beneath is in danger of being caught by a kiss." She stepped hastily away with a look so horrified that he threw back his head and laughed. "'Tis a harmless enough custom, teacher," he added.

"Mayhap," she said, eyeing him warily. "But I think 'tis one tradition I'll decline."

He leaned toward her and whispered, "My nephews just reminded me that as Lord of Misrule, I can order you to do anything I want tonight. They were quite amused by the notion."

She took another step away from him. "You didn't tell them that you had kissed me?" she gasped.

"That I thoroughly kissed you. Twice," he corrected. "Nay, don't worry. 'Tis another secret between us."

"Thank you," she said, looking relieved.

"But if the Lord of Misrule should kiss you tonight, no one will think it amiss."

"Then perhaps I should return to my chamber and avoid the evening altogether."

He grabbed her hand and tucked it into his arm, then began walking with her to the great room. "You can't leave," he said firmly. "The Lord of Misrule won't permit it. Now come and let me show you the Nollaig candle in the front window."

Nine

Maura tried to remember if her father or Nonna had ever had stories about Christmas, but she didn't think so. Everything was new to her. She tried not to act surprised at customs that the rest of the household seemed to be taking for granted. If she was the daughter of an Irish schoolmaster, she surely would know that the Nollaig candle was to provide light to guide the Holy Family. She would have known that the little figures that emerged from the Christmas tarts, much to the children's delight, represented Mary, Joseph, baby Jesus along with the shepherds and angels who watched over them that long ago Christmas Eve.

But to her, it was all foreign . . . and quite wonderful. At times she was even able to stop thinking about Eamon, though he was ever-present during the evening playing his role as host. When he began a game of Blind Man with himself as the target, the children raced around the great room and out into the hall, dodging his grasping hands and shouting with glee.

She watched with the other adults, smiling fondly.

Eileen's presence no longer bothered her. In fact, she had the sense that Eileen knew that the two young women shared the bond of having set their hearts in a direction that may not be possible to follow.

"They will never settle down to sleep after this," Claire protested as the Blind Man finally cornered all three of his victims in the front hall and, scooping them up in one giant embrace, carried all three of them shrieking and squirming back into the great room.

"'Tis only once a year, *chara*," Cormac replied, grinning at his offspring.

"Aye, once a year, but we've fifteen more days of the season yet to go," Claire replied with a little sigh, but she was smiling, too.

"Shall you be with us through the holidays?" Eileen asked Maura. The two were seated side by side on the trestle bench near the great room hearth.

"Aye," Maura answered. "Your sister has been kind enough to say that I am welcome."

"Of course you are welcome," Eileen replied warmly. "I trow, the entire family has fallen in love with you. Since I arrived, I've heard little else but the virtues of the new tutor."

"Lord, that must be quite tedious," Maura answered with a little grin.

"Nay, 'tis naught but the truth. Even Eamon seems to have fallen under your spell."

Maura looked for any sign of the jealousy she herself had felt, but the young woman's statement seemed to lack any rancor. "We've been teaching the children together," she explained. "It's meant that he has to be around me each day, whether it pleases him or not."

Eileen's cheeks dimpled, and she cast a glance across the room where Eamon, blindfold removed, was now rolling on the floor with the three children on top of him. "Ah, it pleases him, I've no doubt of that."

It was hard for Maura to believe that the sister of her employer would mention the match so freely. It was almost as if something between her and Eamon was not beyond possibility. She felt a lightening in her heart that had nothing to do with the nutmeg posset they'd been drinking since supper.

"It pleases me, too," she confided.

Eileen reached over to give Maura's hand a squeeze. "I will light a candle for your happiness and Eamon's as well," she said in a low voice. "Let us pray that the new year will bring all of us our heart's desire."

There was fervor in her words, and Maura remembered Eamon's explanation that Eileen had fallen in love with a man her father had not deemed suitable. She could not light a candle for Eileen's match—it was not the Romany way. If she were still with the Gypsies, she would give Eileen a potion of crushed hemlock or tell her to wish on a crescent moon, but in this new life, her former customs had to remain hidden. "Aye," she said finally. "We'll hope for a good year for all."

Eamon had risen from the floor, breathing hard from the exertion. The children still clung to him, but his gaze was on Maura. Eileen leaned toward her once again. "See how he looks at you. The man is besotted."

"I hardly think that's possible," Maura protested.

"Why not? You know 'tis said that whatever transpires during the twelve days of Christmas will determine the course of the year to come. And Christmas is a time of miracles."

Eileen gave her a last smile, then stood to help her sister bundle the children off to bed.

•　•　•

By Christmas Day, Maura had grown accustomed to the idea of being accepted as part of the Riordan family. The children had insisted that she be present for every meal, both noon and evening. She'd played the Christmas games, burned her mouth trying to grab raisins from the flaming bowl of snapdragon, searched the holly bushes for signs of the tiny faeries who might live within. She could not remember a time when she had laughed as much or felt so lighthearted.

Eamon's presence throughout the days just added to her giddy mood, though he had not again come to her room or tried to be alone with her.

The long Christmas mass had been an odd and quite wondrous ritual. The entire family had made the trip to Kilmessen for the services. She'd managed to follow along with strange motions of the priest and the parishioners, and she didn't think that anyone realized that the supposed daughter of a traditional village schoolmaster had never before been inside a church.

After mass Maura had spent the afternoon in the kitchen with Claire and Eileen and some of the servant women helping Molly prepare the Christmas feast. She'd never seen such a parade of food. Besides a magnificent boar's head, there was stuffed goose and spiced beef, puddings with brandy sauce and sweetmeats and currant cakes.

"Is it possible for one's stomach to burst?" Eily asked toward the end of the meal, her tiny hands clasped around her middle.

Maura, seated next to her, leaned over and answered, "I hadn't thought so until tonight."

"Then it might?" The little girl looked concerned.

"Nay, silly," Ultan answered. "Mistress Maura is teasing. Stomachs can't burst." He paused a minute and then asked, less certainly, "Can they?"

Maura put her arm around each of the children and hugged them. "Nay, for if 'twere possible, we surely would already have popped like a fool's pig bladder."

All three of the children were giggling when Eamon looked at them from across the table and demanded to be let in on the joke. "Aha!" he said when they had repeated Maura's words. "I do believe that the Lord of Misrule might have some new tricks for next Christmas."

"I know some children who'd best be off to bed if we're all going to make it through *this* Christmas," said Claire from the end of the table.

After some murmurs of disappointment that the happy day was over, everyone at the table stood and began moving away to their respective evening activities. Claire and Eileen ushered the children upstairs. Dermot and Cormac headed to the parlor for mulled brandy. Molly and the two servant girls who had been helping in the kitchen that afternoon came in to begin clearing the table.

"Let me help you clean up, Molly," Maura said quickly, partly out of a desire to assist the friendly cook and partly to keep from noticing that Eamon's gaze was on her again with that odd expression that made her stomach flip.

"Aye, Molly, me sweet," Eamon agreed. "We'll all pitch in and 'twill be done in no time."

"Lord love ye, Master Eamon, but ye don't need to be doin' that," the cook protested as Eamon lifted a heavy platter full of leftover plum puddings.

"Nonsense," he answered. "Many hands make light work. Isn't that in one of your books, teacher?" he asked Maura with a wink.

She made no reply, but she was smiling as she continued clearing off the crowded table, transporting the dishes out the back door to the washing shed. Molly directed the proceedings, and within minutes the big dining board was clear and had been wiped down with sand, ready for the next day's feasting.

"Mistress Maura and I will douse the lamps in the hall, Molly," Eamon told the cook as they placed the last load in the big tub where Molly would let the dishes soak until morning.

"Thank ye, Master Eamon," the cook answered with a grateful smile, her hand rubbing a crick in her back. " 'Tis a long day it's been, and that's the truth."

It seemed as if the other servants had disappeared, leaving Maura and Eamon to return to the dining hall alone. Eamon began walking along one long wall, turning the wicks of the wall sconces. After a moment's hesitation in which every instinct was telling her that she should flee up the big front stairs, Maura went over to the far wall and began to do the same along the opposite side of the room.

They met at the door. The dining hall behind them was now dark, but light shone through from the front hall putting Eamon's face half in shadow. He was standing very close, watching her. The palms of Maura's hands had grown moist.

" 'Twas a long day, but a marvelous one," she said. Her tone had a husky edge to it.

"Aye," Eamon agreed. He smiled down at her. "The first day of Christmas. Partridge in a pear tree." At her look of confusion, he asked, "Do you not know the carol?"

"Nay."

He seemed surprised. " 'Tis a carol they sing for the twelve days of Christmas, though 'tis really a kind of catechism devised to remember the true religion. You should ask the children to sing it for you."

"I shall." He was really *very* close. She could smell the sweet ale on his breath. She made a move to leave, but he put a hand up to the doorframe and blocked her exit. "I—er—I'll bid you good night, then," she said with a dry swallow.

"Do I not get Christmas wishes?"

"We all exchanged Christmas wishes before church this morning," she pointed out, suddenly short of breath. Was it her imagination or had he somehow managed to draw even closer without seeming to move?

"Ah, but that was for everyone. Now you must say them especially for me."

"*Nollaig shona duit,* Master Riordan," she said obediently offering the traditional Christmas wish.

He paused a moment, studying her. "I think you must call me Eamon," he said after a moment.

"'Twould hardly be proper—"

He put two fingers on her lips. "You forget, 'tis the Lord of Misrule says what is proper at Christmas."

"That's not fair," she said. "The Christmas activities are over for the day."

"Let me hear you say it," he urged. "'Tis not so hard. If you can twist all that Latin around your tongue, surely you can manage my name."

She knew that he was being outrageous, but she could not help smiling. "Very well. *Nollaig shona duit,* Eamon."

He nodded. "Aye, I like the sound of it."

His arm still blocked her way from the room. "Now I should leave," she said.

He shook his head.

"'Tis late and—"

He removed his arm from the doorframe and pointed up. She didn't need to follow the direction of his finger to know what was above her head. "I should be a sorry Lord of Misrule if I did not claim at least one kiss under the kissing bush," he said.

She could think of no answer, but felt the instant heat in her cheeks.

He leaned toward her and put his lips on hers briefly. It was over in an instant. She felt a mixture of relief and disappointment. "Happy Christmas, teacher," he said.

Her smile was shaky. "Thank you."

Once again she turned to leave, but this time he reached out to pull her back into the darkened room, out of the light of the hall, and folded her in his arms. "That was the Lord of Misrule's kiss," he said, his voice rough. "Now here's mine."

She didn't know how many minutes they clung to each other, mouths and tongues meeting in a passionate dance. At some point he had moved so that he held her against the wall of the dark room, his body pressed intimately into hers. His hand moved to one of her breasts, gently pressing, fingers searching for the raised tip. The other hand was at her waist, urging her softness against his midsection.

Maura's knees grew weak and she made a moan at the back of her throat.

Eamon pulled his mouth from hers and put his forehead on hers. "This is not going to go away, Maura— this thing between us. You know it as well as I."

She nodded, moving both their heads.

He moved his hips against her gently, allowing her to feel exactly the state of his desire. "What are we going to do about it?" he asked.

She had no idea. Miracles happened at Christmas, Eileen had told her. But she had seen no miracle come to change anything about the situation between her and Eamon. She still was the Gypsy thief. He still was the

powerful nobleman. Would giving in to the desire that
they obviously both felt do anything to close that
chasm?

Before she could answer, the voices of Cormac and
Dermot could be heard in the hall. Eamon straightened
up and released her. She smoothed her dress nervously.
"Don't worry," he said softly. "They won't see us here."

"You must let me go."

"I'll let you go if you promise to ride with me in the
morning."

Ride with him? The idea was exhilarating. She'd
grown up with horses. Her father's band had been
skilled traders. Other than her father and her friends in
camp, riding was the thing she had missed the most
during her years in Dublin. "Nay," she said, realizing
with a sinking heart that it was the only answer she
could give. "I can't go out with you. What would your
family say?"

"They'd say that the Lord of Misrule had ordered
the teacher to ride with him." His voice was light, but
he was not smiling, and she could see the passion still
in his narrowed eyes.

" 'Twould be impossible," she said.

"Then I shan't release you. And when Cormac
makes a final check of the house, he'll wonder why his
brother is holding his children's tutor pressed against
the wall of his dining room."

"You wouldn't dare."

He grasped her upper arms again and moved her
back against the wall. "I would," he said firmly.

She didn't truly believe that he would keep such a
threat, but finally, against her better judgment, she gave
in. "Very well, I'll ride with you. 'Twould feel that good
to be on a horse again."

He stepped back, releasing her. "Midmorning, then? Meet me at the stables?"

She nodded.

He looked at her, his face shadowed and stern. "That's a promise, teacher."

"Aye," she agreed. "I'll come to the stables at mid-morning."

For a moment when he heard the knock at his door, Eamon wondered if it could possibly be Maura. He instantly dismissed the idea. Though it had been clear that she had been as affected as he by their encounter in the dining hall, he also knew that she was nervous as hell about what it all meant. So was he.

He hadn't yet undressed, figuring that sleep would be long in coming this night. When the knock sounded again, he walked over and pulled open the door, seeing the person he expected on the other side.

"What are you doing up this time of night?" he asked his brother, not keeping the irritation out of his tone.

"I wanted to talk with you for a minute," Cormac replied. His gaze swept the room almost as if he were searching for someone.

As usual, there was almost no need for spoken communication between them. Eamon knew his brother well. "She's not here, if that's what you're thinking," he said.

Cormac walked over and sat on the bed. "But you admit that you've considered the idea?"

"None of your bloody business."

"Now that's where you're wrong, brother mine. The girl's in my employ. She teaches my children."

"Aye, but she's not indentured. She's free enough to make her own decisions." Eamon felt his temper rising as it always did when Cormac tried to act like the scolding big brother.

Cormac's tone stayed even. "Granted. I'm just concerned that she'll be hurt."

"I won't hurt her."

"How can you know that?"

Eamon gave a sigh and walked over to sit on the bed beside his brother. "I can't," he conceded. "But I'd not willingly hurt her."

"Are you in love with the girl?" Cormac asked abruptly.

Was he? Eamon didn't know how to answer. The very notion of love had always seemed preposterous to him, but he couldn't stop thinking about her. And he couldn't stop wanting her. If that was what it meant to be in love, then perhaps he had finally succumbed to the mysterious malady that had afflicted each of his brothers before him.

"Truth is, Cormac, she's got me in a muddle," he said.

Cormac smiled sadly. "I don't want *you* hurt, either, Eamon. 'Twould be best if you could forget about her. Mayhap you should plan another trip when the holidays are past."

Eamon leaned forward and dropped his head into his hands. "I'm not sure I want to leave just now."

"Which is exactly why you should," Cormac said firmly, standing. "At least think about it. 'Tis rumored they've found O'Neill's treasure."

Eamon straightened up at this piece of news. "The lost gold?"

"Aye. It could mean that they will launch a new campaign against the English. We need you to go north and find out what's happening. That should keep your mind off your beautiful, but poor-as-a-church-mouse teacher."

Eamon knew that his brother's concern was due to the many differences between him and Maura, not the state of her wealth. The Riordans had always prided themselves on looking at all men as equals. Of course, if Cormac knew the whole truth about Maura's past, he would no doubt be horrified that his brother had grown so close to her. But his brother was right about one thing. If the war with England was to start up again, it would mean that there would be little time to think about dalliances of any kind.

"I'll make plans to go north after Twelfth Night," he said soberly.

Cormac looked down at him with a gleam of sympathy in his eyes. " 'Tis for the best, brother."

"Aye."

Cormac waited a minute more for his brother to speak, but when Eamon remained silent, he turned and walked quietly out of the room.

Eamon tried not to feel guilty as he saw Maura walking up to the stables toward him. His brother's late-night visit had compounded the confusion he was already feeling. What was he intending to do anyway? he asked himself. There was no way to escape the question. He wanted her, and she wanted him. The signs were unmistakable. With women he had known previously, that had always been enough. But there had been no one like Maura in his past.

She was wearing a brown wool riding dress that showed off her trim figure. At least it covered her up, he thought ruefully. She'd been wearing Claire's old low-cut Christmas frocks all week, exposing much of her tantalizing white breasts. The riding dress exposed nothing, covering her chest up to a high-necked collar. Perhaps he could behave himself after all, he thought.

She looked a bit wary as she neared, but her expression turned into a smile when he greeted her with a casual tone. "'Tis a beautiful day for a ride, fair lady. Shall we choose you a gentle mount?"

"Oh, please, nay!" she exclaimed at once. "That is, you may of course give me any mount you like, but I'd much prefer one with spirit. The more spirit the better," she added.

She looked so much like a child asking for a sweet that he couldn't help laughing. "A spirited one 'twill be, then," he said. "I didn't realize that you were skilled at riding."

"I rode all the time when I was with . . . when I lived with my father."

As usual, there was an odd note in her voice when she talked about her childhood, but he let it pass. "I do remember thinking once that you were a good judge of horseflesh. You judged Cormac's horse superior to mine when you were deciding which one to *steal*."

"I stole the lesser one."

He gave her an amused glance. "Aye, I remember."

"Could we not talk about that time?" she asked, looking up at him with pleading eyes.

He discovered that he was so focused on the up and down sweep of her long eyelashes that he'd almost forgotten the topic already. "If you really like spirit, I'll put you on Lightning," he told her, taking her hand and leading her into the cool stable. They walked along the stalls until he came to a halt in front of a medium-sized gray mare.

Maura looked disappointed. "Will you be riding your stallion?" she asked.

"Aye." He nodded his head toward the stall where he kept his horse.

"What is his name?"

"Rioga," he answered, not mentioning that he had named the horse after the one she had stolen from him.

"Could I not have a stallion as well?" she begged, once again sounding like a little girl.

Eamon gave the gray a pat. "Trust me, teacher. You'll like Lightning. She'll give you as much spirit as you could ask for."

Maura gave a wishful glance toward Eamon's big horse, then nodded agreement and said nothing further as she helped him get both horses saddled. He threw the saddlebags he'd prepared over Rioga's rump, then turned to help her mount, only to find that she'd sprung up on the horse's back without assistance.

He couldn't remember when he'd seen such a broad smile on the tutor's face. "She does feel good," she said, smoothing a hand along Lightning's flank. "We'll see if she lives up to your promise."

"She will," Eamon said, swinging up onto his own mount.

They headed out of the stable side by side, their horses walking in apparent harmony.

"How long shall we be able to ride?" Maura asked. "I warrant 'tis a full two hours before the noon meal."

Eamon gathered his reins. "Aye, but we'll not be back for dinner. I want to show you Tara Hill, and 'tis nearly a two-hour ride. I got some food from Molly this morning and told her to inform Cormac not to expect us at the table."

Maura frowned. "Won't people know that we've gone off together?"

"Aye."

"What will your brother say?" she asked cautiously.

Eamon's temper surged. His brother's opinion was the last thing he wanted to think about at the moment.

"I don't give a bloody damn what he says," Eamon snapped. Then without asking if Maura was ready to ride, he gave Rioga a nudge that spurred the horse into a gallop and headed around the stables and up the hill.

Ten

Maura had been taken aback by Eamon's sudden burst of temper, but after a startled moment, she gave Lightning a gentle kick and turned her in the direction Eamon had gone. She was pleased by the animal's quick response and easy gait as they mounted the hill. In moments they had caught up to Eamon. He turned toward her with a rueful smile.

"Forgive me, teacher," he said. "I didn't mean to bark at you. I suppose the irritation comes from a lifetime of always having to listen to my big brother."

"And from the fact that you know your brother would not be pleased that we've come out together," Maura added.

He shrugged. "Mayhap. But 'tis too beautiful a day to worry about it. It hardly seems possible that it could be Christmas."

Maura looked around the hill. The unseasonable warmth had left a few hardy fall wildflowers still in bloom, and the normally sere winter grass was still green. The temperature was brisk, but there was a bril-

liant sun, and after several moments of riding, she felt
she hardly needed the cape that was part of Claire's old
riding ensemble.

"What made you decide to go all the way to Tara
Hill?" she asked him. "That was where I first met Ultan,
you know."

"I thought you met him at O'Donnell House."

"Nay, 'twas on a day we were both wanderers and
happened to come together in a magical little glen."

"That would be Cliodhna's Glen," he said with a
frown of disappointment. "That's where I'd planned to
take you today."

"Aye, I believe that's what Ultan called it. 'Tis a
beautiful place, and I'd love to see it again."

"Did they show you around Tara Hill while you
stayed at O'Donnell House?"

"Nay. After I brought Ultan home that day, we didn't
go back."

"But you were there the day you rescued me in the
woods."

"Aye." Maura hesitated. His words implied an unspoken question. Now that they were alone and away
from the house, it would be a perfect time to tell Eamon
more about her past. Perhaps she could even tell him
who she really was—the true nature of her family and
her childhood. She looked over at him as they rode
side-by-side. They had let their horses set their own
easy pace. He looked relaxed and happy.

And powerful and wealthy, she reminded herself.
Though his clothes were plain enough, they were made
from rich materials sewn by the finest hand. He wore a
heavy gold ring with the Riordan swan symbol. His riding boots were beautifully tooled, made of a leather
finer than any she'd ever seen in the Gypsy encamp-

ments her family had sometimes attended. They fit over his muscled legs as if they were part of his body.

She gave a little sigh. No matter how much in harmony they seemed riding along together, she'd never be able to tell Eamon the truth about her heritage. It would be the end of everything between them.

Staying with a safe topic, she said, "Little did I know that the mischievous nephews who left you trussed up that day would become so dear to me."

He grinned at her. "They are lovable scamps, aren't they? But I think everyone in the family is happy to see that they have settled down with a tutor who can turn some of their energy to books rather than pranks."

"I fear I'll not be able to help them much longer. Soon they'll be past what I can teach them."

"Not for a good many months, I warrant," Eamon argued. "And you're teaching them things that they can't get from books."

His words warmed her and helped dispel the slight gloom that had threatened to mar her day. She looked around again and took a deep breath of the crisp winter air. She knew that her stay with the Riordans could not last forever, but at the moment she was riding a fine horse on a beautiful day with a man at her side who made her senses alive as they had never been before. Nonna always said, "Tomorrow does not exist. Live today."

That was exactly what she intended to do.

They had reached the edge of a broad, gently sloped meadow. "I believe it's time to see if your claims about this horse are justified," she told him with a laugh. Then before he could reply, she gave Lightning the signal and held on as the beautiful little mare took off like the flash her name implied.

They reached Tara Hill in much less than the two

hours Eamon had predicted, but neither mount seemed overly tired.

"Did I not tell you?" he asked. "Riordan horses are the finest in the county. Even the females."

"*Even* the females? Fie on you, sir," Maura answered, pulling up beside him. "As I recall, my female beat your big male across the meadow back yonder."

"Only because you declared the race by surprise. You'd shot halfway across before we could get started."

They grinned at each other like children in a friendly rivalry. "I've enjoyed the morning," she said.

"So have I. Are you hungry yet, or should we wait to bring out the food when we get to Cliodhna's Glen?"

Maura wasn't the least bit hungry. She was already full to brimming with the joy of the morning—the ride, the laughter, and Eamon's presence at her side. She felt as if she'd drunk a pitcher of ale all by herself.

In the end they decided to wait for their meal, and Eamon led the way as they climbed the hill beyond the broad plain of Tara to make their way to the sheltered grove where Ultan had caught Maura talking to the still waters of the pond.

She smiled, remembering that day. Once again she'd been fleeing Pietro, running away. She'd had no idea where to go or what was to become of her. But fate had had a plan for her. It had brought her to the Riordans and to Eamon. As they dismounted next to the little pond, she wished the tranquil waters could tell her where fate planned to lead her next. A chill breeze ruffled the hair on the back of her neck.

"Are you cold?" Eamon asked. He was removing the saddlebags from his horse. "Mayhap 'tis too cold to lunch outside. We could head back and stop at O'Donnell House, if you prefer."

"Nay," she answered with a smile. "I'm not cold. 'Twas but a passing chill."

"I've a blanket," Eamon said, pulling a roll from behind his saddle. "If need be, you can drape it around your shoulders."

"Nay, truly, I'm fine," she assured him. The chill had passed, though a slight foreboding still lingered. Maura tried to ignore the feeling as she helped Eamon spread the blanket and lay out the food he'd brought.

When they were finished, they sat on opposite ends of the blanket, facing each other. "When you asked Molly for all this food, did you tell her who you would be riding with?" Maura asked, wondering just how open Eamon intended to be about their escapade.

"Aye," he answered. "I told her I was kidnapping you because you'd spent too many hours with your books and needed the outing."

"What did she say?"

"Molly's a wise little lady. She doesn't say much, but she fixes you with those gray eyes of hers and makes you feel as if you would be the lowest form of scoundrel if you ever did anything to disappoint her good opinion."

She studied him. "And does taking me riding threaten her good opinion of you?"

"Nay, Maura," he answered gently. "But she's fond of you. 'Twould threaten her opinion of me if I hurt you in some way."

Their gazes held. Neither one elaborated on what form that hurt might take.

"I promised her that I would take good care of you," he added. "And I intend to keep that promise."

Once again some kind of pull was happening between them that she didn't understand. She didn't know

how to fight it or if she wanted to fight it. Her mouth
had gone dry.

Eamon spoke more loudly than usual. "I do know
that Molly will be disappointed if we return with all this
food uneaten. Let's see what we have here."

He unwrapped a cloth and pulled out a chicken leg,
which he handed to her. She took it and brought it to her
mouth, scarcely recognizing what it was until the
greasy meat touched her lips.

Once she had taken the first couple of bites, she realized that the fresh air and the long ride had made her
hungrier than she had imagined. She managed to forget
about the odd sensations zinging back and forth between her and Eamon and concentrate on the meal. Besides the chicken, Molly had packed bread and cheese
and leftover Christmas cake. They finished it all, along
with most of the skin full of wine Eamon had brought.

When they were done, Maura wiped her mouth with
the back of her hand and flopped backward on the blanket with a contented sigh. "'Twas a veritable feast," she
said.

Eamon grinned down at her. "'Tis the banquet hall
that makes the banquet," he said, sweeping his arm to
indicate the vivid blue sky.

"Aye," she agreed. "This is a beautiful place. Did
you say you and your brothers came here as children?"

"We often had to come to Tara Hill for clan meet-
ings. Since we never found our elders' wranglings all
that interesting, Cormac and Niall and I would ride up
here to see if we could spot any faeries in Cliodhna's
pond."

"Did you ever see any?"

"Nay." Eamon grinned. "In truth, I've never much
believed in faeries. Cormac swears that a mysterious
woman appeared here once on the wall of that old altar

across the pond, but 'tis more likely that he was so besotted by Claire that he was seeing visions of her everywhere he looked."

"Now, that is a very romantic notion, Eamon Riordan," Maura declared.

"I reckon. Though 'tis no more than the truth."

He had cleared away the remains of the meal from the blanket between them and had moved next to her, leaning on one hand while he looked down at her as she lay on the blanket. Maura realized that she'd forgotten to breathe for several moments. She sucked in a ragged breath and managed to say, "They are much in love, those two."

Now he'd moved so that his head blotted out the sun over her. "Aye," he said. " 'Tis a treat to watch them together. They always seem to have trouble keeping their hands off each other. She's forever fussing about him, smoothing his hair back from his forehead or straightening his doublet."

"I've noticed," Maura agreed. "And he is constantly putting his hand at the back of her neck or touching her leg as they sit side by side."

"There are moments when they look at each other and you just know that they are both wishing the rest of the world would disappear for an hour or two."

"Wishing they could be alone."

"Aye."

The winter sun was suddenly hot. Maura swallowed and started to raise her head, but Eamon pushed her gently back. Though he continued to talk about his brother, the words were causing her insides to churn. "I remember when Cormac first took Claire to his bed," he was saying. "He complained that the wench had him in a constant state of need. 'Twas like a fever, he told it."

"That"—she licked her lips—"sounds unpleasant, don't you think?"

"I remember thinking that at the time. But only now am I beginning to understand what he meant." He leaned closer and lowered his voice. "I'm finding *myself* in a fever much of the time these days."

She looked up and saw nothing but his dark eyes. "And is it . . ." Her voice became almost inaudible. "Is it unpleasant?" she finished.

"I can't say. 'Tis a kind of wondrous torture."

She nodded, since she knew the feeling exactly. Just as she knew that he was going to kiss her.

At first he merely leaned down and touched her lips in a gentle, dry kiss, but her body was already so primed that the light contact sent flutters all the way to her fingertips. Without thinking, she reached her arms up around his neck to draw him down to her, and then he was lying beside her, pressing his body close to hers, his tongue making erotic explorations of her mouth.

She shifted and one of his legs moved on top of her, pressing her tender core, allowing her to be aware of his private part stiffening against her thigh. She tried to make her mind remember all the reasons that this could not be. All the impossibilities she'd lain awake at night considering. But her mind refused to think about anything but the feel of his hard body and soft mouth.

She turned toward him, letting him enfold her in his arms so that her breasts were pressed against his chest. She could feel them swell, pulling tight against the wool of her riding outfit. Heat went up her neck in waves, and she fumbled to find the fastening of her cape. "I'm warm," she told him.

"Not warm, teacher—burning. So am I." He gave her a hard kiss, then pushed her hand aside and took over the task of unhooking the clasp. " 'Tis this thing between us. It has bewitched us both, and I fear neither of us will find peace until we've given into it."

For the first time in her life, she knew what it felt like to have lust licking at her loins. Her head was a jumble and she wondered if she'd ever be able to think straight again. Eamon was right. It *was* like a fever. None of her questions had been answered, but she suddenly didn't care. "I don't know what to do," she murmured.

His eyes kindled with a smile and something stronger. "I *do* know what to do," he told her wryly. "But I could do it a lot better if you wouldn't mind ridding yourself of all this wool." He gestured to her riding frock. "Would it make you uncomfortable to remove it?"

She shook her head. Now that the decision had been made—by no will of her own, she would swear—she was eager to continue. She had already experienced a closeness with Eamon that she'd not known existed. Now she wanted to belong to him completely, if only for a few moments on this glorious winter afternoon.

They stood and together made short work of ridding her of her dress, leaving her clad only in a thin shift. Then Eamon, too, disrobed and stood before her naked. He was not the least bit ill at ease, but she felt some shyness as she let her eyes roam over his body, trying not to show surprise at the flagrant state of his manhood. After a moment he drew her against him, and she could feel the hard warmth of him at the juncture of her thighs. Her body throbbed against him.

While her sensations seemed to be pooling between her legs, Eamon was kissing her, and making gentle circles on each of her breasts through the thin fabric of her shift. "Your breasts are perfection, sweetheart," he murmured. "Sometimes when you've been bent over your books in the schoolroom, I'd watch them and ache to feel my hands on these little tips." As he spoke he began to twist her nipples gently with his fingers. Rays of feeling shot straight downward to her already swollen center.

"You watched my . . . my breasts?" she asked in wonder.

"'Tis what men do, my innocent. If we can't have our hands or our mouths on them, we watch them."

Her eyes had closed as his rhythmic ministrations continued. He pushed the straps of her shift off her shoulders, leaving her breasts bare. She could feel the sun on them. Out of some kind of age-old instinct, she lifted one full globe toward his face and let him take the nipple in his mouth.

The gentle tugs were exquisite, yet just on the edge of pleasure and pain. She made a slight move, and instantly he switched his attention from one breast to the other. Once again the sensation was soaring, and he stopped just when she felt the first threat of discomfort.

Suddenly he lifted her in his arms and deposited her back on the blanket. With an impatient sweep of his arm he sent the remains of their lunch scattering. She was on the ground and he was on top of her, and somewhere from deep in her mind came a brief moment of panic. Without thinking, she pushed hard against his chest.

He looked down in surprise. "What is it, *macushla*? Have you changed your mind?"

The endearment warmed her. This was simply too new, she told herself. She was nervous. "I don't know what I'm supposed to do," she said again.

"Don't fret, Mistress Maura," he reassured her with a relieved smile. "Today I'll be the teacher."

For the next several minutes he covered her face so thoroughly with kisses that she didn't have time to think of anything else. The brief moment of fear was forgotten. She lay back against the blanket and gave herself up to his skilled caresses. Then his hand was covering the soft hair at her thighs, his fingers searching the dampness there. They settled on a spot and began a gentle massage that made her gasp in wonder.

"You feel wet and welcoming, love," he whispered in her ear. His words made her wanting intensify. Since childhood, she had known more or less what transpired in the ritual of mating. She'd seen it enough times among the horses. The idea had never held much appeal for her. But now that it was Eamon beside her, she felt an overwhelming kind of primitive need to feel him within her. She wanted to *mate* with him.

As if he had read her thoughts, he moved over her again and nudged her opening with the tip of his penis. "Tell me if I hurt you, sweetheart," he told her as he entered her, but all she felt was liquid heat and a tremendous surge of emotion. They were one, truly and fully. She felt him as part of her body, and as he began to move, slowly at first and then with more force, she rocked with him. Her mind went blank as the feelings spiraled ever more intensely until finally he hissed an intake of air and clutched her waist. Then she felt his faint pulses deep inside. It was an experience so amazing that she burst into tears and felt her body quake with completion.

For several long moments she drifted. Then she was aware that Eamon was kissing the tears from her temples and murmuring, "*Macushla,* are you all right? I've done no harm?"

She opened her eyes and little by little the world came back into focus. She felt the rough texture of the blanket under her back. Above her the sun was still high in the bright winter sky. Eamon's face looking down at her was strained with anxiety.

She smiled up at him, and immediately his expression cleared. "I was afraid something was wrong," he explained. "You were crying."

"I didn't mean to be." She wiped her eyes with the back of her hand. "In truth, I wasn't even aware of the tears until—until afterward."

He grinned. "That's as it should be. Caught up in the moment, as they say."

"Caught up, indeed. I had no idea. It's no wonder people like it so."

He laughed and flopped down beside her on the blanket. "You found it pleasing, then?"

"Aye." Her eyes closed and she felt overwhelmingly sleepy. The same feeling seemed to have overtaken Eamon. For several minutes, neither spoke.

Little by little, she realized that she was lying outside with her shift bunched around her waist leaving her legs and breasts bare. She sat up and looked around. "What if someone should come by?" she asked.

Eamon's eyelids fluttered open. He grabbed her arm and pulled her back down beside him. "No one will come, sweetheart. This is our private world today."

"Are you sure?"

He grinned at her without lifting his head. "Would anyone dare disobey the orders of the Lord of Misrule?"

"Apparently not," she answered with a rueful smile. "You had little enough trouble bending me to your will."

At that he sat up. "Oh ho! Is the maiden trying to claim that she was not a willing participant? For I had ample evidence to the contrary." He softened the words with a smile, but there was a question in his eyes.

"The maiden was willing," she admitted.

"Good." He lay back down beside her. "The Lord of Misrule is a mischievous fellow, but he'd not order someone to act against their own will. Nor would I," he added more seriously.

She gave him a smile of reassurance. "'Twas my own body telling me how to act."

He turned and pulled her into his arms, lightly kissing the tip of her nose. "Tell me you do not regret it, *macushla,* for I swear 'twas the sweetest lovemaking I've ever known."

She settled her head against his shoulder. Did she regret it? Except for the one brief moment of panic toward the beginning, the entire experience had been amazing and wonderful. Whatever was to follow, she was grateful she had had this day. "Nay," she told him. "I don't regret it."

He gave her a squeeze. Now that the desperate urge was past, she was better able to concentrate on little details such as the feel of his bare skin against hers. Experimentally she moved her hand up and down the muscles of his arm, then down his back and over the curve of his hard buttock. Looking down, she saw that he had hardened again. She let her hand linger behind him, as his erection grew against her. It gave her a delicious feeling of power.

With a growl at the back of his throat, he reached back to pluck her hand off his backside. "Careful, sweetheart, or you'll find your lovemaking lessons prolonged."

The mere thought that she had been able to make him hard again had started her own juices stirring. Looking down at herself, she could see her nipples had once again grown stiff and pink. With a smile she said, "I believe lessons should be taught thoroughly, lest the pupil forget the teaching before the next class."

"Do ye now?" he asked, his voice instantly husky.

"Aye."

"Well, we've all afternoon. Are ye tryin' to tell me we needs must repeat the lesson until ye know it by heart?"

The gentle waves had already begun again in her midsection. "Aye." A whisper was all she could manage. "I'd want to be sure that my teacher is satisfied with my progress."

"Ah, sweetheart, your teacher is already *very* satisfied," Eamon said, his eyes narrowing. Then he flipped her over onto her back once again and moved over her. "And he's about to be satisfied again."

Eleven

Maura was not sure what to expect as she went for the requested meeting with Claire in the ladies' solar. It had been three days since she and Eamon had ridden off together, not returning until well after suppertime. Eamon had made no attempt to hide the fact that they had been together the entire day, nor that he had become entranced by her.

Maura was the first one he sought out at every holiday gathering, and she was well aware that he was standing closer, leaning nearer, and smiling more intimately than would be considered proper for a gentleman of the household and the children's tutor. He even touched her occasionally, guiding her from room to room with a hand at the small of her back or taking her hand to help her up from her chair.

Then there was her own reaction—the flaming of her cheeks when he approached, the sparkle in her eyes every time he smiled at her. The couple had made no effort to be alone together again, and the children did not seem to notice anything different, but any of the adults would have to blind not to see what was happening between them. And Claire was not blind.

Maura knocked softly on the half-open door, then went in. Claire looked up with her usual pleasant smile, and Maura breathed a little more easily. If she was to be dressed down for her behavior with the younger brother, at least it appeared the reprimand would be without rancor.

"Have a seat, Maura," Claire said, motioning her to a small tooled-leather chair. "I'd like to speak to you about a couple of matters."

Maura nodded and sat down, clasping her hands tightly in her lap.

Claire gave a little laugh and set aside the tapestry square she'd been sewing. "Don't look so worried, my dear. You've committed no crime. This isn't a tribunal."

Maura tried to smile. Claire and all the Riordans had been kind to her. She didn't want to think that she had repaid their kindness by deceiving them, but of course that was exactly what she had done. And now she'd become involved with Eamon in a way both he and she still had yet to understand.

The afternoon they had spent in the glen, it had seemed as if every other consideration had ceased to exist. It was just the two of them in that magical place. But the truth was that there were other things to think about. There were people who loved him and wanted to see him properly wed. There were rules of society that made matches between people of different stations impossible.

She voiced part of her thoughts. "You've been kind to me, Lady Riordan. I'll never forget it. If you think 'tis best for me to leave, I'll do so at once."

Claire's eyes widened. "Leave? What nonsense is this? Surely you know that Eamon's fallen in love with you? I'd thought . . . I had reason to hope you felt the same about him."

Maura's jaw dropped. "But . . . such a thing . . ." She could not even form the words. "'Tis not possible. He's a . . . the Riordans are rich and powerful and I . . ."

Claire leaned forward. "You are a lovely, bright young woman whom he would be lucky to win," she said.

Maura could not have been more surprised if Claire had slapped her. "I . . . is that the way *Lord* Riordan feels about the matter?"

Claire made a dismissive gesture. "Men are always slower to come around to accepting these things when it comes to romance. You're not denying that you do love Eamon, then?"

Maura shook her head slowly. "I . . . I believe I do love him, milady. Though I have little enough experience to know."

"Experience is not usually a requirement, Maura," Claire said, smiling. "People have been falling in love without any experience at all for hundreds of years, I'd imagine. Suddenly one day you just look at him and you know. 'Tis nothing you'd ever planned."

"Aye," Maura confirmed, her tone gloomy. "That's exactly how it is. But, begging Your Ladyship's pardon, I warrant Lord Riordan may be less likely to accept such a notion than you think."

"You may leave Lord Riordan to me. Besides, Maura, you may be every bit as suitable a match for Eamon as anyone in the county. We haven't found your mother's family yet. Mayhap you're a countess with every right to lord it over the rest of us."

Though Maura had had a similar fantasy, she knew in her heart that such a thing was unlikely. And even if she did find out that her mother was from a genteel family, that fact would really have nothing to do with her. She'd grown up a Romany, and in her mind, that was what she would always be. Would it make a difference to Eamon? she wondered. If her mother was from respectable Irish society, would he be more likely to consider marriage to her?

Of course, he'd never said anything about marriage, and it could well be the farthest thing from his mind. The only thing she knew for certain was that he had wanted her body, and that was something that many men had wanted before him.

The thought brought a slight shiver of discomfort. Since her afternoon at Tara Hill with Eamon, she'd had a flash or two of unwanted memories from the day she'd run away from Pietro years ago. At the time she'd been an innocent, horrified child, and she'd worked hard to put aside every recollection of the things Pietro had tried to do to her. Until this week, she'd been successful in blocking most of it from her mind.

"Would that bother you?" Claire asked with a puzzled frown.

Maura had lost the thread of the conversation. "Would it bother me . . . ?" she asked.

"To find out that you come from a noble family," Claire prompted.

"Ah." She hesitated. "Nay, I . . . it wouldn't bother me. 'Tis just that I don't feel that would have too much to do with the real me."

"Exactly," Claire said, pleased. "Which is why it shouldn't matter that what we *do* know is that your father was a humble schoolmaster. Where you come from is not important. What matters is who you are—which is a dear girl who has my brother-in-law walking around the house whistling for the first time since I've known him."

Maura gave an inner groan at the mention of her schoolmaster fable. Should she tell Claire the truth? Would this amazing tolerance that seemed to be a characteristic of the Riordan household extend to Gypsies—the most outcast group in Irish society? Somehow she didn't think so. Even tolerance had its limits.

"Eamon and I haven't talked about . . . about anything of that nature," she said finally. "Most likely, this is a passing fancy that—"

Claire interrupted with a snort. "Eamon doesn't have passing fancies. He's too serious. I don't mean to tell you that he's lived the life of a monk, but as far as I know, no woman has ever reached him the way you have." She paused a moment, considering, then said firmly, "Nay, if this isn't love, then neither will the sun rise in the east tomorrow."

Maura felt a tremendous surge of happiness. She hadn't dared hope that what she and Eamon were experiencing was love. She hadn't even voiced the notion to herself. But Claire's certainty made her heart sing.

"What do you think I should do?" she asked Claire.

"Why, 'tis fairly new this thing between you, is it not?"

Maura nodded.

"Then there's no help for it. You still have to suffer the agony."

Now Maura was thoroughly confused. "The . . . er . . . agony, milady?"

"Aye. We've all had to endure it. It's that terrible time when you're not sure of him and he's not sure of you. You don't know how much to say or when to say it. He doesn't know how much to show or how to show it. I swear, 'tis the faeries set things up this way for their amusement."

Maura joined in Claire's laugh, but she had a feeling

that there was a great deal of truth in her employer's words. She'd already had a sample of the kind of agony she was talking about it. "Is it worth it?" she asked.

Claire's expression became tender, and Maura knew instantly that she was thinking of Cormac. "Aye," she said. "It's worth every bit of the suffering when you can end up with the kind of strong and enduring love that I've found. 'Tis what I most heartily wish for you and Eamon."

Maura's eyes brimmed with tears as she gave her employer a grateful look. "I thank you, milady."

Claire leaned over to pick up her sewing. "I think you'd best begin to call me Claire. I only wanted this chat to reassure myself that you were feeling the same way as he. And the light I see shining in those blue eyes of yours leaves me with no doubt. Now go on and find him, if you like. Tell him that his sister-in-law is matchmaking again, and this time he may find the notion more to his liking."

After her talk in the solar, Maura went looking for Eamon, but was just as glad to learn that he had ridden out with his brother and cousin and would not return until late. She needed time to absorb what Claire had told her.

Claire had seemed so certain that Eamon was in love with her, and for a moment, Maura had dared to believe it. Was it possible? She sailed through the rest of the day, happier than she could ever remember being, yet feeling some of that agony Claire had cautioned about.

Should she tell Eamon what Claire had said? What if Claire had been mistaken and he hadn't even considered the notion of love? They'd had one afternoon together. Did that mean he loved her? They'd made love. Did that mean he wanted to marry her? And if he did, could she continue to deceive him? Could she accept an offer of marriage knowing that she was living a lie?

By supper she was exhausted with the sheer weight of unanswered questions. When Cormac, Eamon, and Dermot had not returned by the end of the meal, she excused herself and went up to her room, intending to try to let sleep free her from the incessant thinking.

Of course, her mind had its own plan. The questions continued while she tossed and turned on the bed, rose to attend the fire, then returned to the bed to toss and turn some more. She had no idea of the hour when she finally gave up the attempt. She would do better to be reading a book than trying to sleep, she decided, slipping from her bed. Drawing a wrap around her thin night rail, she started toward the door.

She was halfway across the room when she heard the knock. The fast beat of her heart told her who it was before she opened the door to find Eamon standing outside holding a candle.

Beyond him, the hall was dark and there was no sign of any other light or activity. To all appearances, the rest of the household had retired. "What are you doing here?" she whispered.

He grinned at her. "I've come to spirit you away to Cliodhna's Glen or, that not being practical"—he stepped inside the room and closed the door firmly behind him—"we could create our own little faerie cove right here."

"It's past midnight," she protested.

"Aye. Cormac and I didn't come in until late. Did you miss me, teacher?" he added, giving a teasing tweak to her nose.

"Aye . . . I mean, nay. That is—" All at once she felt as tongue-tied with him as she had the first few days in the schoolroom. He had not changed from when she had last seen him that morning, but after what Claire had told her, everything was different. Finally she blurted, "I met with Claire today."

His expression sobered and he walked around her to put his candlestick on her nightstand. "And it appears to have distressed you," he observed with a frown. He sat on her bed and reached a hand toward her. "Come and tell me about it, sweetheart. What did she say to you?"

She avoided his gaze as she walked over to take a seat next to him on the bed, carefully avoiding contact. She remembered one of Nonna's sayings: "Plain speaking is the shortest road to understanding."

Hoping that Nonna's advice would prove to carry its usual wisdom, she took a deep breath and said, "Claire seems to think we're in love with each other. She says 'tis plain to the others."

Eamon's tense expression relaxed into a smile. "I should think so. I've done everything but holler it from the Kilmessen church steeple."

She looked at him, dumbfounded, her mind a jumble of elation and irritation. More of the agony Claire had mentioned? she wondered wryly. "You might have tried hollerin' it to *me*, Eamon Riordan. Then I might have been more prepared to hear it from your sister-in-law."

He grinned and reached over to lift her into his lap. "I was hollering as loud as could be four days ago in Cliodhna's Glen." He put his mouth close to her ear to whisper, "Mayhap ye didn't hear me because ye were doin' a bit of hollerin' yourself that day, as I recall."

She could feel his breath tickling her neck, and it made chills run down half her body. "That's not what I'm talking about," she said, still not satisfied with the casual way he was handling what was to her such a momentous revelation.

"Ah, *macushla,* I don't mean to tease you. The truth

is, I received a bit of a talking-to myself from my big brother and my cousin today."

She stiffened. "What did they say?"

He voice was studiously casual. "Probably much the same as Claire. They said 'tis plain as a turnip that I've fallen for you, and if I don't intend to do the proper thing by you, I'd best own up to it right now before they have to intervene to defend your honor. Being as how you've no family to defend it for you," Eamon added with a rueful grin.

"Truly?" she asked in wonder, relaxing again in his arms. "They said all that?"

"Aye."

Something about the way his glance slid away from her made Maura think that Eamon was not telling her the entire story about his conversation with his brother, though she couldn't be sure. Perhaps it was just that it was hard to believe that things could be this easy. "What would your brother say if he knew that I had once tried to steal his horse?"

Eamon nuzzled her neck. "I think we may best forget to mention that little detail," he said.

"It might make him see me in a different light."

He stopped nuzzling her and looked into her eyes. "It matters not how Cormac sees you, sweetheart. I'm the one who's fallen in love with you. Cormac mentioned that he wanted to find out a little more about your father's school and so on, but I told him not to bother with inquiries. I fell in love with *you*, not with your father's daughter."

Now the half-chill had crept over her whole body. Cormac had actually mentioned making inquiries? It would not be hard for them to discover that the village where she had placed her fictitious schoolmaster father knew of no such person.

Things had gone too far, she realized. It was time for her to tell Eamon the whole truth. If that ended things between them, so be it, but she simply couldn't let this deception continue. Eamon had told her more than once that her background made no difference to him. It was time she took him at his word.

"I *am* my father's daughter," she began slowly. "If we are truly to be together, you need to know more about me. I need to explain where I came from and—"

He put his fingers against her lips and gave a kind of groan. "Sweetheart, do you mean to keep me talking all night or will you let me kiss you the way I've been wanting to every waking minute since we left Cliodhna's Glen?"

As if worried that his words weren't convincing enough, he moved his fingers from her lips and replaced them with his mouth.

"But 'tis important," she murmured against him.

"So is this," he whispered back.

Then his tongue was seeking entry and she could no longer speak. She let him deepen the kiss, and all thoughts of trying to continue the discussion fled. She'd tell him later, she promised herself. For now, she had suddenly grown as impatient as he.

The kisses lasted only a short time before he was pulling at her wrap, then lifting her night rail over her head to leave her lying naked against the clean linens of her bed. The fire had almost died out, but by the light of the one flickering candle, she could see the bronze gleam of his skin as he, too, disrobed. Once again his erection drew her attention immediately, and this time she was bold enough to reach a hand to touch him there.

He gave a pleased gasp, then cupped his own hand around hers to show her how tightly to hold him. "The teacher is a fast learner," he said with a shaky laugh. He

knelt beside her on the bed, allowing her easy access to
explore the private places that were so different from
her own. Maura's natural curiosity combined with her
own rising desire to make her examination thorough
and erotic. Finally she looked up at him and saw him
watching her with hooded eyes, nostrils flared. It gave
him a fierce expression. Looming over her with his
broad chest and strong arms, he had every aspect of an
ancient warrior, full of the bloodlust of battle.

For just a moment she felt the swift rise of panic. The
same thing had happened briefly back at Cliodhna's
Glen, she remembered, but it had been fleeting.

Swallowing back the unreasoning fear, she reached
up to pull him against her. This was no wild warrior in
her bed, she told herself. It was Eamon. The man who
had just declared his love for her. He came willingly,
stretching his body along the length of hers, his hands
seeking her breasts.

"Cliodhna herself could not have been more beautiful, *macushla*," he murmured, bending to take one
peaking nipple in his mouth.

The goddess and the warrior—a fitting couple, she
thought, still trying to push aside the moment of fright.
She allowed him to lave her breasts for several long
moments until all memory of the panicky moment had
fled. Then she took his hand and guided him down to
the place he had massaged with such skill on their previous encounter. Once again she was already wet, and
this time he had barely begun touching her before she
stiffened with a sudden climax.

"Oh!" she cried. "Forgive me. It's not supposed to
happen that way, is it?"

Eamon threw back his head and laughed. He had
stopped the rhythmic attention of his fingers, but his
hand still lay against her there, warm and comforting.

"Sweetheart, it's supposed to happen any way and every way it feels good. This just means that I was not the only one who was eager."

He looked up and down her body. "Now you've turned a rosy pink for me."

She felt her already flushed face grow warmer still with embarrassment. "It somehow doesn't seem respectable," she told him.

"Everything's respectable when two people love each other, sweetheart. I rather like you in pink," he teased. "And I do believe I'm going to kiss every inch of your pretty pink skin, starting here." He kissed her forehead, then her nose, her cheeks, her mouth, then the tip of each breast.

She lay still, giggling, and let him work his way down her body, all the way to her toes. When he had wiggled his tongue along the bottom of each foot, she said, "You've reached the end, I believe. That's every inch of me."

He slid back up against her, his expression once again intense. "Nay," he said softly. "I missed one spot."

One of his hands was between her legs, but she couldn't believe that he could mean to kiss her there. Yet to her amazement, he slid down, moving his fingers to open her. Then his mouth was there, gently licking the most sensitive hidden folds, and moving up to encircle the tiny center of sensation. He lingered there, sucking gently, until she thought her body would surely ignite into flame.

Just as she felt herself about to go over the edge once again, he quickly moved up and entered her, driving deep inside, his rhythm matching the waves of her climax.

For several moments afterward, she couldn't move.

Her arms and legs seemed impossibly heavy. The weight of Eamon's body pressed her further into the billowy mattress. Her head spun in endless circles.

Finally Eamon moved to one side and gathered her in his arms. "Now that that's taken care of," he said wryly after several long moments of silence, "you can continue telling me those things that were so important a few minutes ago."

She gave a dreamy smile. "I'm not sure my mouth will move anymore," she said. "I'm quite certain none of the rest of me will."

Her head was against his warm chest and she could feel his chuckle. "Faith, sweetheart, are ye afflicted with some kind of strange malady?"

"Aye," she said. "Strange and wonderful."

She could feel him kiss the top of her head. "You have that right. Strange and wonderful, indeed. 'Tis what we are together," he told her fervently. "How can you think that anything else in this world could matter?"

She wanted to believe him. She wanted to think that what she and Eamon had found together was so perfect and so complete that they could have a life together no matter what had come before.

"Maybe it doesn't," she said finally. "Maybe it doesn't matter."

Without letting her go, he reached down to pull a cover over them. "Then if there's no more need for discussion, I'd suggest we go to sleep, for unless we intend to scandalize your three charges, I need to be away from this room before dawn."

He was right. As comforting and warm as it felt to be held by him like this, the children often came to wake her in the morning, and she wouldn't want them to discover him here. "Perhaps you should leave now," she suggested with reluctance.

He put his head up and looked down at her with a sleepy grin. "Do you really want me to leave?"

"Nay."

"Good," he said, settling back down beside her. "For I intend to let you wake me in the morning."

She snuggled against him. "How would you like to be awakened, sir?" she asked archly.

He gave her a light pat on the bottom. "I have a feeling you know exactly how I would like to be awakened, minx. But if you don't stop that squirming, we'll neither one of us ever get to sleep."

"In truth, I'd given up on sleep for the night. I was on my way to fetch a book when you came."

Once again he pulled away to look down at her. "Truly?"

"Aye."

He appeared to be considering as his hand made a slow path along the curve of her side. "I've never been one to be overly fond of sleep, either," he said finally. Then he brought his mouth down on hers once again.

Twelve

In spite of her earlier statement, Maura had fallen into a deep sleep almost instantly after their lovemaking. Eamon continued to hold her against him, still enjoying the sense of oneness. He was finding that the tender feelings Maura engendered were like nothing he had ever before experienced. Though there had been no lack of love in the Riordan household, the love had been expressed through the rough screen of male camaraderie. After his father's third bride had died giving birth to Eamon's brother Niall, the elder Riordan had refused to consider marrying again, choosing to raise his boys without the soft influence of a woman.

He looked down at Maura in his arms, watching the even rise and fall of her breasts. Her cheeks had lost the rosy flush of their lovemaking. In the dark room they looked an alabaster white and finely chiseled, as though by the hand of an expert sculptor.

She belonged to him, he thought, feeling an odd swelling in his chest. This spirited, brave, beautiful creature was his. Or would be, if he had anything to say about it. He had not told her the entire truth about his conversation with Cormac and Dermot. While it was true that they had warned him against causing her hurt, they were also concerned that he himself might suffer.

"What do we know of this girl?" Cormac had asked.

Eamon wasn't at all sure that his brother would give up his efforts to find out more about her. And while Eamon believed her story about her thievery being an action taken in desperation after the death of her father, Cormac might not be so understanding.

He sighed. At least it appeared that Claire was on his side. He could always count on his sister-in-law to take up the cause of happiness, even if that meant going against the rules prescribed by society.

Maura stirred slightly in his arms, and he cradled her like a child.

Perhaps he should just marry her, he thought suddenly. Once the vows had been spoken, neither Cormac nor anyone else could do anything about it. Maura and he would be together, till death, and anything that might have been disturbing about her past would no longer matter.

Once the idea had surfaced, he couldn't stop thinking about it. It was almost Twelfth Night, a fitting and romantic time for new lives and sacred promises. He'd ask her then, he decided. It would be the Lord of Misrule's last and finest Christmas trick.

Once again she shifted position, more restlessly this time. Her legs moved against him. He looked down at her, concerned, as she gave a moan.

"Sleep, *macushla*," he whispered, trying again to rock her gently back into slumber. But her agitation continued. She twisted against him as if trying to escape from his embrace. The moans continued, becoming stronger, more frightened. Her eyes were still closed, and she appeared to be having some kind of bad dream. He held her more tightly. "Everything's fine, sweetheart. Go to sleep."

"Stop!" she yelled, and then her fists began pummeling his chest.

Surprised, Eamon released her at once and moved to give her space on the bed. He was sure she didn't know that it was him she was hitting. He tried to decide if he should wake her fully.

"Stay away from me!" she cried, and then she said a foreign name that sounded like "Pietro!"

Alarmed, he took her shoulders in his hands and shook her, but still she did not awaken. "Don't touch me! I'll kill you!" she said, quite plainly.

A chill went through him. Was this truly a nightmare, or was Maura reliving some horrible moment from her past? Did this have anything to do with the reason she'd stolen his horse? It had been done out of desperation, she'd told him.

"Maura," he said, speaking more loudly. "Wake up, sweetheart. You're having a bad dream."

Finally his words seemed to penetrate. She turned her head from side to side with another fearful whimper, then her eyelids fluttered open. She stared at him with a terrified expression, as if she didn't recognize him.

"'Tis I, sweetheart," he assured her. "You're safe in your bed. Nothing can happen to you."

Gradually the fear went out of her face. "I was dreaming?" she asked, dazed.

"Aye, a bad one, from the sound of it. Do you remember what it was about?"

She averted her eyes. He had the sense that she *did* remember, but she didn't want to tell him about it.

"Was it a bad experience you once had?" he pressed. "Was someone trying to harm you?"

She shook her head. "I-I don't know. I don't remember. 'Twas a dream, as you said."

Her answer was nervous and forced. He frowned. What could she be remembering that she didn't want to tell him? They'd just declared their love for each other and spent much of the night in each other's arms. Surely she should feel comfortable to confide in him, even if the memories were painful?

He waited another few moments, hoping that she would change her mind and talk to him, but she remained silent, lying next to him tensely, and watching him with wary eyes, as if worried that he would continue his questions.

Finally he sighed and leaned over to kiss her on her cheek. It was cold as marble. "Sweetheart, if something is disturbing you, you can tell me about it."

"Aye," she said.

Once again he waited, and once again she remained silent. "I should be leaving," he told her. "It will be dawn soon and the servants will be stirring."

She nodded stiffly.

"Are you going to be all right?" he asked.

"Aye, I'm fine."

He wasn't satisfied with her answer, but the faint light through the window told him that he had little time to make his way to his own room. He rose from the bed and pulled on his hose and boots, then bundled the rest of his clothes under one arm.

"Will the dream come back?" he asked her.

She sat up. "Nay, I'm getting up. I'll get some reading in before the children are up."

He was displeased at the ending to what had been a momentous evening. She seemed tense and distant. All the closeness they had had together had disappeared. But he could now hear activity below in the hall. "I'll see you later today," he said quickly, forcing a smile.

"Aye," she said, but had no answering smile for him. With a puzzled frown, he turned and left the room.

The dream had been much more vivid than the memories she retained of that horrifying night. All the years that she'd spent away, she'd pushed those memories away, until they stopped threatening to surface. She'd worked to wipe away any trace of that vision of Pietro as he had come into her wagon that night, his eyes glazed and leering. He'd smelled of garlic and hard liquor. They'd buried her father that same morning, and she was weary with grief, but when he had seized her, she'd fought him with every bit of strength she could muster.

Maura looked around the fine chamber the Riordans had given her. She smoothed her hands over the expensive linen sheet of her bed. She'd moved on to a different life. No doubt, Pietro and his band had moved on as well. She'd never have to be afraid of him again. Still, now that the images had been resurrected, she couldn't seem to get them out of her head.

"Don't worry, little Maura," he had slurred that night with a drunken smile. "Your father's dead, but Pietro will take care of you now." He'd wrenched her to the floor of the wagon and pinned her there with his arms and legs. Then to her horror, he'd shoved his hand under her skirts and pushed his fingers into her most private places. She'd fought waves of nausea while she struggled, kicking at him and pushing against his chest. When she was finally able to land a solid kick to his left shin, he'd pulled back and slapped her across the cheek so hard that it had made bright lights explode in her eyes.

She'd never forgotten that slap, all those years in Dublin. Even after she'd been able to push the rest of the dreadful encounter to the deep recesses of her mind, she'd remembered the slap. Now the entire scene came flooding back—how he'd bruised her breasts trying to tear the dress from her body and bloodied her lip mashing his mouth against hers.

If it hadn't been for Momo, he would have completed the rape. Maura was never sure how much Momo had understood about what was happening when he had poked his head into the wagon to ask indignantly, "What are you doing to her, Pietro?"

The interruption had startled the drunken Pietro long enough for Maura to escape from underneath him. Then she'd scrambled out of the wagon, grabbing Momo's hand to pull him along with her as she fled into the woods.

"What's wrong?" Momo had asked.

She'd merely shaken her head and told him, "Pietro's drunk. We need to leave him alone."

"You're crying," Momo had observed with alarm. "Did Pietro hurt you?"

Maura had merely shaken her head. Momo sometimes considered himself her champion, and she hadn't wanted the boy getting any ideas about trying to go up against Pietro. Now, still lying in her bed in Riordan Hall, she could remember every detail of that night. She remembered crouching in the woods with Momo, watching her wagon to be sure that Pietro would not come out in search of her. She remembered the rustling of the leaves above them as the night wind became cold. She remembered sending Momo back to his wagon to fetch her a set of his clothes, then walking deeper into the woods to retch violently. When Momo returned she had dressed herself in male garb. Then steeling herself

against the misery in his dark eyes, she'd bid him farewell and crept away from the Gypsy camp.

What had triggered the memories? Why now? she
wondered. Her lovemaking with Eamon had nothing to
do with what had happened between her and Pietro that
night, yet for a moment in her sleep, she'd thought that
Eamon was Pietro, holding her against her will. There
was no comparison, she told herself firmly. The one
was beautiful; the other was obscene.

She lay in bed for several minutes longer, willing
away the bad memories. Finally, feeling as though she
hadn't slept at all, she got up from her bed and went to
splash water on her face from the bowl on the wash-
stand.

Last night she'd felt ready to tell Eamon everything
about her past. Now she wasn't so sure. She knew that
Eamon had wanted a fuller explanation of her dream,
but she couldn't imagine telling him or anyone about
that shameful night with Pietro. Not ever. Even now,
thinking about it, she could taste the bitter bile rising at
the back of her throat.

*I'll wait until after the holidays to tell him about my
real family,* she decided. She would not spoil the magic
of these Christmas days by bringing up the shadows of
her past.

For as long as anyone could remember, Riordan Hall
had celebrated New Year's Day by inviting the Kilmessen villagers and anyone else who should happen along
for a special celebration. The men were served cups of
ale, and the children were given gingerbread cakes and
marzipan sweets in the shape of stars and angels. Molly
and her kitchen girls had been working on the treats for
a week.

Maura was relieved to be swept up in the busy

preparations. It meant that she could take her mind off the disturbing end to her night with Eamon. He had sought her out that morning with a worried expression, but when she had managed to give him a smile of reassurance, he seemed to forget about the incident and joined in doing his part to get ready for their visitors.

New Year's Day dawned bright and warm, so tables were set up out of doors to allow more space for people to mingle and enjoy the Riordans' annual bounty.

The children had been waiting eagerly for the event. They'd followed the progress of the marzipan in Molly's kitchen, and had been the beneficiaries of the occasional treat "just to test the batch," as Molly had told them with a wink.

The morning of New Year's the three were all up early, dressed in their finest clothes. After the briefest of knocks, they came tumbling into Maura's bedchamber, each vying with the other for the right to speak.

"You must get up, Mistress Maura. It's New Year's!" Ultan shouted. "You must choose your best frock for today. 'Tis the custom."

By now Maura was used to their morning visits. Though she still wore her night rail, she didn't feel the least self-conscious as the three piled on to her bed. "You must help me, then," she told them. "For your mother has given me so many lovely things that I'm not sure I know which is the best one."

"The green!" Eily shouted.

"You want everything green," Ultan told her with some disdain.

"I like green," Eily said, subdued.

Maura reached to give her a hug. "So do I," she said. "And I think you may be right. The green it shall be. Now you must give me a moment to change, and then we'll all run down to the kitchen and see if Molly needs help with the treats."

"I get to cut the gingerbread this year," Ultan said proudly.

"Do I?" Dylan asked Maura, who had no idea.

"Nay, you can't use the cake knife until you're nine like me. Isn't that right, Mistress Maura?"

Maura looked from one eager face to the other. She sensed that the use of the cake knife represented some kind of milestone. "Boys, Molly is in charge of the kitchen. Whatever rules she makes, the rest of us have to follow."

"Even you?" Dylan asked.

"Aye. Everyone."

"Even Papa," Eily added with a giggle. "Molly told us that she used to slap his hand if he tried to steal a tart before supper."

"Molly's in charge," Ultan parroted, sending his brother a smug little smile. "And Molly says that this year I may use the big knife."

"Your turn will come," she said to Dylan, giving his shoulder a pat.

"Papa lets me hold his sword," Dylan said defensively.

"Only when he's watching," Ultan retorted. "And the cake knife is sharper even than a sword. Molly told me."

Maura sighed. The Riordan boys were good children and she knew that they cared about each other. But sometimes their incessant brotherly rivalry was wearing. "If you don't scoot out so I can get dressed, Molly will have the gingerbread all cut before we even get down to the kitchen."

At that, all three of the children trooped obediently out of the room.

At least their squabbling took her mind off her own concerns, Maura thought with a smile. It promised to be a happy, busy day, and if she was lucky, she would not have time to think about what she should or shouldn't tell Eamon about the shadows of her past.

Watching the Riordans mingle with the people of Kilmessen was a delight. Maura already knew that the family was not at all like some of the wealthy landlords she'd heard about. They were kind and generous and without pretensions. They were all wearing their finest clothes today, as though a visit from the village cobbler was every bit as important as one from the most powerful earl in the land.

The children were having a wonderful time playing hosts. They plied their village counterparts with gingerbread and sweetmeats until what had seemed to Maura an enormous supply had been totally devoured.

"This has always been one of my favorite days of the year," Eamon said, coming up from behind her as she stood along the stone wall of the house surveying the scene.

She turned around to him with a smile. "I can see why. The Riordans are giving happiness to everyone and, from all appearances, receiving it back in full measure."

"Aye, we're fortunate. We reap more than we sow."

To her surprise, he put his arm around her. She looked around the yard, wondering if anyone was watching them. Even after knowing that both Claire and Cormac knew of their affection, it was hard to believe that Eamon would want to show it so openly. But after the initial surprise, his gesture gave her a warm glow inside. She leaned against him. "I believe the Riordans have sown a great deal. The people on your estate are content."

He frowned. "Aye. I just hope they can stay that way."

"What do you mean? Why wouldn't they?"

Eamon gave his head an impatient shake. "It's nothing. I shouldn't have brought it up to dampen a joyous day."

She stepped out of the circle of his arm and turned to face him. "Nay, tell me. What makes you think things will change?"

He gave a rueful smile. "Ah, sweetheart, things always change. Surely you have learned that with the twists your life has taken. But what I was referring to specifically was war. War can wreak the most dramatic of changes."

Maura remembered the earlier conversation when Claire had mentioned that talk of war was heating up, which might mean that Eamon would have to travel after the holidays.

"Are the English sending more troops?" she asked.

He nodded. "All the time. And taking over more Irish estates. While we've sat without response for lack of leaders to organize the opposition and lack of funds to fight with."

"And now?"

"Now a new O'Neill is emerging to take on the leadership of his fallen uncle, Shane. His name is Hugh O'Neill, the Earl of Tyrone. And the rumor is, Tyrone has his uncle's gold."

Eamon was right. The talk of war was dampening the merry spirit of the day. "Will you have to leave?" she asked.

"Not if I can help it, *macushla*. Normally, I'd not mind the travel, but these days I have a good reason to linger at Riordan Hall." He took a quick look around the yard, then bent to kiss her.

Maura returned the kiss briefly, but then did her own search of the yard. She still wasn't completely comfortable with his public attention. In particular, she wanted to explain things to the children before they saw her exchanging caresses with their uncle. Her gaze scanned the crowd. Though the food was gone, many of the villagers remained, still enjoying the festive mood and the company.

Suddenly she saw a face among the revelers that made her freeze in shock. Pietro. The blood drained from her face and she felt instantly cold. Quickly she turned back to Eamon, positioning herself so that she would be hidden from the crowd behind them.

"Shall we go see if there might be one or two of Molly's marzipans at the bottom of one of the trays?" he asked, reaching to take her hand. She snatched it away, and he looked down in surprise. "What's wrong?"

Pietro. It couldn't be. She wanted to turn around to be sure that her eyes were not playing wicked tricks, but in her heart she knew that it had, indeed, been he. This was not the face of her restless dreams. It was Pietro, real and near.

"Is something amiss?" Eamon asked again.

She swayed slightly, realizing that it was not at all difficult to pretend a sudden affliction. " 'Tis a megrim," she said. "It came over me of a sudden."

Eamon looked concerned. "We should get you out of the sun."

"Aye, but I can go inside by myself. You stay until the festivities are finished."

"Nay," he said firmly. "I'll see you safely to your bed. You need to lie down until you feel better."

She tried protesting, but he insisted on accompanying her to her bedchamber and sitting with her there until she told him that she was feeling better and only required a little time to rest. When he finally left her, she turned and pushed her face into the pillow.

What devil's luck had made Pietro show up at Riordan Hall? Did he know that she was there? Maura thought not. If he had known where she was, she believed he would have sought her out before this. She took some deep even breaths to try to slow her heart, which had been drumming inside her since the moment she saw his face.

It meant nothing, she told herself. His appearance today had been mere chance. He had simply come upon the gathering and had seen a chance for some free drink. The New Year's celebration was over. By now the crowds downstairs were leaving and Pietro with them. There was no reason to think that he would ever find out she was here.

She grabbed the pillow and rocked back and forth miserably, trying to rid herself of the memories that were threatening to surface once again.

She repeated her reassurances. It was mere chance that had brought him here. It meant nothing. And then, unbidden, she could hear Nonna's voice with another of her favorite sayings. *"There is no such thing as chance."*

Thirteen

Something was wrong, Eamon decided gloomily as he came in from his brisk twilight ride.

He'd known from the beginning that Maura was not a typical woman. The first time he'd met her, she'd been stealing his horse. She claimed her father was a schoolmaster, yet she came to them not knowing how to read. Granted, she had learned quickly, but at the beginning there had been no doubt—she was new to the skill.

He finished taking the saddle off Rioga, patted the animal, then turned to walk out of the stables. Aidan, the stableman was just finishing up feeding the horses. "It were a fine New Year's, Master Eamon, were it not?" the man said with a grin. "One of the finest we've had. The day could've passed fer summer."

"Aye," Eamon agreed, though in his current mood nothing seemed fine to him. Maura had insisted that he leave her alone after her spell in the yard, and he'd had the feeling that she'd sent him away more to escape his questions than to rest.

"I didn't think ye'd want to be ridin' today or I'd have come up afore this. I figured everyone would be well nigh done in after the celebration."

"I just felt the need for a ride," Eamon explained. "I didn't expect you to be here, Aidan. 'Tis a holiday for you, too."

The stableman was a distant Riordan cousin and, as such, sometimes took more liberties than the typical servant. He cocked his head and studied Eamon. "Looks to me as if ye were ridin' off a problem. Did ye manage to rid yerself of it?"

Eamon gave a little chuckle at the stableman's perceptiveness. "I'm not sure, my friend. I'm not even sure I know what the problem is."

Aidan nodded and turned to close the stall of the last horse he'd been tending. "Ah," he said, "then 'tis a woman fer sure. The lassies are the only ones that leave us poor gents in that much of a muddle. 'Tis that teacher, then?"

The question didn't surprise Eamon. He calculated that everyone in the household knew by now. "Aye," he confirmed.

"Well, if 'twere a female horse, I could give ye some help, but I ain't much good with the human kind."

Eamon laughed. "I reckon 'tis my puzzle to work out for myself."

"I'd thought it might be something about the O'Neill."

"The O'Neill?"

"Aye, did ye not hear? Your brother got word this afternoon that he's near, meeting with the Hennessys in Fingarry."

This was news, indeed. If Hugh O'Neill had come all this way to meet with one of the strongest of rebel families, it meant that things were getting serious. Perhaps the rumors about O'Neill having his uncle's gold were true. Something had made him decide to move now.

Aidan was watching him with a concerned expression. "What do ye think it'll mean? War again?"

"It's very possible."

"'Tis a sad thing, then."

"Aye," Eamon said gravely. "At least we had a happy New Year's."

"Aye, we did that," the stableman agreed with a smile.

Eamon gave him a little wave, then turned to run down the hill toward the house in search of his brother.

He found both Cormac and Dermot in the great room, staring gloomily into the fire.

"What's happened?" Eamon asked, out of breath.

Cormac looked up. "Where the hell have you been?"

Eamon was surprised at his brother's unusually harsh tone, but he didn't take offense. Obviously, Cormac was upset. "I needed a ride," he answered. "I was gone little more than an hour."

Cormac grimaced. "Forgive me, brother. I've no right to be taking my temper out on you. 'Tis this bloody war. I fear it's about to start up again, and it's come right here to the gates of Riordan Hall." He motioned for Eamon to help himself to ale and take a seat with them.

"I'll be riding north tonight to alert the rest of the family," Dermot added.

"What about Niall in Killarney?" Eamon asked. "Will he need help from us?"

"More likely *we'll* need help from *him,*" Cormac corrected. "I tell you, 'tis here on our doorstep."

There was a note of urgency in his voice. "What do

you mean?" Eamon asked, taking a seat next to his brother.

Cormac leaned close and lowered his voice. "I mean the O'Neill's gold. It's here."

"Here?" Eamon's question was loud, and Cormac motioned him to silence.

"The fewer people who know about it the better. It's only temporary, of course. Evidently Hugh O'Neill decided Riordan Hall would be a safe place to keep it where no one would look. We're a Midlands family that has managed to stay neutral through much of the conflict."

"And one who tried to broker the peace with Elizabeth when Hugh's uncle Shane was alive," Dermot added.

The youngest Riordan brother, Niall, had been Shane O'Neill's representative to the court of Queen Elizabeth herself before his attraction to one of her beautiful ladies-in-waiting had landed him in the Tower of London.

"But . . . you mean, right here? At Riordan Hall? Where? Is someone guarding it?" Eamon still couldn't believe what he was hearing.

Cormac sighed. "Two of O'Neill's men brought it in quietly, just after twilight. Then they rode off again. They said the O'Neill didn't want any guards around to alert people to the possibility that the treasure might be near. According to his men, the O'Neill's words were 'If no one knows it's there, no one will try to steal it.'"

Eamon sagged back in his chair and took a long drink of ale. "How can he be sure that he can trust us? What if we want to use it for our own ends?"

"Is there a family in Ireland whose word is trusted more than the Riordans?" Dermot asked. "Is there a man more respected than your brother?"

"Nay."

"Hugh O'Neill knows we won't betray him," Cormac agreed. "I'm just not as sure about his judgment in leaving it here unguarded."

"Where is it?" Eamon asked, looking around the room as if expecting to see gold bars under the furniture.

"In the armory. 'Tis rare that anyone goes there." The armory was an old shed full of broken pieces of armor and weapons, many of them obsolete. The building had been used little since the end of the last fighting eight years ago.

"How long will it have to stay here?" Eamon asked.

"O'Neill is negotiating with the Dutch for the purchase of new weapons. The English soldiers have muskets. We can't fight them with pikes and arrows anymore," Cormac explained. "When the deal's done, someone will come for the gold."

"I mislike the thought of that kind of money sitting here in our very household," Eamon said.

"As do I," his brother agreed. "But until I can speak with the O'Neill himself, I'll let it stay. With luck, no one will ever know that it's here. I've told only Claire."

Eamon's thoughts were on Maura. While Cormac could feel free to share this secret with his wife, Eamon realized that it was something he would not feel comfortable confiding in Maura, especially not now after her odd behavior of the past couple of days. Did it mean he didn't trust her? he asked himself. She'd been a thief once. He'd thought he'd been able to forget that, but suddenly he wasn't so sure.

"Ultan and Dylan sometimes play around the kitchen, which is near the armory," Eamon pointed out.

"We've thought about that. Claire will tell Maura to keep them away."

Eamon shifted in his seat, wondering if he should voice his doubts. He had never told Cormac about Maura having once been a horse thief. Did he dare continue to keep this secret? "Will you tell Maura about the gold?"

He tried to make his question casual, but he could tell from his brother's sharp look that Cormac wondered what his brother was thinking.

"You're the one who's claiming to be in love with the girl. Do you think we should tell her?"

Eamon hesitated. "Nay," he said finally. "As you said, the fewer people who know, the better."

To Eamon's relief, Cormac did not question him further.

"I need sleep, if I'm to ride north in the morning," Dermot said after a moment of awkward silence.

The three men said their goodbyes, and Eamon left to go upstairs, feeling tired and confused. He had been planning another visit to Maura's room, but her odd behavior and his reaction to her knowing about the gold made him reluctant to face her. In four days it would be Twelfth Night, the day he had been planning to ask her to be his wife. But all at once he was no longer certain of what had seemed so clear to him a couple of days ago.

What did he know about the woman who had come to them calling herself Maura Roman? He knew only one thing for certain about her life before she had come into the Riordan household. She had once been a thief.

And at the moment, a fortune in gold lay unguarded within easy reach.

Even the children seemed to be wearying of the holidays. Though Maura had tried to do a little reading each day, she missed the long hours in the schoolroom.

The last golden days of fall that she'd spent with Eamon and the children had been among the happiest of her life.

Would there be more days like that once the holidays were over? she wondered. Suddenly it seemed as if nothing was the same. For one thing, things had somehow changed between herself and Eamon. For another, each day the talk of war grew. Eamon had remained vague about whether he would have to leave once Christmas was over.

With only one day left before Twelfth Night, the end of the festivities, Maura felt oddly unsettled. She still hadn't gotten over the sudden appearance of Pietro on New Year's Day. She still hadn't entirely banished the old memories from her restless sleep.

She wished she could curl up on top of the barrel in Nonna's wagon, as she had so often in the past, and ask the old woman to give her assurances that everything would come out all right.

Perhaps a ride would help, she decided. Eamon had told her that she was free to take a horse out any time she wanted. Earlier she'd seen Aidan the horsemaster working around the stables. She'd ask if he would help her saddle Lightning. A swift run across the plains would be just the thing to clear her head.

With sudden decision she went to her room to put on her riding frock, then ran out of the house and made her way up the hill to the stables. She glanced at the sky. It would be at least an hour before sundown, she decided. She would have plenty of time for a nice ride.

There was no sign of Aidan as she neared the big barn, she noted with a frown. If she couldn't find him, she'd have to figure out how to saddle the big horse by herself. In the waning afternoon light the inside of the stable was nearly dark. "Aidan?" she called, the sound echoing.

She entered the big building, waiting for her eyes to adjust to the lack of light. Lightning's stall was at the far end, she remembered.

"So ye've become one of 'em, have ye? All dressed like a lady in yer fancy riding togs?"

She whirled around with a gasp.

Pietro stepped out of the shadows. "Ye've not told them who ye are, I warrant," he said. Then he reached a thick hand to knock off her neat black riding cap. Her hair tumbled loose around her shoulders. "No one knows ye're just a tramp Gypsy girl."

There was the distinct garlic odor and fetid breath, the smells of her nightmares. The stables were too far from the house for anyone to hear her if she screamed, but she knew that it would be a mistake to allow Pietro to see her fear.

Straightening, she asked coldly, "What are you doing here, Pietro?"

"Why, I come to see ye, girl," he answered with the leering grin that she'd never been able to totally erase from her mind.

"I'm not interested in seeing you, Pietro," she said. "I've a home here and people who can protect me against the likes of you."

He looked around the stable. "Where are they, then, these protectors of yers?"

She would *not* panic, she told herself firmly. "I'm meeting someone here any minute."

She winced as he took a painful hold on the tender part of her upper arm. "Aye, 'tis a Riordan ye'll be meeting, from the rumors in the village. Ye've come up in the world. Ye were too good to lift yer skirts fer the likes o' me, but I reckon when the Riordan came snif-fin' around, ye were ready enough to spread yer legs."

She wrenched away from him and looked toward the door, gauging whether she could run fast enough to get within sight of the house before he could reach her. But he followed the direction of her gaze and grabbed her again, this time pushing her against the wall of a stall. He fastened his hand on the collar of her riding frock and ripped it away. "Mayhap I'll take me a sample of what the gentry's been gettin'," he said.

She could begin to fight, but she had the feeling that a struggle would inflame him more. Instead, she used her most contemptuous tones and said, "Take your hands off me, Pietro, or I swear when the Riordans get up here, I'll have them throw you in the gaol."

To her surprise, he let her go and took a step back. She didn't know if it was her new clothes or a new confidence, but somehow Pietro sensed that she had changed. She was no longer the Gypsy girl he could bend to his will.

"Riordan can have ye fer all I care," he said sourly. "I came fer the gold, and if ye know what's good fer ye, ye'll tell me where it is."

Maura's eyes widened. She remembered Eamon mentioning something about rebel gold, but she had no idea why Pietro would think she knew anything about it. "What gold?" she asked.

He put his forearm against her upper chest and slammed her against the stall. "Don't play coy with me. The gold yer lover is hiding fer the rebel leader."

Tears stung her eyes at the sudden pain. It felt as if he had broken her neck. She gave a little cough and gasped, "I have no idea what you're talking about."

His eyes were like two black beads. "It's here some-where. Everyone in the village is saying it. The O'Neill is in Fingarry, the next village over, and everyone says his men brought the gold to Riordan Hall for safe-keeping."

Maura rubbed her neck. It was hard for her to imag-ine that there could be any truth to the story. She'd seen no strangers at Riordan Hall, and the family had been busy with celebrations, right up through yesterday's New Year's festivities. "I don't believe it," she said. "There's no gold here. And even if there were, what is it to you? The gold belongs to someone else."

"Only until I find it."

" 'Tis against the Kris, Pietro. We take only what we need, remember? And pay in kind."

"To hell with the Kris. That gold will take us out of this wretched place, back to Spain, where the weather is warm and the wine is cheap."

Maura frowned. She remembered Pietro's arguments with her father about leaving Ireland. Like other Gypsy bands, they had been wanderers, but her father had always wanted to stay in Ireland. Maura had often thought it was because here he could still feel close to her mother.

"Nothing's stopping you from going back to Spain, Pietro. You don't need the gold to do it. Just sell a few more of the leather—"

"Aye, sell our trinkets," Pietro interrupted her, "sell our leather, fix their pots, shoe their horses, all so that they can throw us a penny now and then. 'Tis no way fer a man to live. I mean to end it—*now*."

He was sweating profusely, and the crazed expres-sion on his face scared her. Yet she didn't think he was drunk. She decided to try reasoning with him once more. "Pietro, listen to me. I swear—I swear it on my father's grave—there's been no gold brought here. 'Tis Christmas here. I've been with the family every day, celebrating. I-I'm close to them now. If there were any gold, I'd know about it."

Her words seemed to reach him. "Then where is it?" he asked.

"I don't know. I only know it's not at Riordan Hall."

His eyes narrowed. "If ye're lying to me—"

"I'm not," she said firmly.

Suddenly a figure was silhouetted at the rear door of the stable. "Is that you, Mistress Roman?"

It was the stablemaster. "You'd best leave," she told Pietro quickly.

He looked down the row of stalls toward the far door, then back at her. "I intend to find that gold," he said, leaning close. "And if I find ye've lied to me, ye'll be sorry ye ever lived."

Then as suddenly as he had appeared, he was gone.

"Who was that?" Aidan asked, walking toward her.

Maura smoothed her dress, pulling up the bodice to cover the loss of her collar. "Ah—'twas no one. A passerby."

The stablemaster came closer. "He didn't bother ye, did he, Mistress Roman? Ye do look a bit distressed."

"Nay, he didn't bother me."

"Are ye waiting fer Master Eamon?"

Did everyone on the estate know about her and Eamon? Maura wondered. She tried to smile, but found her lips were too shaky. "Nay, I was thinking about riding out myself, but it's growing late. I've decided to wait for another day."

"I be glad of that, Mistress Roman. Beggin' yer pardon, but ye shouldn't be travelin' out alone. I warrant Master Eamon'd not like that."

"I'll wait to go when he can accompany me," she said, turning to leave.

"Aye, 'tis best. Good day to ye, then."

Maura managed to give the man a nod and a brief smile and maintain the expression while she walked out of the stable. But as soon as she started down the hill toward the house, the tears poured down her face.

Eamon knew that the only way he and Maura were going to get things straight between them was to spend some time together. Time alone, so that they could talk freely. Yet for the past two days it seemed that she was always with the children or with Claire or helping Molly in the kitchen. And now this afternoon, when he'd gone in search of her, she seemed to have disappeared entirely. He'd asked every member of the household, and no one knew where she'd gone.

He'd just decided to head up to the stables to see if she could possibly have gone riding when he saw her through the window of the great room. She was walking toward the house, and even from a distance, it appeared that she was crying.

He frowned. His first instinct was to run out to her to see what was wrong, but the way things had been between them, he hesitated. Instead, he went to stand in the door of the great room where she couldn't fail to see him as she came into the hall.

When she came through the front door, she was not only crying, she was sobbing, her shoulders shaking with great wrenching gasps. All uncertainty forgotten, he strode over to her and pulled her into his arms. "Sweetheart, what is it? Are you hurt?" he asked.

She shook her head, but didn't seem to be able to speak. "Ah, *macushla*," he said, letting her bury her face against his chest. "Whatever it is, we'll take care of it. Don't fret so."

For several moments she simply clung to him as her sobs subsided. Eamon held her slight body against him and felt such a wave of protectiveness that it nearly brought tears to his eyes as well. All his doubts of the past couple of days fled. Perhaps it was true that she had secrets. There may be things in her past that were shameful or dark. But as he felt the tremor of her chest against him and heard the dying whimpers of her tears, he knew that whatever it was, he was willing to face it. He loved her, as he had never thought to love anyone. He wanted to keep her safe and make her happy and prevent anything from hurting her ever again.

Finally the storm seemed to have subsided. He held her away so that he could look into her eyes. "What is it, sweetheart? Tell me. What has distressed you so?"

"You don't know who I am," she said in broken gulps.

He was right. This thing that was shadowing her—that was shadowing *them*—concerned her past.

They were still standing in the middle of the hall, which was not the best place for this conversation. "Let's go to your room, teacher," he said. "We need to talk. And after we've talked, I intend to make love to you until you are finally convinced that whatever you have to tell me is not going to make any difference between us."

Fourteen

Even though Eamon's arm was around her waist supporting her, Maura felt as if she were walking up a gallows stair instead of the grand staircase of Riordan Hall. Though he hadn't spoken the words, she sensed that Eamon was ready to offer her a new life and with it his love and protection. She had only to reach out and take it. But she knew that in order to do so, she had to tell him the whole truth about who and what she was.

Even before the appearance of Pietro today, she had realized that she needed to tell Eamon about her past. Now she had no choice. Pietro knew she was here. Once he realized his search for the rebel gold was fruitless, he'd no doubt be back to finish what he had tried to start with her.

Eamon smiled down at her. He had sworn that nothing she could tell him would make a difference between them. But he didn't know the enormity of the lie she had been living.

When they reached her room, he let her go long enough to throw a couple of logs on the fire. "Shall we

sit here on the hearth?" he asked. At her nod, he
scooped the pillows off the bed and threw them on the
floor. The bark on the new logs caught suddenly and
sent up a shower of sparks.

It was appropriate, Maura thought, taking a seat in
front of the blaze. The most important talks she'd had
growing up with her father and Nonna had been sitting
around the fire at their camp.

Eamon picked up a shawl from the end of the bed
and walked around to drape it over her shoulders. Then
he sat down beside her. Without touching her, he leaned
back against the pillows and said, "Now, tell me. What
disturbed you just now? What has been bothering you
these past three days?"

She took a long time, trying to decide where to start.

He misconstrued her silence. "You have reason to
trust me, teacher," he pointed out. "Have I not kept all
your secrets?"

"Aye," she said slowly. "I've made you a conspirator
in my many deceptions against your kind and generous
brother and sister-in-law."

He frowned. "You may have overstated your creden-
tials as a tutor, but you did the job they hired you to do.
You helped Ultan tame his wild impulses and you got
all the children interested in their studies. I doubt the
finest London scholar could have done any better."

His continuing generosity only made her guilt
deeper. "Eamon," she said slowly. "I'm not the daughter of a schoolmaster."

"I rather guessed that, teacher. And I like to hear my
name on your lips," he added.

She looked at him, surprised. "You guessed it?"

"Aye." He shrugged. "I couldn't imagine a father
who loved books not wanting to introduce them to his
daughter. I certainly intend to introduce them to ours."

She wasn't sure she had heard him correctly. "Ours?" Her voice was barely audible.

He grinned at her. "Aye. The half dozen daughters you and I will have together. For I've decided that this household needs more lassies."

Maura slipped the shawl off her shoulders as the heat from the fire joined the flush of her neck. "Half dozen?" she asked.

"More or less. We might have a lad or two if you want along the way, but we'll start with the girls."

There was no doubt about it. He was talking about marriage. That thing she had not even dared hope for. His words were almost making her forget what they had come here to discuss, but she forced herself back to it. Pietro was out there. Her life had caught up to her, and she had to tell him.

"We might name the first one after my mother—"

"Stop!" she said sharply.

His smile faded.

"Eamon, I'm a Gypsy."

He stared at her for a moment, then gave a little laugh. "Aye, and I'm a pirate. We'll make a good team. What nonsense is this, sweetheart?"

"I *am* a Gypsy, though we call ourselves Romanies. My father's name was Giacomo. I was born and raised in an open camp. I slept each night underneath a wagon, watching the stars."

Eamon had straightened up from the pillows. He looked as if he'd swallowed a bad piece of meat.

"The stories I tell the children are Gypsy stories," she continued. "The songs are the ones I learned at night around the Gypsy campfire."

"How can you be a Gypsy?" he asked finally. "You have red hair and blue eyes—"

"From my mother," she told him. "You know that

Claire has been trying to find a family in the neighbor-hood."

"A family whose daughter ran away some twenty-three years ago to marry a poor village schoolmaster."

"Aye, but 'twas not a schoolmaster she went to marry. 'Twas my father, Giacomo. She ran away to the Gypsies and became one of them."

Eamon had turned from her to look into the fire. He sat hunched over his knees. "That day when I first saw you," he said slowly. "Were you stealing the horses for them? For the Gypsies?"

She pulled herself up indignantly. "Nay! We don't steal horses. 'Tis not our way to steal anything unless we are in dire need, and then we replace in kind, how-ever we can."

He still didn't look at her. "Why did you leave them?"

"The day I took your horse, I was running away. My father had just died, as I once told you. That part was the truth. And I decided that I couldn't stay." Now was the time to tell him about Pietro's attacks—the one all those years ago and the one this evening. But some-how she couldn't form the words.

"I felt I had to leave," she said finally. "My father was dead, and the only true family I had left would be my mother's people."

Finally he turned toward her, puzzled. "But you didn't try to find your mother all those years ago?"

"Nay, I-I wasn't sure how to survive here, so I went to the city."

"With my horse," he said dryly.

"Aye, with your horse. That money gave me the free-dom to find myself a proper job instead of living on the streets."

"What did you do?" Eamon asked with a slight wince.

She looked him in the eyes. "I served in a tavern."

His eyes widened. She could sense what he was thinking. "Aye, I served ale and food to the rummies of the waterfront. I smiled at them and I returned their sallies. I dodged their pinches and slapped away their hands. But I never served myself. Not once. Not ever."

He was silent for a long time. Finally he said in a strained tone, "You were right, teacher. You've managed to take me aback."

What had she expected? she asked herself. Had she thought he would not be affected by her revelation? She ached to have him turn to her with that crooked grin and pull her into his arms, but she knew that it would not happen. He already knew that she was a horse thief. Now she'd told him that she was a Gypsy and a tavern wench. How much would one man be expected to take from the woman he had wanted to produce him a house full of fine and proper daughters.

"So now you know," Maura said. Unlike earlier after the incident with Pietro in the stables, this time her eyes were dry. Deep inside, she could feel the breaking of her heart, but the sorrow was too deep for the tears to surface.

"Now I know," he agreed softly. Then after a moment he added, "Were you planning to go back to them after you found out about your mother's family?"

"Back to the Gypsy camp?" she asked, surprised.

"Aye. As you say, your life was wandering, living in the open, sleeping under the stars. You must miss it."

She had thought the whole notion would horrify him, but amazingly, Eamon seemed to understand that some parts of her Gypsy life had been appealing, even wonderful. Did she miss it? Sometimes. She smoothed her hands over the fine wool of Claire's riding frock. But she would miss this life more. Not the trappings of this life, but the people—the children, Molly, Claire. She would miss *him* a thousand times more than she would ever miss any life she had once known.

"Nay, I was never planning to go back," she answered.

He was quiet a long time, once again staring into the fire. She had to be patient, she told herself, to let him have time to think about what she had told him. But she wished he would give some indication of how he was feeling. She wished he would look at her. What she wished most of all was that he would draw her into his arms and tell her that he didn't care where she had come from, that he loved her and still wanted to make that family of little girls and raise them together. But she realized it was too much to ask. Though he hadn't appeared as shocked as she had expected, as he started to think about what an odd life she had had, he would probably become more and more distant.

"Did you hope to find a place with your mother's family?" he asked after a long silence.

She shrugged. "Mostly I just wanted to know who she was. After that, I wasn't sure. I was"—it sounded silly to voice the Gypsy words in this Gajo world she had entered—"I was waiting for fate to show me my path, to guide my fortune."

Finally he turned to look at her, his expression puzzled. "Nay, you weren't," he disagreed. "You were making your own fortune. You found yourself a position here. Then you studied and learned a whole new skill in order to be able to continue in that position."

"Which I wouldn't have been able to do without your help."

He waved off her disclaimer. "Which you did by

working hard and using that quick mind of yours.
You've not sat back and waited for some kind of fate to
blow you any which way. As I've told you before,
you're one of the most remarkable women I've ever
known."

Finding her remarkable did not mean that he could
accept her in the same way he had when he'd thought
she was part of the Gajo world. He still had made no
move to touch her. He'd not called her sweetheart or af-
firmed his love for her. His knee was only inches from
her hand, and she longed to make some kind of contact,
but she wouldn't do it without his signal.

"I'm grateful, Eamon," she said. "I'm grateful for
everything you've done for me."

He continued watching her for a few long moments,
then said, "You never told me what had you so upset
earlier in the hall."

If he had taken her in his arms, she might have had
the courage to tell him about Pietro, but as he continued
to sit without touching her, she couldn't bring herself to
do it. "I reckon I was worrying about how to tell you all
this," she answered slowly. "I knew it would make a
difference between us. And you'll be wanting to tell
your brother, which means my days here are most likely
at an end."

"Because you're a Gypsy?"

"Aye. No father in the Gajo world would trust a
Gypsy with his children. Gypsies don't *teach* children—they *steal* them."

His glance slid away from her.

"Tell me you've not heard that," she demanded.

"There may be many who think that way, but my father always taught his sons to judge everyone for who
they are. Cormac and Claire have had ample time to see
who you are with their children and what you mean to

them. I can't see that they would feel any differently about you because of your heritage."

She knew the Riordans were remarkable people, but she couldn't believe that even they could completely overcome all the prejudices that Maura's people had always endured. "So you will tell them?"

"I think they should know," he said gently. "For your sake as well as for theirs. You just admitted how worried you've been about this. You won't feel right until this is out in the open."

She reached behind her to pick up the shawl she had discarded. In spite of the heat of the fire, she once again felt cold. "I'll tell them tomorrow," she said.

"Nay, tomorrow is Twelfth Night. After the holiday has ended will be soon enough." As if he was suddenly eager to be out of her company, he jumped to his feet. "I should go get ready for supper. I'll see you in the dining hall."

She shook her head. "I've no appetite tonight. Will you make my excuses?"

He'd already started walking toward the door. "Shall I have Molly bring you up something?"

"Nay, I'm not hungry. Truly."

He hesitated, regarding her with a look of concern, but when she managed a brief smile, he turned again to leave.

He was just about to open the door when she thought to ask, "Eamon, have you heard anything about rebel gold in the area?"

His hand seemed to freeze on its way to the door latch. "Rebel gold?" he asked, a little too casually.

Her sudden cold turned into a shiver. "I—I heard a rumor that this Hugh O'Neill you told me about has brought his gold to the Midlands. Perhaps even near Riordan Hall."

Without turning back to look at her, he said, "Nay, 'tis not likely. O'Neill's stronghold is in the north. If he has the gold, he would want to keep it safe there."

"Ah, so 'tis just rumor."

"Aye," he said. " 'Tis just rumor. If you change your mind about the food, send word to Molly."

Then he was out the door.

Maura hunched over her knees, clutching the shawl around her and rocking slightly in misery. Eamon was lying. She knew it as surely as if a burning brand had suddenly appeared on his forehead. A sense of foreboding came over her. Pietro had been right. The gold was near, perhaps even here at Riordan Hall, as he had said. And Eamon had not been willing to tell her about it. How could she expect otherwise after she had just revealed that she was a Gypsy, one of those outcast wanderers who would never be understood in the Gajo world? There was no help for it. To Eamon she would always be a Gypsy and a horse thief. He may have loved her once. He may love her still. But she wasn't of his world. He didn't trust her, and he never would.

Cormac looked at his brother in wonder. "A Gypsy?" he asked, unbelieving.

"Aye."

"But what was the story about her father being a schoolmaster?"

Eamon sighed and leaned back on his bed. He'd asked his brother to come to him there so that they could talk with total privacy. "I reckon she thought that if she'd told her true origin, Claire wouldn't have employed her."

"She's probably right," Cormac admitted, still shaking his head. "A Gypsy. Sweet Jesus."

"Are you afraid she'll snatch the children away and

carry them off into the woods?" Eamon asked sarcastically.

"Nay, of course not. 'Twould not fit Maura's character to do any such thing."

"I agree. So in that case, what difference does it make who she is?"

Cormac sat on the end of his brother's bed and regarded him gravely. "That would be for you to say, Eamon. Are you telling me that you're totally comfortable with this news?"

"Nay, but—"

"I saw your hesitation about revealing the secret of the gold to her, and that was before you even knew about this. It seems to me you don't fully trust the lass. I have a feeling that you still haven't told me the whole story."

Eamon wished that his brother did not have such an uncanny ability to read his every thought. "She . . . I'd met her once before," he began slowly, then finally blurted out, "Bloody hell, she's the one—the horse thief who took Rioga."

"All those years ago? The girl who whacked you so hard that you had a headache for a fortnight?" Cormac stood and began to pace the length of Eamon's bedchamber. "God's wounds, Eamon, when did you recognize her? Why didn't you tell me this?"

Eamon winced, but he knew that his brother was fully justified in his anger. "'Twas wrong of me, and if you'd like to take it out of my hide, then wale away. Christ, Cormac, the truth is I believe I fell in love with the chit from almost the first moment I saw her."

Cormac's thunderous expression softened. "I'd figured as much," he said with a glimmer of sympathy in his eyes. "I warrant there have been men made bigger fools for love."

"I don't believe she's made a fool out of me," Eamon protested.

"She deceived you—deceived all of us. She lied to you and came here under false pretenses. Now you tell me that the girl's a horse thief. God knows what else she's done."

He walked back to the bed and sat down, taking hold of Eamon's foot and giving it a rough shake. "Forget about her, brother. There are plenty of pretty wenches around. You don't need one with so many complications."

Eamon pulled his toes out of his brother's grasp. When he spoke, his tone was calm and deliberate. "I decided to tell you the truth about Maura because I don't want the pretending to continue."

"Aye, and I'm glad you did. I'll tell Claire—"

Eamon held his hand up. "But I want you to know something else. Tomorrow is Twelfth Night, and I intend to end the celebrations by asking Maura to become my wife."

Cormac sat back on the bed, stunned. "Eamon, you have to consider—"

"I've considered everything. I've considered that, as you suspect, part of me does not completely trust her with information such as the whereabouts of the gold. I've considered that a part of her will always be linked to the wandering life she led as a child. I've considered that she may have beliefs that will not match mine." Now he swung his legs over the edge of the bed and stood. "I've considered all of it, Cormac, and nothing alters the fact that I love her. She's not like any woman I've ever met."

"I'll grant you that," Cormac said ruefully, still looking astounded.

"You're the head of my family and my clan, but

you're also my brother. I'm hoping that you'll understand and that you'll give me your blessing."

Cormac stood beside him. "I'd not see you hurt."

"I know. That's why I'm asking your support. For
the greatest hurt I could suffer would be to lose her."

The two brothers stood face to face for a long moment, then Cormac broke the silence. "I wish only your
happiness," he said.

Eamon smiled. "I don't want anyone to know about
it before I ask her. Not even Claire."

His brother nodded. "I'll stay silent, though I think
the news will delight my cunning wife."

"You don't think she'll be bothered knowing that her
children are being taught by a Gypsy?"

Cormac shook his head. "Not Claire. And I trow the
children will think 'tis a fine turn of events."

Eamon's smile grew broader. Now that he had told
his brother, a great weight had been lifted. He knew that
there would still be obstacles to overcome. It might not
be easy for Maura to fully adapt to her new life, though
she'd done well enough so far. But they were in love,
and somehow he had faith that their love would be
enough to see them through anything.

She was waiting for fate to show her the way, Maura
had said. Well, fate had spoken. It had led her straight
to him, and now he intended to keep her.

The Twelfth Day of Christmas, Epiphany, was the
children's favorite. Following tradition, they each received little gifts that day to commemorate the visit of
the wise men to the infant Jesus. Ultan and Dylan had
been speculating about what theirs would be for days.

Maura had worked on some surprises of her own for
them. She'd given Aidan a few of the coins Claire had
paid her and asked him to buy her some leather strips,

which she'd used to fashion toys like her father used to
make to sell in the village markets.

Ultan's was a horse whose legs appeared to be running when one pulled back on the tiny reins. Dylan's
was a dog with a similar mechanism, triggered by
pulling its tail. For Eily she'd made a bird that flapped
its wings and bobbed its head. When she'd made them,
she'd been eager for the day to come so that she could
see the children's reaction, but now she retrieved the
items from their hiding place under her bed with a
heavy heart. As things were turning out, these could
well be her farewell gifts to her charges, and today
could be her last day to spend with them.

She hadn't seen Eamon since their conversation the
previous evening. He'd not been around when she'd gone
down to the dining hall in the morning. She wouldn't be
surprised if he was avoiding her. She'd put him in a terrible position with his brother and the rest of the family,
and she wouldn't blame him if he was wounded and
angry.

Dinner was to be another formal celebration. Yesterday Maura had seen the cake Molly had created for the
celebration, decorated with a sweet almond paste in the
shape of a crown to represent the three kings. The children had examined the cake carefully, trying to decide
where Molly had hidden the bean that would designate
the finder as king of the feast.

Eamon would certainly be at the dinner, Maura realized, as she descended the stairs to the dining hall. He
couldn't avoid her any longer, though they wouldn't get
a chance to speak privately.

He and the children were already seated at the table
when she entered.

"Here she is!" Dylan cried. "Mistress Maura, we
were wondering where you were."

"I told them you must be dressing your hair," Eily said, trying hard to sound grown-up.

The little girl was making such an obvious attempt to be included in an adult female circle that Maura couldn't help smiling. When her gaze met Eamon's, she saw that he was smiling, too. It warmed her, even though she knew the smile was for Eily, not really for her.

A couple of the neighboring landowners had joined them for dinner, which meant that the conversation inevitably drifted to the war, which put a damper on the holiday atmosphere. But the children were delighted with their leather toys, and Molly's repast was, once again, magnificent. To his utter delight, Dylan had found the bean in his slice of cake and had been declared king of the feast.

Maura surveyed the merrymaking as though from a distance, wondering once again if this was her last meal at the Riordan table. Eamon had not spoken directly to her, though she'd seen his eyes on her every now and then with an oddly intense expression.

All in all, she was just as glad when Cormac pushed back his big chair and said, "We'll have lamb's wool in the great room."

When he saw Maura's puzzled expression, Eamon leaned toward her and said, "'Tis a kind of apple punch made special for the day."

His tone and smile seemed normal, which reassured her slightly. She felt her heart lifting as everyone began leaving the table and making their way into the front hall toward the great room. They were still milling about when the front door burst open and Aidan stalked in. His face was ashen.

"What's wrong?" Cormac asked at once.

Aidan looked around at the crowd of people. "I—I

reckon I should speak to ye private, milord. 'Tis about the—er—the special item ye was askin' me to keep watch o'er."

Eamon and Cormac exchanged a look of alarm. Maura suddenly felt cold with dread. The Riordans were not people who grew attached to things. There was only one "special item" that would cause this much consternation. The rebel gold of Hugh O'Neill.

Eamon stepped forward and grasped the stablemaster's arm. "What's happened to it?" he asked in a low voice.

Aidan looked bleakly from Eamon to his brother. "It's gone, milord. The whole bloody lot."

Fifteen

Aidan's arrival had effectively put an end to the day's festivities. Cormac made excuses to the guests, though he gave no specifics about the problem that required the immediate attention of the men of the household.

Maura noticed that while continuing to confer with his brother, Eamon kept looking over at her with a troubled expression. Finally he broke away from the discussion with his brother and Aidan and came over to her. "I need to talk with you," he said curtly.

She let him take her arm and lead her into a side room. When they were alone, he said, "Last night you asked me about the O'Neill's gold. Why? What do you know about it?"

Her suspicions were right. It was the gold that was missing. The gold that Pietro had sworn to steal.

"This is important, Maura," Eamon said. His voice held none of the affectionate tone he'd used with her in recent days. "The gold is missing, as you've probably guessed. I need to know if you've been in touch with your Gypsy friends. I need to know if you've had something to do with this."

Maura felt his cold words like needles pricking her skin. Now that Eamon knew that she was a Gypsy, he no doubt believed her capable of anything, even the theft of a treasure from the people who had taken her in and been so kind to her.

"I've had nothing to do with taking your gold," she said, her tone as cold as his.

He looked down at her, his eyes bleak. "Forgive me, but the fortunes of many people are in the balance here. I need to be sure you're telling me the truth."

"You already know that I'm a thief and a liar," she said bitterly, "so what is the point of further questions? There is no way for you to ever trust me."

A flash of anger blazed in his eyes. "I know that you have stolen and that you have lied in the past out of necessity. Now I need to know if you would lie and steal out of greed. I believe that the woman I fell in love with would not do so. But because this involves more people than just us, I need to have you swear it to me."

She knew that she was being unfair to be hurt by his doubts. As he said, he was acting out of regard for others. But it hurt, nevertheless. She should tell him about Pietro's questions, but would that help or would it just make him more suspicious?

She rubbed her hands over her eyes, trying to decide what to do. If she told Eamon about Pietro, the Riordans and their supporters in the neighborhood would quickly descend on the Gypsy camp. If the gold was there, everyone in the camp would be blamed. If Eamon wouldn't believe her, whom he claimed to love, how many of these Gajos would be willing to believe that Pietro alone had been responsible for the theft?

"I don't know where your gold is, Eamon," she said wearily. "I swear it."

He hesitated another minute, studying her. Finally he said, "Very well. I should go back to Cormac."

She nodded, and he left without another word. She had the feeling that he still didn't totally believe her, and with good reason. She'd sworn that she didn't know where the gold was, and that had been the truth. She didn't know for certain, but she had a good idea where it was. In her old Gypsy camp.

The hall was still full of people, though the children had disappeared to play outside. She turned to climb the stairs to her chambers. She would dress in her old clothes, then wait for the opportunity to slip away.

Cormac was at the stables, organizing a search, first of the premises, then of the surrounding area. He'd sent riders to Fingarry to inform the O'Neill of the developments and ask for more men. Eamon ran toward him up the hill. "I need to talk with you, brother," he told him.

Cormac turned from giving instructions to some of the male servants. "What is it?" he asked.

Eamon pulled him away from the other men. "I've just talked with Maura."

"About marrying you?"

"Nay!" Eamon had almost forgotten his plan to ask Maura to marry him after the celebrations. "Nay, about the gold. I—she knows something about it."

Cormac frowned. "Did you tell her about it?"

"Nay. That's just the thing. I never mentioned it to her, yet she asked me about it last night. Just now, when I confronted her, she swore she knew nothing about the theft."

"But you're not sure you believe her," Cormac said.

"I believe her. I don't think she'd lie to me—"

"Though she's lied to all the rest of us."

"Aye, but that was different. I can't believe that she would lie to me, not now. But there was something wrong. I know it."

"Do you think there are Gypsies near?" Cormac asked.

"We need to find out. If there is a camp nearby, we need to search them."

"Would Maura know if there is a camp in the area?"

Eamon paused. "She might, though I'm not sure she'd want to tell me."

"Eamon, I mislike the sound of this. If you and Maura are in love, I don't understand why there is still this mistrust between you. Why would she be reluctant to tell you what she knows about the Gypsies?"

"Because they are her *people*, Cormac." Eamon's voice was angry. "As surely as the O'Donnell brothers were Claire's people. As I recall, there was mistrust and deception both between you two when your families had warring interests."

Cormac gave a reluctant nod. "I'll grant you that. Very well, I leave it to you to sort things out with your Maura. But it wouldn't hurt at least to ask if she knows of a camp near here."

"Aye, you're right. I'll go back to the house and question her further."

But when he went to look for Maura, she wasn't in her room, and no one seemed to know where she was. He remembered that she had also disappeared the day before and had come into the house crying. He'd told Cormac the truth. He didn't think that she would lie to him. But something sure as hell was wrong, and he had an uneasy feeling that if he didn't find out what it was, the results could be calamitous.

•   •   •

Maura found the Gypsy camp up the same little stream. She couldn't believe that they hadn't moved in all this time. Gypsies had to keep moving in order to find new villages with pots to fix or fortunes to tell. Most likely the family had been wandering, and then Pietro had decided to bring them back here. It was not an unusual practice to use the same campsite over and over, especially one that was within easy reach of fresh water.

As she approached through the trees, she could see a number of people moving around busily. It appeared as if they were breaking camp, which *was* unusual. It was nearly twilight. They never moved at night. With a frown, she walked into the clearing.

Momo saw her immediately, but this time, instead of a smile of welcome, he looked frightened. He put his fingers to his lips and waved her to move back into the trees out of sight. She quickly did so, waiting in the shadows while Momo looked around to be sure no one was watching, then came to join her.

"What are ye doing here?" he asked without any greeting.

Something was obviously wrong. Any remaining hope Maura had been keeping that she'd been mistaken about Pietro's involvement with the theft faded. "There's been a robbery at Riordan Hall where I've been staying," she said tersely. "I think Pietro might be responsible."

Momo nodded without surprise. "We all talked against it, Maura. My father and Pietro had a terrific fight, and even Nonna got up from her bed to speak to him."

"He took it then—the gold?"

"Aye. More treasure than any of us has ever seen in a lifetime. And for what?" Momo said with disgust. "So that we can become the thieves people think we are? So that we can be hunted down like animals?"

Maura listened uneasily. *More treasure than any of us has ever seen,* Momo had said. Had he seen it then? Suddenly she realized with growing worry that Pietro would probably not have been able to steal that much gold all by himself.

"How did he find out where it was?" she asked, which was the least of her questions.

"I'm not sure. I believe he heard some servants talking on the Riordan estate. He's been ferreting around for three or four days, then yesterday he came back here all triumphant. 'The bloody fools don't even have it guarded,' he told us."

Momo lapsed into silence. Finally Maura took a breath and asked. "How was he able to bring all that heavy gold here?"

Momo looked her squarely in the eyes. "With my help," he said. "We brought it here in the pony cart."

She felt as if she were going to be sick. "You helped him steal it?" She could hardly believe what she was hearing.

"Aye." Momo gave a long sigh. "I had no choice. He threatened to harm Nonna unless I helped him. He made Aislin come with us, too. He won't let her out of his sight these days."

Maura knew that tactic from firsthand experience. She put her arm on Momo's sleeve. "We have to get it back where it belongs before something terrible happens."

Momo's face was hard. "I think we'd have to kill Pietro to get it back. He's become crazed over it. He talks of nothing else. He's stored it away in his wagon and doesn't leave it."

"So Aislin is still with him?"

"Aye, though not for long. Giorgio, Nonna and I are leaving, and she's agreed to come with us."

"You're breaking up the family?" Such a thing would have been unthinkable in her father's day.

Momo's answer was bitter. "This isn't a family anymore, Maura. If the rest want to go with Pietro and his stolen loot, they can, but we've had enough."

"Momo, we can't let Pietro leave with this gold. You don't understand how important it is in the Gajo world. They won't stop looking until they've found it."

"If we leave now, we should be able to get away before the Gajos find Pietro. Pietro doesn't know yet, but when he breaks camp tomorrow at dawn, we're going in the opposite direction. Once we're gone, the Gajos can come and get their gold, and Pietro with it, for all I care."

"But what about the others? They're likely to blame the entire family. No one will think that Pietro acted on his own."

Momo hesitated. "What are you suggesting that we do?"

"We need to get the gold away from Pietro somehow and take it back to Riordan Hall. And we need to do it now. Will Aislin help us?"

Momo flushed. "I believe she'll do whatever I ask her."

"Good. So we need to figure a way to get Pietro away from his tent, then get the chests back into the pony cart." The pony cart was a small decorated wagon that they used at fairs to give rides to the village children. Maura had helped paint it years ago with twining flowers and gaily colored birds.

"My father will help us," Momo said.

"Aye, perhaps you should go back into camp and tell

Giorgio that I'm here. I won't show myself to the others just yet."

"You mustn't," Momo agreed. "I don't know what Pietro would do if he saw you. I tell you, he's gone crazed."

"I'll stay right here," Maura promised, then watched as Momo crossed the clearing back to his wagon.

After some chaos while plans were put into action, Cormac and Eamon had finally organized the search. They had men from the estate and the village combing the countryside late into the night. Word had been sent to the rebels in Fingarry and to the local authorities. The two brothers had not yet joined the search themselves, since they wanted to wait to hear from Hugh O'Neill.

They'd set up a makeshift search headquarters in the great room inside the house. A large map of the area had been found and was now laid out in the middle of the floor. "They could be anywhere from here to Tara Hill," Eamon said. "'Tis a lot of territory to cover."

"Aye," Cormac agreed. He looked at his brother in concern. "Do you think she's gone to them?"

Eamon nodded. "Aye. Where else would she be?" Eamon had continued to hope that there would be some logical explanation for Maura's absence. He'd tried all evening to push away the feeling of dread, but as the hours wore on, it became more and more clear that Maura was gone and was not coming back. In his misery, he could put only one interpretation on her disappearance.

"It doesn't necessarily mean that she's involved in the theft," Cormac pointed out. "She could be trying to find them on her own to see what has happened."

"I should have seen that she was hiding something from me yesterday," he told his brother. "Yet I continued on like a blithering fool, thinking the best and planning to live happily ever after."

Cormac gave him a bittersweet smile. "It's called love, Eamon. Don't apologize for it. And, who knows? Things may still turn out for you. We don't know the facts yet."

Eamon was surprised. It appeared that Cormac had gone from being the suspicious one to suddenly becoming one of Maura's supporters. "We know enough of the facts to make things appear damning," he said gloomily. He wished he himself could regain some of the faith he'd had in her. For weeks he'd known certain dubious aspects of Maura's past, yet he'd continued to help her, continued to keep her secrets. Now it appeared that she'd played him for a fool. Had she been planning to go back to her Gypsy family all along, since the first day she came here? She couldn't have known about the gold, but perhaps they had planned to rob the estate of whatever other riches they might have been able to find. At the moment he'd believe anything was possible.

Cormac was watching him with an expression of troubled sympathy. "Just remember that things are not always what they appear. I doubt any couple had more misunderstandings to overcome than Claire and I, yet today we are one soul, as surely as if we had been forged together by an ironsmith."

Eamon made an attempt to smile. "I'm grateful for your concern, brother, but some metals simply can not be forged, and I fear that is the case with Maura and me. It wasn't our *fate,* as she would say."

There was a stirring in the hall as Claire, who had refused to go to her own bed if her husband was not going to sleep, opened the front door to a new contingent of men. Unlike the villagers and servants Cormac had sent out earlier, these men were armed with swords and breastplates.

"It's O'Neill's men," Cormac said, standing.

Eamon followed his brother into the hall, where they greeted the newcomers.

"Has your leader come with you?" Cormac asked.

"Nay," answered a burly guard who appeared to be the head of the contingent. "I'm his captain, Ronald O'Hara, at your service, gentlemen. Hugh O'Neill is staying in Fingarry and will keep track of things from there. We'll be sending him word of any progress. I hardly need tell you, but it's imperative that we recover this money."

"We know," Cormac said grimly. "And recover it we will. I suggest we give you men some food, Captain, then we all get a few hours sleep and start first thing in the morning."

The man shook his head. "There's not time to sleep. We've heard that there were Gypsies camped near Tara Hill. We want to get over there to check them out before they have a chance to leave the area. Gypsies can be slippery bastards."

Eamon winced at the man's description. "Are you going there now?"

"Aye," the captain confirmed. "If we don't find the gold there, we'll come back here and talk about another plan."

Cormac glanced at Eamon. "We'll ride with you to Tara Hill," he told the captain. "We can help you find the way in the dark."

"That's not necessary if you have other leads you want to pursue—"

"Nay," Eamon interrupted. "We'll ride with you to find the Gypsy camp."

Captain O'Hara shrugged and turned toward the

door. "As you like, gentlemen. I'd ask you to hurry, then. My men are ready to leave."

"We must figure out a way to get Pietro to leave his wagon long enough for us to remove the gold," Maura said. Momo had brought Giorgio to meet with her in the woods. By now it was totally dark and a chill night wind had arisen. Maura pulled her shawl around her. It wasn't likely that she would have a warm bed to sleep in this night.

"Shall we wait until morning?" Momo asked.

"I think it has to be tonight," Giorgio answered. "Pietro has told everyone that we're leaving before dawn."

"Aye, the sooner the better," Maura agreed. "There are already men from Riordan Hall out searching for the gold, and who knows when they might find this place?"

"I could tell Aislin to walk away from the wagon," Momo suggested. "Pietro never lets her be long out of his sight. When she doesn't come back, he's bound to go out looking for her."

"Will that give us long enough to get the gold out of his wagon?" Maura asked Giorgio.

"It will have to be long enough. If he comes back and catches us in the act, we'll just have to deal with him."

Momo looked at his father with a grim expression. "I hope he does catch us," he said.

Giorgio shook his head. "Nay, if it can be done without violence, 'tis the best way."

They agreed that Momo would send Aislin out to where Maura was waiting so that she could help the girl find a hiding place. "I want to be sure she's out of danger," Momo said firmly. "She's been through enough with that monster."

"I'll be sure that Pietro doesn't find us," Maura told him.

Momo nodded, then he and Giorgio crept quietly back to the camp.

It seemed as if she was waiting hours, but it was probably less than half an hour when she heard the trees rustling and looked from her hiding place in the bushes to see the slender girl she'd met weeks before in Pietro's wagon.

She stood and called to her in a loud whisper, "Aislin, over here!"

The girl stumbled toward her, and when she reached her, to Maura's surprise, fell into an embrace. Maura held her there briefly in her arms. She could feel every one of the girl's bony ribs.

"Did you have trouble getting away?" she asked her. "Did Pietro see which direction you came?"

Aislin shook her head. "Nay, I'm free. I'm truly free this time!" Her chest was heaving with dry sobs.

Maura helped her take a seat on the ground within the shelter of the bushes. "Aye, you're free, Aislin." She knew something of the emotion the girl was experiencing. She knew how cruel and overbearing Pietro could be, though she'd only had glimpses of it. Aislin had been with him for what must have been several terrible months. "You never have to go back to him now," she told the girl.

"Momo's going to take care of me," Aislin said shyly.

In the moonlight Maura could see a special shine in the girl's gray eyes. She smiled. "Are you in love with him?"

"Aye. I think so. He's so very handsome and kind and—" She stopped and tucked her head down.

Maura reached to squeeze the girl's hand. "I think he

returns the sentiment," she said. "And I'm so happy for you both." It was true. Though it seemed odd to think of her little shadow Momo all grown-up and in love, she could feel the young couple's happiness. It was similar to what she had had with Eamon for a few brief days. She blinked away the sudden sting of tears.

"What's going on?" Aislin asked suddenly, standing and trying to look toward the camp in the distance. There were sudden shouts and they could see someone running.

"Have they found us?" Maura asked, jumping up. Her first thought was of Eamon. Had he come looking for her?

Cautiously the two women crept closer to the clearing. Now in the distance was the distinct sound of approaching horses.

Maura's heart sank. If the men from Riordan Hall found the gold now, everyone in the camp would be blamed for the theft. She'd probably be blamed as well. "We should go tell them that there's no need for force," she said quickly. If she could find Eamon among the new arrivals, she should be able to convince him that the Gypsies would surrender the gold peacefully. Maybe he'd even be willing to let them go, but she didn't think so. He'd once been willing to forgive her for horse theft. She couldn't expect that he would be so charitable again.

Aislin held back, so she left the girl in the woods and ran toward camp. Riders had made their way into the clearing, and her gaze went immediately to the two black-haired men in the middle, each mounted on a magnificent stallion. It was the Riordan brothers, armed and wearing light armor. They looked grim and fierce—nothing like the kind family men with whom she'd just celebrated a joyous Christmas season.

Eamon saw her, but he gave no sign of recognition.

Some of the other men in the group were going through the wagons, one by one, pulling out any of the inhabitants and forcing them to stand in a circle in the middle of the camp. Giorgio and Momo came out of their wagon, half carrying Nonna. Maura ran to her.

"So ye've come back to us a third time, child," the old woman said. "Third and last. Third and last."

Maura didn't have time to ask the meaning of her words. "Aye, I've come back, Nonna," she said, taking Momo's place at the old grandmother's side.

She could see no sign of Pietro. Had he gotten away? It would be the height of irony if their ploy to draw Pietro away from his wagon had enabled him to escape justice for his thievery.

Then there was a shout from the direction of Pietro's wagon and an excited young soldier jumped out of it, calling, "The gold's here!"

Cormac, Eamon, and the man they had been riding with turned their mounts toward the far end of the caravan. Maura followed them toward Pietro's wagon.

The man who had searched the wagon held a gold bar in his hand. His young face was glowing with excitement. "Two chests full," he said, raising the bar so everyone could see. "And someone has saved the trouble of a hanging, Captain," he said to the mounted man.

"What do you mean?" the rider said.

The young man shrugged. "If your thief is the man inside that wagon, he's already dead. Someone has cut his throat."

Sixteen

Pale streaks of dawn were lighting the sky, and Maura could feel her eyes burning from the smoke of the campfire and the long night of no sleep. She looked around the circle to see that her friends looked little better off. Momo was blinking hard and looked exhausted as he sat with his arm around Nonna. The old woman herself appeared to have held up remarkably well throughout the long night. Maura had tried to speak to Eamon about letting Nonna return to her bed in her wagon, but the soldiers who had been guarding the Gypsies would not let her leave the circle.

She was still trying to absorb everything that had happened. Pietro was dead. She couldn't say that the news made her unhappy, but what had her sick with dread was the knowledge that someone in the camp had been responsible. She scanned the circle of faces, most of whom had been dear to her since childhood.

As usual, steady, dependable Giorgio was doing his best to keep everyone calm. Giorgio and Pietro had been adversaries for years, since before her father's death. Had Giorgio finally gotten tired of Pietro's bullying ways and decided that something had to be done about it? Perhaps Pietro had told him that he wasn't going to let him take his family and leave, as Giorgio had planned. But somehow, she just couldn't picture Giorgio giving into violence.

Deep in her heart, Maura knew that the most likely suspect in the killing was her dear old childhood friend, Momo. She looked over at him again. There was a hollow expression in his eyes that she'd never seen before. Could it be possible that the carefree little boy who had been her constant companion could have killed someone? She remembered that Momo had actually said that they would have to kill Pietro to get the gold back. And there had been hatred in his face when he had talked about what Pietro had done to Aislin.

But what about Aislin herself? She'd been obviously distraught when she'd run out of the camp to meet Maura in the woods. "I'm truly free this time," she'd said. Would frail, slender Aislin have been capable of killing a big man like Pietro? There was no way to ask her, for she had disappeared. Even though the soldiers had made a cursory search of the woods around them, there had been no sign of the girl, and Maura assumed that she'd decided to make her freedom complete by running away from the scene.

New riders had ridden into the camp. Maura gathered that one of them was some kind of local magistrate who had arrived to take over the investigation of Pietro's murder. The men who had come with Eamon and Cormac had already unloaded the gold from the wagon and had taken it away. Maura didn't know where they were taking it and she didn't care. She wished she'd never heard of the rebel treasure.

One of the soldiers was leading the magistrate to

Pietro's wagon. As they started up the wagon steps, Eamon emerged and made his way down. His gaze met Maura's, and after a moment's pause, he started walking toward her.

"I don't see any reason for keeping these people here like this," he said to one of the guards. "Let them go to their wagons or get themselves some food."

The guard gave a respectful bob of his head but said, "Captain O'Hara said we should keep 'em until the local authorities took over here. It appears they've arrived, so we'll just wait to see what they say."

"I need to talk to this woman in private," Eamon said, indicating Maura. "I'll vouch for her presence here."

The guard shrugged. "I reckon Captain O'Hara wouldn't be likely to naysay a Riordan, sir. Do as ye like."

Eamon walked over to where Maura was sitting in the circle and leaned down to take her elbow to help her up.

"'Tis Nonna who needs to get up from here," Maura told him, pointing to the old woman. "She's not well, and shouldn't be sitting so long on the ground."

Eamon looked back to the guard. "Let this woman go to her wagon. I'll vouch for her as well."

The guard shrugged again, and motioned to a couple of his men to help the old grandmother to her wagon. Eamon waited until they were done, then said to Maura, "Come with me. We need to talk."

She took a deep breath and let him lead her away from the circle toward the edge of the woods where they could not be heard by the milling soldiers. When he turned to her, she could see both suspicion and pain in his expression.

"You've got to tell me what you know about this,"

he urged in a low voice. "Who was this man? Was he responsible for taking the gold? Who killed him?"

His eyes were shadowed and he was unshaven. Obviously, he'd had as little sleep as she. If only she could feel free to step into his arms and tell him all the events of the past couple of days, she thought, but his stiff demeanor kept her at a distance. He gave no indication that he had the least memory of the love and tenderness they had so recently shared.

"The man was called Pietro," she said finally. "He was head of this band."

"Of *your* band," he clarified.

"Of the family that was once led by my father. I've not been part of it since he died."

"Why not?" he asked bluntly.

She was surprised. She had thought he would question her more about Pietro and the gold, not about herself. "As I once told you, I felt I had to leave."

"Aye, you told me you were desperate, but you never told me why. Nor did you ever tell me why you have nightmares when I hold you in my arms. I want to know if all this had anything to do with the man who lies dead in that wagon."

Her eyes widened as she realized the motive behind his questions. "Do you think I *killed* him?"

She was aghast at his suspicions, but did she have any right to blame him? He already knew that she was guilty of lying and theft. From there, was it such a short step to murder?

Eamon gave a long sigh. "I don't know what to think anymore, teacher. Yesterday I was going to ask you to become my wife."

Though the use of his old name for her gave her a glimmer of hope, she knew that her words sounded bitter as she said, "And now you think you might be considering marriage to a murderess."

"Are you one?"

She would not cry, she told herself. "If you don't know the answer to that, Eamon Riordan," she said, "then there is little point in continuing this discussion. Now, if you don't mind, I'll go rejoin my Gypsy family."

She turned to leave, but he reached for her arm to hold her back. His fingers closed exactly over the area Pietro had bruised on his visit to the stables. She gave an involuntary gasp of pain.

"What is it?" Eamon asked, dropping her arm as if he had been burned.

Her hand briefly rubbed the tender spot, then she forced herself to straighten up and ignore the pain. "'Tis nothing."

"Like hell," Eamon swore. He pulled her into the trees where they couldn't be seen, then turned her toward him and pushed the shoulder of her dress down. The entire top of her arm was a sickly blue gray. She watched his face go grim as he slid down the material over the other shoulder, where the skin looked much the same.

"He did this to you, didn't he?" he asked. "This Pietro. He was the one you were running from all those years ago—the one who still lives in your nightmares."

Maura straightened up and looked at him directly. "Aye, 'twas Pietro."

He winced. "Did he . . . how did he hurt you?"

"He didn't hurt me the way he intended. I didn't let him. Now it appears he's received a just reward for his cruelty." She searched Eamon's face for some kind of sign that would allow her to seek the comfort of his arms, but he merely looked uncomfortable with her revelation. With a bitter laugh she ended, "I should thank him, really, for he taught me to be wary of men."

"Did he force you to tell him where the gold was?"

"I told you, I didn't know where the gold was. I didn't even know if there was any gold."

"Then why did you ask me about it the other night in your bedchamber?"

She bit her lip, wishing they could be alone together someplace far from here, wishing he would look at her with that special light she'd seen so often in his eyes. But his face remained stern and cold in the shadows of the trees.

"Eamon!" It was Cormac's voice.

Eamon pushed her dress back into place and took her arm again, carefully keeping his hand lower than her elbow. Once they moved out of the trees, he dropped his hold on her entirely.

"Captain O'Hara and his men are leaving," Cormac said to his brother with a glance at Maura.

"What about the people in the camp here?" Eamon asked.

"O'Hara has the gold back, and he says the Gypsy's murder is a matter for the local authorities."

"Don't they care who stole the gold?"

Cormac shrugged. "They're saying the victim was the thief. He was evidently the leader of this troupe, and by all accounts his death will not be widely mourned."

They looked over to the campsite, where the Gypsies had now been allowed out of the circle. Two men were bringing what must have been Pietro's body, wrapped in a blanket, down from his wagon. Maura shivered.

Cormac spoke again. "There's no need for us to stay

here, either. We should ride back to Riordan Hall to let everyone know that the search is over."

Eamon looked from his brother to Maura, uncertain. "What's to become of the people here? Are they being held?"

"Not for the time being. The magistrate says he'll conduct a proper investigation. The new leader, a fellow named Giorgio, has agreed that the camp won't move until permission is given." He turned to Maura. "Apparently you're free to leave. Are you returning with us?"

She looked over at the camp. Nonna was out of her wagon again, sitting by the fire with Momo. Giorgio was at the far end of the camp talking with the magistrate. She glanced at Eamon, who stood stiffly at her side, his expression unreadable.

"I should stay here," she said.

"Is that what you want?" Eamon asked, his voice strained.

"Aye."

There was a flicker of pain in his eyes, but he nodded, then turned to Cormac and said, "Let's be off, then. Claire will be worrying over you."

Cormac glanced uncertainly from his brother to Maura. Finally he asked her, "Are you sure you'll be safe here?"

"Of course I'll be safe. These are my people."

"So be it," Cormac said. Then the two brothers turned and made their way across the camp to their horses.

Claire was waiting for them in the front hall. The instant they entered, she ran into Cormac's embrace. Eamon watched as his brother kissed her thoroughly.

"Now tell me all about it," she said when Cormac

finally released her. "They found the gold in the Gypsy camp?"

Cormac nodded. "The gold and a murder victim." At Claire's raised eyebrows he explained what had transpired during the evening.

"And where's Maura?" she asked when he had ended his recital.

"She's staying with the Gypsies," Eamon explained curtly.

"For how long?" she asked.

"How long? For good, I presume. Forever. As she herself said, they are her people."

Claire frowned. "Aye, but so are we. So are the children."

"Not in her mind, evidently." Eamon knew his words sounded cold, but he was tired and dispirited and his back ached from the long ride. He had no humor for one of his sister-in-law's lectures.

Which did not deter Claire in the least. "Did you try to convince her to come back?" she asked, indignant, looking from Eamon to Cormac. "Did you even *ask* her to return with you?"

"I asked her if she planned to come back," Cormac answered, a little defensive.

"Well now, that sounds like an irresistible invitation if I ever heard one," Claire snapped. "I don't suppose that you two imagined that she was frightened and feeling lost and uncertain of her welcome here?" She looked from one brother to the other. "Eamon? I thought you had professed to love this woman."

"She made her choice, Claire," he answered. "She made it yesterday afternoon when she left to be with them. For all we know, she's only been here all along to spy on Riordan Hall for the Gypsies."

"Rubbish!" Claire said. "You don't believe that any more than I. I'm ashamed of the both of you."

Cormac looked sheepish. "One thing I've learned, brother," he said, "is that my wife is right more often than not. Perhaps we should have tried harder to persuade her to come back with us."

Eamon felt as if voices were warring in his head. Part of him wanted to believe what his brother and Claire were telling him. But part of him was remembering that Maura had lied to him, that she'd been unwilling to tell him the full story of the gold, even this morning. Whatever had been her involvement, they could have faced it together. But it seemed that she did not trust him or love him enough to confide in him.

"We all need some rest," he said finally. "We'll think more clearly after we've had a few hours' sleep."

Then he turned to climb the staircase, leaving Claire and Cormac watching him with worried eyes.

He had slept the night through, Eamon realized as he awoke to bright sun. He'd gone to sleep before supper the previous day, but he'd been exhausted in both body and spirit. Though it now seemed ages ago, it had only been a couple of days since the world had seemed a wonderful place. He had been full of hope and elation over his plans to start a new life with Maura. Now she was gone, and nothing would ever be the same.

He needed to get up. There was much to do. There would be work to be done around the estate after the Christmas holidays. He needed to check with Aidan about which horses they were going to take to the Dublin sale. Cormac no doubt would want him to ride to Fingarry to make contact with the O'Neill and hear the latest news on that score. Instead he continued to lie in his bed, staring at a small crack in the ceiling plaster.

What was she doing at this moment? he wondered. What was being done about the murder in the Gypsy camp? Was she really planning to return to that roaming life she had once abandoned?

He might have never gotten the energy to get up if someone hadn't knocked on his door. Grumpily he pulled himself out of bed and threw on a robe to answer it.

It was Claire. "Cormac said you were up here hiding," she told him, "but I said it was just weariness. There's nothing that saps the spirit quite like doubting the one you love."

Eamon gave a slight smile. She never gave up. "I've just awakened," he said. "Tell Cormac I'll be down shortly. I know there's much to be done today."

"More than you think, brother-in-law."

He looked at her questioningly.

"Maura's been arrested."

"Arrested?" He felt a pounding behind his ears.

"Aye," Claire said grimly. "For murder."

Kilmessen jail was not a particularly stalwart structure. Eamon had seen the building hundreds of times, but had never been inside. He wasn't exactly sure what he intended to do here, but he only knew that he had to see Maura and be sure that she was all right. He hoped he could finally get her to confide in him, as she had so far seemed unwilling to do.

Cormac had had to ride to Fingarry to get special permission for Eamon's visit, since a murderer was not usually allowed visitors other than the accused's own solicitor.

A sallow-looking guard admitted him, asked for his

sword, then grabbed a ring of keys from a hook on the
wall and motioned Eamon to follow him. They went
through a door and into a narrow, dark corridor that ran
along the edge of three tiny cells. It smelled unpleas-
antly of damp and sweat and other odors Eamon preferred not to identify.

The jailor's lantern was the only light in the win-
dowless area. The first two dark cells they passed were
empty. But as they neared the third and the jailor lifted
the light, Eamon could see what appeared at first to be
a heap of clothing on a cot. At their approach, the
bundle moved and Maura sat up, facing them, blinking
at the sudden brightness. Her eyes were red and her
cheeks blotchy. She looked at him for a moment without recognition.

"Maura?" he gasped. It had been only three days
ago that he'd left her at the Gypsy camp, only two days
since they'd heard about her arrest. He'd not expected
to see this much change in her.

"Eamon. Good morning," she said hoarsely, then
asked, "Is it morning?"

He nodded. "Aye."

"How long have I been here?" she asked.

He shook his head. "Three days."

She gave a ghost of a smile. "I had it right," she
said.

Had she gone out of her head? he wondered. He'd
expected her to jump up to greet him with questions
and plans for her defense. He'd expected the energetic
Maura he had come to know. This dispirited wraith was
nothing like the woman he had fallen in love with. She
made his heart ache.

He walked up to the cell bars. The guard stood in-
differently nearby, waiting. "Are you all right?" he asked.
"Has anyone hurt you?"

She shook her head, but made no move to get off the
cot and walk over to him.

"Maura, we need to talk about what happened. What
do you know about that man's death?"

There was a flash of the old spirit in her eyes as she
said, "From what you said at camp that night, you believe that I killed him."

He felt slightly encouraged at her spark of anger.
Anger was better than resignation. "I believe nothing. I
don't know what happened. But if you did kill him, I
assume you had good reason."

"That's charitable of you, Master Riordan," she
said. Finally she stood and walked over to the bars.
"I'm afraid your Gajo justice system may not be as understanding. From what I understand, they plan to hang
me."

Eamon flinched at the words, but tried to keep his
voice even. "They can't hang you without a trial."

Her chin came up in the way he remembered. "Have
you ever seen a Gypsy on trial? Is a trial even necessary when everyone already knows in advance that we
are sneaks and thieves and stealers of children and,
aye, may as well add murder to the charge?"

Her words were disheartening, partly because
Eamon knew that there was a great deal of truth to
them, but he was at least happy to hear some force in
her voice. "I've come to help," he told her.

"Why, when you think me as guilty as they?"

Did he think her guilty? He had to admit that there
had been moments over the past two days when he had
considered the possibility. But in his heart he simply
couldn't believe it.

"Nay, I don't," he told her calmly. "But 'tis not important what I think. I'm not the one who will be sitting in judgment. So you have to confide in me. You

have to tell me everything you know about what happened."

"I have nothing to tell you," she said. Once again the light had gone out of her eyes, leaving them dull.

Had the differences between them already split them so far apart that they couldn't even talk to each other? he wondered in desperation. "You must be able to tell me something about that night, Maura," he urged. "Why have they charged you?" He turned to the guard. "Do you know what evidence they have against this woman?"

The man rolled his eyes. "I just guard 'em; I don't try 'em," he said. But then he added, "But I reckon 'twas the collar."

"The collar?" He looked sharply at Maura. "What's he talking about?"

After a moment's pause she answered reluctantly, "They found a linen collar in Pietro's wagon. It had his blood on it. Pietro had ripped it off me the day"—she paused to glance at the jailor, then continued—"the same day he made the bruises you saw."

"And then there was the knife," the jailor said casually, lifting the lantern so that he could scratch his armpit.

"What knife?" This time it was Maura who asked the question.

"The knife what killed him," the jailor said. " 'Twere a big cake knife that they say do come from Riordan Hall."

Maura looked shocked.

"You know nothing about it?" Eamon asked.

She shook her head, looking dazed.

"Beggin' yer pardon, sir," the jailor said. "Ye was only to have five minutes with the prisoner, and I reckon the time's nigh done."

Eamon turned to her to make one last plea. "Can't you tell me anything more? Who else could have gone into that man's wagon? Who in the camp had reason to harm him?"

It was as if a mask had settled over her face. "I'm sorry, Eamon," she said, her tone steely. "I appreciate your coming today. I hope you'll tell your brother and Claire how much I appreciate all the kindness they showed me. But I can tell you nothing about that night. Nothing at all."

Seventeen

Truly Fitzpatrick had long ago left his homeland for the high style and political games of the London court, but Eamon had never met a shrewder man in a trial. The very morning Claire had come to him with word of Maura's arrest, he'd sent an urgent message to the barrister offering him whatever fee he named to ride at once for Riordan Hall.

He was fairly certain that the Riordan name would bring Truly, even if the fee meant nothing. Still, he waited in a fever of impatience for the lawyer to arrive.

"He'll be here, Eamon," Cormac had reassured him. "Truly has a way of being where you need him precisely when you need him. Not a moment before."

It was two days before Maura's scheduled trial, and Eamon was preparing a desperate ride to Dublin to find a substitute when Truly's comfortable carriage came trundling down the Riordan Hall driveway.

The two Riordan brothers went out the front door to meet him. "Do you think he can learn enough about the case in two days?" Eamon asked as they walked down the steps.

"Being Truly, he can probably learn enough about the case in two *hours*," Cormac told him.

"Gentlemen!" the lawyer said, stepping out of the carriage with a reserved smile. He didn't look the least bit travel worn, Eamon noted, trying hard not to gape at the man's attire. Truly was known for always adopting the latest court fashion. His purple jacket had huge shoulders that narrowed into a pleated waist, then flared out in a gathered skirt. His hose were bright green. In the middle of the Meath countryside, he looked nothing short of foppish. But Eamon had seen Truly in action when his brother Niall had been imprisoned in the Tower of London. He knew it was a mistake to underestimate the man.

Nevertheless, this was Maura's life, and he found himself growing impatient as Truly and Cormac exchanged pleasantries and discussed the lawyer's trip from London.

"Could we go inside and talk about the case?" Eamon asked finally, his tone a little harsher than he had intended.

Truly cast him a look of sympathy. "I take it this girl is more than just a former household tutor," he drawled.

Cormac answered the unspoken question. "Maura and Eamon became . . . very close."

"I suspected as much from the tone of your letter," the lawyer told Eamon.

"I'm in love with her," Eamon said bluntly.

Truly smiled and pulled a silk handkerchief from his belt. "Ah, love," he declared, using the cloth to dab at his upper lip. " 'Tis a strange and wondrous thing, is it not?"

Eamon was uncertain how to reply. "Er . . . I warrant

'tis both, though I've been having difficulty with the wondrous part lately."

"Did she do it?" Truly asked, his eyes suddenly sharp.

"Nay." Eamon said. This time there was no hesitation in his answer.

Truly nodded. "Then we'd best figure out how we're going to prove that to a judge." He motioned to the carriage behind him. "I trust you'll have someone see to my trunks." He turned to mount the stairs.

"Trunks?" Eamon mouthed silently to Cormac. His brother shook his head with a grin. Then they followed the lawyer's green tights up the stairs.

"You admit to seeing these bruises on the girl. Isn't it possible that she killed the blackguard in self-defense?" Truly asked as the three men and Claire lingered at the table after a late supper.

Eamon shook his head. "Nay, 'tis not her nature."

"We know that she's a thief," Truly pointed out.

"I believe that she stole precisely because she was running away from this man," Eamon said.

"Which would make her guilt seem all the more likely," Truly told him gently. "The man's been a problem to her for years, and finally she decided to rid herself of him. The judge would likely be lenient."

"There may be something to that," Cormac agreed. "Remember, Eamon, you're not exactly objective about this matter."

"Love is blind, as they say," Truly added with a hand flourish.

Eamon looked around the table. "I'll admit that my faith in Maura has not been without moments of doubt. But I've thought of little else since her arrest. I've examined everything I know about the kind of person she is. And I've come to the conclusion that she is innocent of this crime."

"Eamon is right," Claire agreed firmly. "Maura did not kill that man."

Truly turned to her with a bow of his head. "Then we shall be pleading her 'not guilty.' I always trust the instincts of a lady."

"Instincts aren't going to help us make our case," Eamon said, trying to restrain his irritation. Truly had asked for a bath after his arrival, then had taken an inordinate amount of time to dress, and now was prepared to sit at the table half the night. He couldn't see that anything was being done to advance Maura's cause.

Truly's eyes narrowed slightly. "Nay," he said. "The word of a lady as beautiful as Lady Riordan will always convince me, but I doubt 'twill impress the judge. Which is why I have no choice but to go tomorrow and talk to the other lady in question."

"You'll see Maura?" Eamon asked.

"Aye."

"I hope she'll talk with you,"

"Why wouldn't she? I'm her lawyer."

Eamon hesitated. How could he explain in a few words how he and Maura had lost the closeness they had just begun to develop? How in just a few days things had changed from love to suspicion and hurt? "It might be best if she didn't know that I was the one who hired you," he said finally.

Truly's eyebrow raised, but he made no comment.

Cormac shot his brother a look of sympathy. "You may tell Maura that Claire and I hired you," he told the lawyer.

Truly shrugged and curled his hand around his glass of port. "Whatever you say, gentlemen."

•　•　•

Her jailor was a dreary-looking fellow, but at least
he had made no inappropriate gestures or comments.
Sometimes when he brought one of her two daily meals,
he even exhibited a measure of rough kindness. One
day he'd added an extra piece of bread to her plate. On
another occasion he'd brought in a candle and allowed
her to keep it for a few precious hours of light.

Most of the time she sat in the dark, and she had now
finally lost count of the days. She'd had plenty of time
to go over and over the night of Pietro's murder, but she
could come no closer to an answer to who had killed
him. Momo still seemed the strongest suspect. Whoever
it was, she would say nothing that would help the authorities find the culprit. Whoever had killed Pietro had
done the world a favor.

Eamon had not visited again, but she had not really
expected him to. Though she believed he truly had
loved her once, the series of events beginning with the
revelation about her heritage and ending with the murder of Pietro had surely caused any feeling he might
have to die. Hadn't he as much as admitted that he believed her guilty of murder?

A shaft of light at the end of the corridor brought her
abruptly upright on her cot. Unless she'd finally lost all
sense of time, it was not yet time for a meal. She looked
down the corridor eagerly.

"Yer lawyer is here to see ye," the jailor said, approaching the cell. Behind him came a tall, elegantly
dressed man Maura had never seen before.

"My lawyer?" she asked, confused.

The man stepped around the jailor and bowed at the
waist. "Truly Fitzpatrick, at your service, mistress. I understand you've a trial to attend on the morrow, and I'm
here to represent you."

Maura stood, walked across the cell, and grasped the

bars, looking out at the newcomer. "But . . . I've hired no lawyer," she said. "Who sent you?"

"I've been employed by the Riordans to defend you, m'dear," the man said with a smile that held such warmth she forgot his fancy clothes.

"By Eamon Riordan?" she asked with a sudden shaft of elation.

He studied her a long moment, then said, "Nay, by his brother, Cormac, and Lady Riordan, of course."

Maura swallowed back her disappointment. "I'm grateful," she said. "Though I fear they may have signed you on to a losing cause."

Her hand was curled around one of the bars. The lawyer covered it with his own and gave it a squeeze of reassurance. "I make it a practice never to sign on to losing causes," he said.

He released her hand, then motioned to the jailor. "Give me the lantern and leave us." His voice was once again the gentleman. "I have the right to talk with the accused in private."

The jailor shrugged and handed over the lantern, then went shuffling down the corridor to the door.

"Now," Truly said softly. "Suppose you tell me about your friends in the Gypsy camp."

Maura tensed. "I don't want to talk about that night," she said.

He nodded agreeably. "I just want you to tell me about the camp," he said. "Tell me about the people you grew up with. We'll simply have a little chat. Is that satisfactory?"

She nodded warily. She had no intention of saying anything of her suspicions about Momo, but if this unusual man could think of any way to save her without that, she'd try to help.

•   •   •

The courthouse in Kilmessen was a modest building, nothing like the grand chambers in Dublin. Evidently it had been decided that a quick trial to condemn a poor Gypsy girl accused of murder did not merit any more elaborate attention. Truly, however, had come dressed for the occasion as if he were arguing a case before the greatest London chamber. He'd brought an entire case from London just to hold his judicial wig.

"If Maura wouldn't talk to you, how could you find out any information to help her?" Eamon asked as they made their way into court with Claire and Cormac a few moments before the time appointed for the trial.

"I didn't say that she wouldn't *talk* to me," Truly replied calmly. "I said she wouldn't talk to me about the night of the murder. We spoke at length about other topics."

"But what good—" Eamon started to interrupt.

Truly held up a languid hand. "And the people in her camp told me a great deal more."

"You went to the Gypsy camp?" Eamon asked.

"Aye. Whenever possible, one visits the scene of the crime. Often it will tell you a lot more than any of the people involved will."

It was the first time in anyone's memory that there had been a murder trial in Kilmessen. The fact that the accused was not only a woman, but a beautiful *Gypsy* woman, added to the appeal of the event, and the small courtroom was full. Three of the Gypsies Eamon had seen that night at the camp were sitting in the front row near Truly. He recognized the old woman whom he had allowed to go to her wagon and the young man who had been sitting with her that night. An older man who resembled them both sat between them.

There was a sudden hush over the crowd as a jailor brought the prisoner in from a side door. Eamon felt his heart constrict. Maura's normally shining hair hung in greasy strings around her face. She was pale and much thinner than he remembered. There was a smear of dirt along her jaw and her lower lip was dry and cracked. To Eamon's horror, her slender wrists were weighted down with heavy shackles.

The jailor held her arm until she stepped into the prisoner's dock, then he stepped back and took a position behind her.

The judge had been brought over from Fingarry to try the case. He looked bored through most of the preliminaries, then straightened up sharply as he said to the prosecutor, "Get on with it. Tell your story, sir."

One at a time the opposing attorneys presented their versions of the events of the fateful night. Then the prosecutor called the magistrate who had been present at the scene to describe the evidence of the bloody collar and the Riordan Hall kitchen knife.

"Your Lordship," the prosecutor concluded. "We have testimony that this man was unkind to his women. Undoubtedly the accused was the recipient of his brutality. But this is not justification for his vile murder by her hand. We ask that in the interests of a civilized society, she be declared a murderess and sentenced to death."

There was total silence in the courtroom as the man ended his speech on a ringing note and sat down.

Eamon looked at Maura, who stood stiffly in the prisoner's dock. He wished she would look at him so that he could at least give her a reassuring smile, but she never once glanced his way.

Truly rose slowly to his feet.

"Your Lordship," he drawled with an exaggerated bow to the judge. "I find myself almost embarrassed to return to my country to see how low the state of justice has fallen." He glanced contemptuously at the prosecutor, whose face became blotchy with anger.

"My esteemed colleague here," Truly continued, "is asking us to believe that this young lady coldly murdered a man. On what does he base that belief? On a scrap of cloth with the man's blood? On a knife that anyone could have removed from the Riordan kitchen? We know that at least some of the Gypsies were in the vicinity of Riordan Hall. We know that they were there helping themselves to Hugh O'Neill's gold."

He turned to Cormac. "Lord Riordan, is not the armory where the gold was kept next to your kitchen?"

At Cormac's nod, Truly threw up his hands in exaggerated disgust. "There you have it, Your Lordship. Anyone could have taken that knife. The state has not a shred of *solid* evidence that my client is guilty of this crime. I'd ask that Your Lordship dismiss this travesty of justice and let us go about our business."

The prosecutor jumped to his feet and for several moments both lawyers and the judge conferred in low voices that couldn't be heard by the rest of the room.

When they were done, the prosecutor, who was still puffing with indignation, took his seat. Truly faced the judge. "I accept your decision to continue, Your Lordship. Yet I feel a couple of witnesses can soon help us resolve the matter."

Eamon noted that Truly seemed neither surprised nor upset by the judge's unwillingness to dismiss the case out of hand. Undoubtedly the lawyer had known all along that the evidence was strong enough for trial. Truly looked relaxed and confident. Eamon began to breathe more easily.

"I call as my first witness Momo the Gypsy."

In the prisoner's dock Maura swayed slightly, and one hand went to her throat.

The young man Eamon had noted earlier walked to the witness dock. He looked over at Maura and gave her a smile of reassurance.

When Momo appeared ready, Truly asked, "Tell us, if you will. What is your relationship to the accused?"

He appeared surprised at the question. "Maura and I are family. At least, er, that is in the Romany sense."

"You were in the same Gypsy family or troupe?" Truly clarified.

"Aye."

"And was this the same relationship you held with the deceased?"

Momo paused, then after a moment said, "Aye, as much as I'm ashamed to admit it."

Truly's eyebrows went up. "Ashamed to admit it? Now, why would that be, Master Momo?"

"Because Pietro was a cold-blooded bastard," Momo spat.

Maura clutched the rail of the prisoner's dock and closed her eyes. Suddenly Eamon wondered if her reluctance to talk had had something to do with protecting this young man.

"Ah," Truly said calmly. "Was he such a bastard that he deserved killing?"

"Aye." Momo looked defiantly out at the crowd, who appeared to be hanging on every word.

Truly walked over to Momo and leaned close to him. "And was that killing a task you took upon yourself to accomplish, Master Momo?"

Momo hesitated, then looked bleakly over at Maura. "Nay," he said finally.

Once again, Truly did not seem in the least surprised. He gave a kind of satisfied nod, then asked the prosecutor, "Do you have questions of this witness?" When the opposing lawyer shook his head, Truly said, "That will be all, Master Momo."

As Momo made his way back to his seat, Truly turned to the judge and said, "Your Lordship, I'd like to call one more witness. Aislin of Burley."

Eamon had no idea who Truly was talking about, but the name caused a commotion among the Gypsies. He saw Maura straighten up in surprise as necks craned toward the back of the courtroom.

The rear doors opened and a slight young woman entered. Momo stood up from his seat and started moving toward her until the judge cautioned him to remain where he was.

The new witness was a pale, fragile-looking creature who appeared to be not much older than sixteen. Truly walked over to help her up the step into the witness dock, and waited patiently for her to compose herself before he started his questioning.

Finally he stepped back and asked her the same question he had put to Momo. "What was your relationship with the deceased?"

The girl ducked her head. "He were my lover," she murmured.

"Did you love him?" Truly asked gently.

"Oh, no!" she said, raising her eyes. "He never did aught but hurt me!"

Truly nodded. "So Mistress Aislin, you would agree with Master Momo that Pietro was a man deserving of killing?"

She gave a vehement nod. "Aye! 'Tis a better world without him."

"And were you the one who undertook to do the world this favor?"

Aislin looked directly at the three Gypsies sitting in

the front of the court. Her eyes held fright and something more, but she shook her head and said, "Nay."

"Well then, if neither you nor your friend Momo had
anything to do with this killing, what do you think
could have happened that night?"

The witness looked down at the floor. "I . . . I don't
reckon I . . . I can't rightly . . ." She let her voice trail
off, before again bringing her gaze up to the three
Gypsies.

Truly waited without pressing the question through a
long moment of silence. His sharp gaze was also on the
three Gypsies. Finally the old Gypsy woman smiled.
Then she put a hand on Momo's arm and pushed herself
up from her seat.

"Don't worry about it, child," she said, looking directly at Aislin. Her voice was scraggly with age, but
strong and confident. "It's time to put this matter to
rights. If they want to hang an old woman like me, I
reckon it won't be much of a loss to anyone. My life has
run its course."

The courtroom erupted into chaos. The two Gypsy
men both jumped to their feet, and the younger shouted,
"Nonna!" At the witness dock Aislin burst into tears.
Eamon looked over at Maura. She stood frozen as a
statue, her face a mask of shock.

Eighteen

"How could you know the old woman was the one who killed him?" Eamon asked Truly as they all sat together finishing a late supper. "She was never at Riordan Hall. How did she get the knife?"

"And where did you find that girl, Aislin?" Claire added.

Truly smiled and brought another spoonful of frumenty pudding to his mouth. "You know, London is an abysmal place for cooking. I haven't had such delectable dishes since the last time I visited home," he said. "I congratulate you, Lady Riordan."

Eamon could tell that Claire's smile covered impatience with the lawyer's delay in answering their questions, but she answered graciously, "I have a wonderful cook named Molly."

"Ah. Perhaps she would reveal her ingredients for this piece of heaven," he said, delicately spooning another bite.

"About the trial—" Eamon pressed.

Truly put down the spoon and dabbed at his mouth

with a napkin. "Simply elegant, my dear lady," he said again to Claire. Finally he turned back to Eamon. "It was the girl, Aislin, who brought the knife from Riordan Hall. I believe she may have actually been planning to use it on Pietro. Or at least use it to defend herself. But I doubt if the feeble little thing could ever have pulled it off. I never seriously considered her as a suspect."

"The old grandmother was even more feeble. How could she have killed him?"

"There are different kinds of strengths," Truly explained. "I could see the strength in the woman they all call Nonna the moment I talked to her. She was, perhaps, the strongest person in the camp. And she had the strongest sense of destiny, which is often what is necessary to have the kind of resolve needed in this case."

"Yet she was willing to see Maura charged for her crime?" Cormac asked.

Truly smiled. "It's odd speaking with the old woman. She nods calmly and appears to know everything that's going to happen. She guessed that it was Eamon who hired me and the notion seemed to please her."

"So she let the trial continue," Eamon clarified.

"Aye. Apparently at first she had wanted to tell the authorities the truth, but her son and grandson convinced her that there was not enough evidence to convict Maura. They feared reprisal against the entire Gypsy camp if she turned herself in."

"She would never have let Maura be convicted," Claire put in.

"Nay. She made sure that I knew enough to find the girl Aislin. I believe she intended all along that the truth would come out if it seemed that Maura was in any danger of being judged guilty."

Eamon shook his head. He'd felt in a daze since the trial had ended so abruptly earlier that day. After the old grandmother had stood up to make her confession, the entire courtroom had turned into an uproar, and all the efforts of the judge to quiet it had been unsuccessful. In the end, Maura had been released. She'd glanced at Eamon briefly, then had run into the arms of Nonna, who held her calmly, murmuring words of comfort to the younger woman.

"Why did she do it?" Eamon asked Truly. "They'd evidently put up with Pietro's cruel ways for years. What made it different that night?"

"Apparently the grandmother's family was planning to leave the following morning with the girl. Pietro had discovered the plan and was starting to beat her. As usual, the poor creature could put up little defense, but the grandmother heard the commotion, somehow climbed up into the wagon, took the knife, and did the task."

"So this poor little Aislin was a witness?" Claire asked.

"Aye. That's why she ran that night. But she had nowhere to go. She'd been living out in the woods since the murder. When she saw me at the Gypsy camp questioning people, she decided to come forward. After a bit of questioning I was able to get the truth about what had happened."

There was a long moment of silence at the table as everyone absorbed the story. "What will happen to her—to Nonna?" Claire asked finally.

Truly shrugged, pushing back his chair to rise. "She's apparently got the lung disease. I don't think the prosecutor has the stomach to try an old woman who will be dead within the year in any event. Especially when it seems impossible to find a living soul to mourn the victim."

Eamon had more questions about the trial, but the question that was most on his mind was one that the lawyer would not be able to answer.

Maura had not looked his way as people started leaving after the trial. The same jailor who had brought her into the courtroom had taken the old grandmother into custody, over the protests of the two men who were apparently her son and grandson. Maura had watched with anguish while they led the woman away, then she had slowly walked over to Truly to thank him for his help. Eamon had overheard her say something to the lawyer about giving her gratitude to the Riordans, as well, but before he could make his way through the crowd toward her, she and the Gypsies had disappeared.

"All in all, it has been a satisfactory day," Truly said as he paused at the dining hall door. "I shall bid you all a very good night."

Eamon pulled his thoughts away from Maura long enough to remember that he owed this man a debt. "We're grateful to you, Truly," he said, rising to walk over and give the lawyer's hand a heartfelt shake. "I'm not sure how to repay you."

"Never fear," the lawyer told him with a twinkle in his eyes. "We'll think of some way. I hope you and your pretty little Gypsy will have a smoother path from now on."

Eamon grimaced. "I fear she's not mine any longer, my friend. She left with them, as you know. I would wager that I'll never see her again."

Truly gave one of his unrevealing smiles. "If I were a betting man, Riordan, that is one wager I would take."

•   •   •   •

Giorgio wanted to move the Gypsy camp as soon as possible, this time clear out of the country. "I know you've always felt that you might find your mother's family if we stay here in Ireland, Maura," he told her apologetically. "But the truth is, the place has brought ill luck to us. Your father died here, and now all of this. As soon as the magistrate gives us clearance to leave, I want to get as far away from here as possible."

Nonna had been released by the authorities that afternoon. Giorgio had put her immediately to bed in her small cot in the wagon, and since then her family had stayed close by her side. Momo and Aislin were sitting together at the far end of the wagon. It was one of the few joys of the situation to see the two young people so happy, looking at each other with those secret glances that were unique to young love.

She'd probably looked at Eamon in just that way, Maura thought ruefully, then silently chastised herself. She was *not* going to think about Eamon.

"I understand why you want to go," she said to Giorgio. "If Lady Riordan wasn't able to find my mother's family, then I reckon they're not to be found. I'll be ready to leave with you whenever you say."

"Are you sure that's what you want?" Giorgio asked.

She nodded. "Aye. You are my family now, if you'll have me. I've come back to stay."

Nonna had appeared to be sleeping, but now she opened her eyes and said, "My child, how many times have I told you to listen to your heart?"

She'd been held by the authorities for less than two days, but she appeared to be much weaker from the ordeal. Maura reached to take her bone-thin hand. "I *am* listening to my heart, Nonna. My heart is here with all of you."

Nonna smiled. "A piece of your heart will be with us always, Maura, but your destiny lies with another."

She could feel the heat in her cheeks. "Nonna, I know you are wise, but this time I believe you're mistaken. There is no other. I don't belong with those people." She blinked hard. "Or with him," she added.

"We should go and let you rest, Mother," Giorgio said, standing. His head went just to the ceiling of the wagon. "We'll bed down outside tonight so that you may sleep soundly."

Nonna shook her head and struggled to sit up. "I'll have plenty of time for sound sleep soon enough. For now, I want to get things straightened out with this foolish child of ours." She leaned to pat Maura's cheek. "I want a promise from you," she said, her voice suddenly strong again.

Maura had had a lifetime of obeying when Nonna took that tone. "Aye," she agreed. "Whatever you need."

" 'Tis not my need, 'tis yours. I want you to promise that you will go speak with him." Maura started to protest, but Nonna held up a steady hand. "That's the promise I require," she said. "Just to speak with him."

Maura sighed. It would be difficult enough leaving Ireland. Seeing Eamon again would make the departure heart-wrenching. But Nonna was watching her with determined eyes. "I warrant 'tis only proper that I go thank Lord and Lady Riordan for providing a lawyer for me. They had no reason to do that after the way I deceived them."

Nonna sank back on her bed, looking suddenly utterly exhausted. Giorgio leaned over his mother in alarm. "Sleep now," he told her. "Tomorrow is soon enough to speak of this."

Her eyes were closed, but she shook her head and insisted, "I want to hear Maura's promise."

Maura moved close to tuck the blanket around the old woman's neck. "I promise, Nonna. I'll go to Riordan Hall. Just to thank them and say goodbye."

Nonna gave a slight nod, her eyes still closed. "That will be enough," she murmured. Then she appeared to drift off to sleep.

Maura would have liked to postpone her visit to Riordan Hall indefinitely, but she knew that Giorgio was anxious to be moving on, so she set out the next morning, borrowing one of the band's string of horses. While not as fine as the animals at the Riordan stables, the Gypsies had always been good traders, and Maura was able to pick out a respectable medium-sized mount for the ride across the plains back to Riordan Hall.

It was early afternoon by the time she arrived. She told herself that she had planned the timing so that she would be least likely to find Eamon at home. If he were out working on the estate somewhere, she could talk to Claire, extend her thanks, and ask Claire to pass them on to the rest of the family. Then would come the goodbyes to the children, which she had not allowed herself to think about.

Still, as she rode up to the familiar stone mansion, she felt that peculiar sense of *awareness* that seemed to come over her whenever Eamon was near. It would be better if she did not see him, she told herself again. Yet she knew that she wanted desperately to see him.

Not wanting to enter without permission, she knocked on the door. Almost immediately it was opened by Claire herself. "Maura, thank the Lord. Cormac had predicted that we would never see you again, but I knew you would at least not leave without seeing the children."

Maura felt a wave of guilt. If it hadn't been for the

promise Nonna had extracted, she might have done just that. "I would like to see them, Lady Riordan," she told Claire who ushered her inside. "How are they?"

"They miss you dreadfully, my dear," Claire said. "I told Cormac that if there is any way we can lure you back, we need to do it. Is there anything we can do to make you consider it?"

Maura couldn't believe the offer after everything that had transpired. Still, it wasn't Eamon who wanted her here. It was the children. She couldn't stay with them without being forced into daily contact with their uncle. Which would be simply unbearable.

"Milady, I will never forget your kindness to me, and I'll never forget the children, but I can't stay here."

"Because of Eamon?" Claire asked gently.

She nodded.

Claire was silent a long moment. "You know that he's still in love with you, Maura?"

Maura shook her head. "I believe he did love me. I'll cherish that to the end of my days. But there's simply been too much between us—my Gypsy heritage, the misunderstanding over the gold and—" She stopped as the painful memories flooded back. "He could not have still been in love with me when he thought me a murderess."

Claire looked surprised. "Eamon never thought you committed that crime."

"Aye, he did."

Claire put a hand to her cheek. "Oh, Maura, you are so wrong about that. Granted, some people in this household found the evidence against you damning, but Eamon always insisted that you were innocent. That's why he brought one of the best lawyers in all the isles all the way from London—"

"*He* brought Master Fitzpatrick?" Maura asked, her

heart beginning to pound. "I thought you and Lord Riordan hired my lawyer."

"Nay," Claire said. "'Twas Eamon, all of it. And when Master Fitzpatrick began to believe you guilty as well and suggested that you plead self-defense, Eamon continued to adamantly maintain your innocence." She gave a deep, exasperated sigh. "I don't understand why this is so hard for you two mule-headed people to see. You're in love with each other. And if one of you doesn't do something about it, you're going to let the prejudices of the rest of the world drive you apart."

Maura felt a surge of excitement. Claire's words had a pure ring of truth. And Claire was perhaps the wisest woman she had ever known, after Nonna. Nonna—who had also implied that Maura's destiny was with Eamon.

"Do you happen to know—" Maura's mouth had gone dry. "Can you tell me where Eamon is now?"

"He should be up at the stables. He and Aidan are deciding on some horses for a—"

Before she could get the final words out of her mouth, Maura had turned and fled out the door.

By the time Maura had climbed the hill to the stables, her heart was pounding so hard that she could hear each beat in the back of her ears. As she neared the building, she slowed down, suddenly nervous. If Eamon was with his brother or the stablemaster, she had no idea what she would say.

But he was alone. She found him in a stall at the far end of the building. He was kneeling, examining the right front hoof of a small silver mare.

He looked up as she approached. His face registered surprise, but Maura couldn't tell if he was pleased to see her.

"Good afternoon," she said, waiting to take her cue from him.

He nodded, but remained silent, waiting.

She bit her lip. Claire had said that he was in love with her, but she had seen no sign of affection from him since before Twelfth Night. With a touch of irritation, she said, "I came to say goodbye."

He stood, slowly. She thought his face flinched, but his voice was steady enough as he said, "You're leaving with them, then?"

"With the Gypsies. Aye."

"With your family," he corrected gently, and then, there it was. The crooked smile, this time with a tinge of sadness.

The stiffness in her body melted. She tipped her head to one side and said, "I also came to thank Lord and Lady Riordan for hiring me a lawyer." This time there was a definite flinch around his eyes. "However, Lady Riordan informed me that 'tis you I have to thank."

She moved closer to him, close enough to note that he smelled slightly of horses. The pounding began again behind her ears.

"Everyone has a right to a good defense," he said.

"Even a poor Gypsy horse thief who you believe is guilty of murder?"

He shook his head. "I never believed that."

"But you knew I was a poor Gypsy horse thief."

A single shaft of light shone through the high stable window behind them. It lit the hair curling around the base of his strong neck.

This time it was he who took a step closer. "I knew you were a remarkable woman who had overcome misfortune and fought to find a place in the world. I knew that you were determined and caring. I knew that I may

never close my eyes at night without seeing your blue
eyes dancing before me."

Somehow they had ended up so close that she could
feel his breath against her lips. "You knew all that?" she
asked, her voice hoarse.

"Aye," he said. Then he lifted her up against him and
kissed her. The world started to spin. The words she had
rehearsed all the way from the Gypsy camp to Riordan
Hall fled. She no longer needed words.

They kissed for long, long moments, hungry and
desperate and utterly relieved that the separation was
over. Suddenly he lifted her off her feet and started
walking toward the back of the stable. She put her arms
around his neck and let him carry her up a small ladder
to a low hayloft. "What are we doing?" she murmured,
dazed. "Someone will come."

But he shook his head, setting her down, then jumping to the floor of the stable again to retrieve a couple
of horse blankets. "They wouldn't dare," he said. "I've
waited too long for this."

His words made the waves begin inside her. "I have,
too," she whispered.

Then he was beside her on the blankets, kissing her,
moving his hands over her, stroking her through her
clothes. "Did you truly come to say goodbye?" he asked,
continuing his caresses.

She pressed against him, feeling the need rising
swiftly. "Aye," she murmured between kisses.

"So you would leave me?"

His tongue making circles inside her mouth pre-
vented her from answering. He slid her skirt up her legs
and found a path through her underclothes into her center core. His fingers slipped inside her, touching a place
that sent an erotic shock to all parts of her body. At her
gasp he pulled away and grinned down at her.

"You would leave me?" he repeated.

She nodded her head dazedly. His fingers still traced lazy circles inside her.

"What if I won't let you leave?" His speech had turned thick. He moved over her again, gently nipping the lobe of one ear. "What if I just keep you here, making love to you every day and every night?"

She made a whimpering sound at the back of her throat as his fingers once again played over the special place inside her.

"What do you want, *macushla*?" he whispered in her ear. "Tell me."

He pulled his fingers away from her and waited. Maura hesitated only a moment. Then she moved her hand over his stiffened manhood and stroked him through the wool of his hose. "I want this," she answered softly. "I want you."

It was all the prompting he needed. He moved over her and, freeing himself from his hose, pushed into her with an involuntary hiss of satisfaction.

She moved to accommodate the full length of him, then began to match his slow thrusts. After their many days apart, it seemed mere seconds before they were clasping each other in a shared climax.

Maura lay without speaking for several moments with Eamon's head heavy on her chest, her fingers trailing idly through his hair. Her throat began to swell with tears as she realized that for the first time since the death of her father, she did not feel alone.

Eamon had not moved. His eyes were closed.

"Are you asleep?" she asked.

He lifted his head to look at her. "I just needed a minute's recuperation, my love. 'Twas a sudden storm, but fierce," he added with a grin.

"Aye." She blushed. "And if your brother should come—"

Eamon shifted so that he was beside her again on the blankets. "Let him come. I've endured his mooning over Claire long enough. 'Twould serve him right to suffer a little now that I've finally convinced my own beauty to fall in love with me."

"Have ye now?" she asked archly.

He gave a firm nod. "Aye. She may not want to admit it, since she's a stubborn wench at times, but she's in love with me. I know the signs."

Maura grinned and looked up at the rafters of the barn above them. "Nonna always says that a smart woman keeps a man guessing."

"I may need to have a talk with your Nonna one of these days." He gave an exaggerated sigh. "Does she also say that a woman should go running off with a troupe of Gypsies when the man she loves is offering her his home?"

"I believe Nonna would say it depends on whether the man is also offering her his heart."

His expression softened. "That he is, sweetheart," he said. "And if I have to follow that wandering band of yours until I can convince you, I'll start packing."

"You'd follow me?" she asked.

"Aye, sweetheart," he said fervently. "If necessary, I'd follow you to—where did the little Gypsy girl go? The Land of the Moon and the Sea?"

"Aye," she replied with a smile.

He nodded. "I'd follow you to the Land of the Moon and the Sea, my Gypsy. And beyond."

Then their heartbeats joined into a single rhythm. And neither spoke for a long, long time.

Epilogue

For generations, Riordans had been married outside on the plains of Tara Hill, but the curse of the Riordan brides had cast a pall over the ceremonies, and Eamon and Maura had decided it was time for a new family tradition. They would be married in the great room at Riordan Hall, surrounded by family and the people of the estate. Claire had taken over planning as Maura went through the days in a haze of happiness.

They'd waited just long enough for Niall and his family to arrive from his wife's estates in Killarney. It had been Eamon's only request. "I want the three Riordan brothers to stand together at my wedding," he'd said. "We've always been together in sorrow, and now we'll come together in joy."

Niall's wife, Catriona, was not as immediately approachable as Claire, Maura discovered. Of course, the beautiful Cat had her own concerns keeping track of the two lively lads she and Niall had produced without any sign of the birthing problems that had cost the lives of so many young Riordan brides.

Eamon had explained the curse to Maura one night in their bed after she'd expressed the hope that their lovemaking had already created a child within her. Maura had listened carefully as he recounted how each of the mothers of the three brothers had died giving birth, as had countless other Riordan brides, according to the old legend.

He himself had never held much belief in the curse, but he knew that there was a mystical side to Maura's reasoning that might give the notion more credence. She'd been raised by Nonna and her father to believe in the power of fate. It was a faith that gave her both peace and strength, and it was one of the things he'd come to love about his chosen bride.

When he'd finished his story, Maura had been silent for a time, considering her answer. Finally she said, "Claire has three healthy children and Cat and Niall have two. I think I share your brother's opinion that the curse has now been broken forever."

He'd pulled her into his arms and proceeded to ensure that if she wasn't already with child, she soon would be.

Finally the wedding day had arrived. The children had greeted her, as usual, by tumbling into her bedchamber shortly after dawn and jumping up on her bed. "Uncle Eamon says I can sign the wedding book," Ultan announced immediately.

"I can, too," Dylan parroted.

Ultan frowned, then turned to Maura for a ruling. "I'm the oldest," he pointed out.

Maura gathered all three into her arms at once. She was so happy, she felt as if she could gather the entire world up into one huge hug. The only damper on the day was that she had no family of her own to witness her joy. They had had no success in discovering the identity of her mother's people, and her Gypsy friends were by now far away, perhaps even out of the country. The goodbyes had been painful, since she'd known it was likely that she'd not see them again.

"All three of you shall sign the book," Maura proclaimed. "Since you all now write so beautifully."

"I can, too?" Eily asked in wonder.

"Aye, sweetling," Maura said, giving the girl a kiss.

It had taken several minutes to get the children cleared out of the room so that she could begin her own preparations. Claire had had a dress made specially for her as a wedding gown. "Green, of course, to show off that hair," she'd declared. The color had made little difference to Maura. While she was grateful to Claire for all her care over the ceremony, she was not particular about any of it. She'd been raised on the road, with little wealth and few possessions. The wealth she had found in the Riordan household had nothing to do with material things.

She'd hoped to see Eamon before the ceremony, but it was Catriona and Claire who arrived shortly after the children had left to help her don her new finery. They each embraced her as they came into the room. "We've come to help you get ready, sister," Claire told her, and Maura felt a great lump forming in her throat at the word. Momo had been like a brother to her growing up, but she'd never even imagined what it would be like to have sisters.

The ceremony was to take place at noon before the wedding feast, and by midmorning, Maura had been dressed and primped and fussed over to her new sisters' satisfaction. When she'd asked wistfully about Eamon, Catriona and Claire had assured her that he was being prepared with equal care by his two brothers, and that she would not see him before the ceremony, lest it bring ill fortune.

Claire and Catriona each took an arm to lead Maura down the stairs to the great room, which was decorated along every wall with the first spring wildflowers. The bright yellow, blue, and pink blossoms filled the entire room with a delicate scent.

A crowd was gathered—Riordan kin and neighboring landowners, as well as every servant on the estate. But Maura's gaze went immediately to Eamon, who stood near the huge fireplace with Niall and Cormac at his side. The resemblance between the Riordan brothers was unmistakable. All three were tall and brawny and darkly handsome. The trio would appear fearsome, Maura decided, if they were not all watching her with those engagingly crooked Riordan grins.

Eamon took her icy hand as she neared and turned her to face Father Brendan, the old priest who had spent many long hours with her in the past few days as she prepared to marry under the laws of the traditional church. Maura had found him incredibly tolerant of her Gypsy beliefs, which were a mixture of the new and the ancient.

Nevertheless, she was grateful that they had chosen to make the ceremony short. In her heart, she and Eamon were already united.

"You may kiss your bride, Eamon," Father Brendan said with a gentle smile, and then Eamon's lips were on hers.

They'd scarcely finished the kiss before she was swept up in a much rougher embrace by first Cormac, then Niall, who both called her sister, just as Claire had earlier. The two women gave her more dignified embraces. Then the three children, who had been sitting as quietly as possible in the front of the room, jumped from their seats to gather around her. She knelt, laughing, to let them all put their arms around her neck.

"Now we must greet *your* family," Eamon said.

She looked up at him, confused, then gave a little cry as she saw Giorgio and Momo coming toward her, supporting Nonna between them. Tears streamed down her cheeks as she embraced each of them in turn, along with Aislin, who hung behind until Momo reached back for her hand and pulled her forward. "And here's *my* new bride, Maura," he said, beaming.

"What are you all doing here?" she asked, looking around at the dear faces. "I thought you'd be far away by now."

"Your new husband rode after us and asked us to stay for the wedding," Giorgio explained. "He said we were the only family you had to be at your side. And he had an ally in Nonna," he added with an affectionate glance at his mother.

"I'd already seen this day long ago in my dreams, child," Nonna said. "But 'tis good to be here for these old eyes to see it for real. I knew that you'd make a beautiful bride, for you have a beauty that is soul-deep."

Maura took the impossibly frail old woman into a special embrace. "If I do, it is because of the teachings you and Papa gave me," she whispered. "I'm so glad you could be with me here today."

"Giacomo is here with you, too, child, never doubt it. Soon I'll be with him. But neither one of us will ever leave you."

It was several moments before Eamon was able to pull her into the hall away from the rest for a private moment. "Thank you for bringing them," Maura said. "I didn't even realize until I saw their faces how very much it meant to me to have them here."

"They are your family," Eamon said firmly.

She smiled at him. "I warrant most men of your station would be more than a little embarrassed to bring Gypsies into their house and call them family."

"They are fine people," he said, "and they are part of who you are, which means they will always be welcome here." He stopped as tears began streaming down her face. "What's wrong?" he asked.

She smiled through the sobs. "Since I first came to Riordan Hall, I've held out a fantasy that Claire would find my mother's people and that somehow it would make it all right for me to be part of this world. But you need none of that. You've just married yourself to an itinerant Gypsy who once stole your horse, and you seem to be perfectly well satisfied with the bargain."

He laughed and rocked her in his arms. "Ah, my sweet Irish Gypsy, I love you. Now that the vows are said, will you finally believe that nothing else matters?"

She wiped her tears away, sharing his laughter, but she shook her head and said, "Nay, I'll not believe it." At his surprised look, she slipped her arms around his neck, tilted up her head, and offered her lips. "I'm going to need to be convinced," she murmured. "Many times a day."

He grinned at her and said, "My pleasure, Mistress Riordan." Then he proceeded to become as convincing as possible.

About the Author

With family roots tracing back to both England and Ireland, **Ana Seymour** has been a lover of history since childhood. She now loves writing about it in popular romances, which have been published around the world.

Ana lives in the country near one of Minnesota's fifteen thousand lakes. She appreciates hearing from readers at P.O. Box 24107, Minneapolis MN 55424, or by email at anaseymour@aol.com.

HIGHLAND FLING

Have a Fling...with Jove's new Highland Fling *romances!*

The Border Bride   Elizabeth English   0-515-13154-7
No one can remember a time when the Darnleys and Kirallens were at peace—the neighboring clans have been at each other's throats for generations. At last, however, it seems like peace is at hand—Darnley's daughter Maude is to marry Jemmy, Laird Kirallen's son, bringing the bitter fighting to a wary truce.
But things aren't always as they seem...

Laird of the Mist   Elizabeth English   0-515-13190-3
Banished from his clan, Allistair Kirallen is a sword for hire and a man with a dream: to avenge his brother's death. Until a very different dream fires his imagination. She is his heart's desire, his one true destiny—but she is only a fleeting vision...

Once Forbidden   Terri Brisbin   0-515-13179-2
Anice MacNab has just wed her bethrothed, the heir to the clan MacKendimen—a family powerful in both name and arms. In the years she has waited for this day, Anice has dreamed of becoming the lady of the clan and its castle, and of
finding love with her handsome bethrothed. But her dreams of love are brutally shattered on her wedding night...

TO ORDER CALL:
1-800-788-6262